UNSEEN WORLD

SEAN CUMMINGS

snowbooks

Proudly Published by Snowbooks in 2011

Copyright © 2011 Sean Cummings

Snowbooks Ltd.
Kirtlington Business Centre
Oxfordshire
OX5 3JA
Tel: 0207 837 6482
email: info@snowbooks.com
www.snowbooks.com

British Library Cataloguing in Publication Data
A catalogue record for this book is available from the British Library.

ISBN   978-1-907777-03-5

Printed and bound by J F Print Ltd.,Sparkford,Somerset

For Shane, as he begins his journey.

CHAPTER 1

My name is Marshall Conrad, and the world as you know it is a damned lie.

I know this, because when I first started this crime-fighting gig, I was expecting to cleverly engage a costumed super villain, and it didn't happen. It still hasn't happened, and I've been at this for over ten years now. Because bald-headed megalomaniacs with a freeze-ray and homicidal mimes that squirt acid out of a fake flower exist only in the pages of comic books; what I do is largely a form of crime prevention.

If you're thinking that I dress up like *McGruff the Crime Dog* and deliver lectures to children about the dangers of talking to strangers, give your head a shake. I'm not a superhero, despite what the newspapers have been reporting, and I haven't been called on to save the planet. I'm not even sure that I could save the planet, if the opportunity were to present itself. My preference is to work on a much smaller scale, so if you're disappointed by this fact, deal with it.

If journalists are reporting the news as opposed to fabricating it, you will have googled the living crap out of your computer in hope of learning as much about me as you possibly can. Congratulations, you've found my blog. Since you're here, do try to remember that much of what you're about to learn will sound like it came straight from the pages of fantasy novel, and you'll no doubt continue to question the believability of the mainstream news media, whose focus has been on the small City of Greenfield, along with yours truly.

I'm sure you've heard about the one-million-dollar bounty on my head, courtesy of *The National Monitor*—who hasn't? Ever since the *Drudge Report* broke the story about the rescue of Congressman Byron Aldrich's wife, after she was kidnapped from the family cottage at Crystal Beach, the City of Greenfield has become a Mecca for crackpots and conspiracy theorists bent on obtaining proof of my existence.

It wasn't just the rescue of Mrs. Aldrich that grabbed the attention of every media outlet in the country—it was the grainy photograph of a man floating high above the roof of the Greenfield County Hospital that has everyone talking. I believe the headline on Drudge's website read:

WTF??? REPUBLICAN CONGRESSMAN'S WIFE RESCUED BY SUPERMAN?

Charming.

Homeland Security is on high alert, *Fox News* persists in reporting that I'm an Islamic Terrorist, and people are selling t-shirts emblazoned with the slogan "Somebody Save Me!" beneath the now infamous snapshot.

I know the identity of the person who captured my image with her cellphone, and I'll be contacting her shortly to express my displeasure. If that picture hadn't been fired off to Drudge, Marilyn Aldrich's story of being whisked off into the sky by a man with glowing eyes would have been dismissed as the hysterical ranting of a traumatized political wife. Better yet, I would be snoring in my bed instead of writing this blog to set the record straight.

Necessity required that I find and rescue Mrs. Aldrich, as the person responsible for her kidnapping fully intended to murder her at 11:55 PM on Wednesday, June 18th. For the record, I don't normally rescue the damsel in distress while I subdue the bad guy. That might look good in the pages of *World's Finest*, but it's not tactically advantageous, since most victims of crime are bouncing off the walls, and most perpetrators are inclined to shoot at you, possibly injuring or killing the person you're trying to save.

I discovered the barn where she was hidden that night around 8:30 PM, and thankfully, the kidnapper was nowhere in sight. Mrs. Aldrich was stoic throughout her first flight outside a serviceable aircraft. She even asked me if I voted for her husband. God love her.

She told me the kidnapper would be returning to the barn at 11:00 PM to "purify her body." I took this to mean that he intended to eviscerate Mrs. Aldrich and scatter her body parts in selected areas of suburban Greenfield as he's done with three of his eight victims. I would have captured the guy when he returned to the barn, but Drudge posted the "startling" picture of yours truly on his website at 9:45 PM, thereby tipping him off.

By the way, while I appreciate the kind words from Congressman Aldrich, thanking me for saving his wife, he didn't get my vote last November because he is a Republican. Please don't take this personally, Congressman, but you people scare the hell out of me.

As this is my first-ever attempt at blogging, I am mindful that what I am writing is going to piss off comic book enthusiasts.

Good.

You're a troubling pack of nerdish kooks who need to get out of your mother's basements. Seriously, there's more to living than watching *Star Trek* reruns and counting down the weeks until the next comic book convention. Try organized paintball, or maybe find a girlfriend instead of locking yourselves away in your bedrooms and posting your fantasies about *Seven of Nine* to some weird-ass fan fiction website.

Yes, in her day, Jeri Ryan was smoking hot, and the good people who produced *Star Trek Voyager* gave her that tight-fitting bodysuit for a reason—to get people like you away from your role-playing games long enough to watch their program. I should add that your obsession with errors in Hollywood's portrayal of comic book heroes is getting a little old, because nobody but you gives a damn if the big screen *Spider-Man* has organic web shooters instead of mechanical ones.

If you feel like sending me hate mail because you're lumped with the "Trekkies," suck it up. I won't be reading your comments, because I don't publish my email address. You can try snail mail, but don't hold your breath waiting for me to respond, since it's unlikely that I will survive what is about to occur in the next twenty-four hours. Even if I miraculously do pull through, which is doubtful, I won't receive your letters, because my mailman is an asshole.

Frankly, I don't understand America's fascination with superheroes. I know that many thousands of people play online games like *City of Heroes* or *World of Warcraft,* and hey—who wouldn't want epic powers, right? You get a groovy costume, and it's a blast to fantasize about super-jumping over a building or firing laser beams out of your fingertips.

Unfortunately, video games bear little resemblance to how I spend most evenings, and fighting crime isn't all that glamorous. While super strength or the ability to teleport yourself eight city blocks might sound attractive, you have to remember that until last week, most people weren't psychologically prepared to see a grown man floating in the air without mechanical assistance.

You're no doubt wondering why I sound like a prick, and you're probably troubled that I'm not offering myself as an inspiring role model for others. *Why the hell is that my job?*

I've created this blog to explain why you'll be seeing Greenfield residents hacking one another to pieces on the news, should I fail to take out *Grim Geoffrey*. If you're clueless as to what I'm talking about, I recommend that you continue reading, because your neighborhood might just be next on his hit list.

While you're at it, kindly remember that popular culture often portrays crime fighters as god-like beings who swoop down from the sky to thwart a criminal mastermind's evil plan with seconds to spare. Movies and fantasy novels suggest that my kind represents the very best in humanity while ignoring that much of humanity is a cesspool of twisted people with addictions to everything from porn to crystal meth. I'm not a hero. I'm just a guy from the east coast. My hope is that readers will stop slurping on their Starbucks for longer than ten minutes to simply look at the world through my eyes, because it's an ugly place.

You'll see the pedophile that lives down the street busily preparing a lesson plan for his third grade class while the little boy he molested grows up to become damaged goods. You'll learn that your golfing buddy regularly beats the crap out of his wife, and that she's mastered the art of disguising a shiner with liquid foundation while he jokes with you about missing that last putt on the ninth hole. Frankly, it's depressing.

I have no wish to motivate others with a sense of community responsibility or to act as a mentor for at-risk youth. I like to come home when my work is done, and more often than not, I just want to go to bed. I'm a solitary person by choice and the only person whose opinion I value nearly as much as my own is Walter's—and *he's* a cat.

I don't possess an excessively muscular physique that should be immortalized in marble, though I do look good in my outfit. *It's not a costume*, got that? Spandex tights aren't practical, and because I work exclusively at night, primary colors generally attract gunshots – or worse, cops. I hate cops.

Don't get me wrong, I completely respect their profession, but they have the bargaining power of a union and are paid for protecting you, whereas I'm on my own. When it's pouring rain outside, they can take shelter in a squad car and watch everyone else get soaked. If it's the middle of January, and the weather office has issued a wind-chill advisory, they can crank up the heat, while I zip around town freezing my ass off.

There are over fifty-thousand people in Greenfield, and I'm suspicious of every single one of them. I'm not motivated to protect the city and its citizens for noble reasons, and I sure as hell don't pursue truth, justice and the American way. I'm a crime fighter primarily because of migraine headaches. More on that later.

The summer solstice will soon be here, and I've left instructions for a news release to go to *CNN* along with conclusive proof that a flying man resides in Greenfield. I doubt *The National Monitor* will be paying out the million-dollar reward, because if anyone is reading this, it means that a supernatural phenomenon is underway, one that makes my existence seem like a fart in the hurricane. With this in mind, we'll start at the beginning and take it from there. Don't look for me to disclose too much information about my abilities, and don't assume I am the lone survivor of a long dead planet like *that other guy*. I was born in Vermont and raised by a single mom. Okay, here goes...

CHAPTER 2

Marnie Brindle lives one floor above my apartment and bugs the hell out of me. I should add that she's causing my cat Walter to present with some kind of feline neurosis, as he's taken to scratching my new sofa whenever he hears her irritating gangsta rap mix pounding from the ceiling at all hours. I can't confirm or deny whether Walter actually dislikes Marnie, because whenever she comes downstairs for one of her unannounced visits, he usually hides under my bed and won't come out until she leaves. I had considered that he might actually be afraid of my nosy neighbor, but he is a treacherous bastard, and he's recently allowed himself to become corrupted with her bribes of *Pounce*, those vile-smelling nuggets that cats love.

Marnie didn't know I existed for the first few months she lived in my building, which at the time was my preference, since we have less than nothing in common. In hindsight, I'm glad we met, because even though the picture she emailed to Drudge has turned Greenfield into a veritable Roswell, she's always broke, and I would imagine that she'll be a rich woman when she auctions off the cell phone she used to snap my picture.

At twenty-three years of age, Marnie Brindle's life is consistent with most people in her demographic. She is addicted to *American Idol* and has been through a string of boyfriends, all of whom she unceremoniously dumped via email. She complains bitterly about her failing grades at Chesterton College and swears that her Women's Studies professor is out to get her.

I've never really understood why women feel a need to study themselves, but I can see Marnie's point. It's probably very easy for a fifty-something professor who authored three books about female body image in the media to hold a grudge against any woman who fits into that ten-percent of the population best described as "beautiful people." Then again, show me a college student who doesn't bitch about their grades, and I will show you a bald-headed sheep.

Are we friends? I guess so. Am I in love with her? Not sure on that one—ask me later.

My first encounter with Marnie was after I received her copy of *Elle* in my mailbox. Did I mention that my letter carrier is an asshole? He pulls this crap all the time. My Apartment number is 112 and Marnie lives in 212 . He's delivered mail to my building for the past eight years, and he knows damned well that the only magazine I subscribe to is *Fly Fish America*, so this was clearly an act of pure spite.

It seemed reasonable for me to return the magazine to its rightful owner, so I wandered up the stairs and opened the grey metal door leading to the hallway on the second floor. When I found apartment 212, I planned to slide the magazine under the door, so I wouldn't actually have to come into contact with my neighbor, but the door sweep thwarted my efforts. Realizing that I had no choice but to meet the person who'd become my cat's nemesis, I knocked on the door, hoping that our encounter wouldn't last more than one minute.

When the door opened, a strikingly beautiful young woman wearing gym shorts and a pink t-shirt with the words "Old Navy" across her chest stood before me, clutching a mason jar filled with a grayish looking substance in an oven mitted left hand. Her eyes were green, with a touch of amber, and she wore a puzzled look on her face as she glanced down both sides of the hallway, then back at me. My stomach growled loudly, as the scent of cinnamon and fresh apples filled my nostrils. She looked me over, presumably to ensure I wasn't some pervert standing at her door,

"Hello, are you Marnie Brindle?" I asked politely.

"Yes, I am. Are you a courier?"

"No, just a good Samaritan," I said, presenting her with the magazine. "I live downstairs in one-twelve, and your apartment is obviously two-twelve. The mailman knows I don't generally read fashion magazines—not my area."

She swept her long red hair back with her right hand and chuckled, still looking amused. "No, I guess you don't, do you? Well, now that you know my name courtesy of the US Postal Service and Elle magazine, who might you be?"

Rats.

I hate questions like that. I like being a hermit, and random introductions of this nature generally lead to boring conversations about the weather, when I would rather be lying on my couch looking at the weather through my living room window.

"I'm Marshall Conrad," I said, hoping she wouldn't want to shake my hand.

"Wait a minute," she said, cocking an eyebrow. "I've seen you before. You're the guy who walks that Siamese cat in a harness every night."

It had begun.

She'd cornered me into a conversation, and I instinctively knew that from this day forward, every time I bumped into her, there would be an inquiry about Walter's health, which would inevitably lead into a subsequent chat about what happened on the last episode of some mind-numbing reality show, or worse, twenty-something angst.

"Uh, yeah, that's me," I said, trying to sound polite. "My cat is on an exercise regime, because the vet told me he'd die of a heart attack if doesn't lose ten pounds."

"Aww, that's so sweet." She smiled, and her voice lilted up an octave, immediately causing the hair on the back of my neck to stand on end. "I'd get a cat, but he'd probably move out, just like all of my other roommates."

"Roommate troubles, huh?" I offered, hoping our conversation would be ending soon. "Not a lot of fun, I would imagine."

"Yeah… Arnold was the last roommate I had. He sold cars for a living when he wasn't complaining about his boyfriend troubles. All he did for the three months he lived here was bitch about my hair in the bathroom sink and make deals on his cellphone. Every other gay man I know is either a hairdresser or an interior designer—but a car salesman? What's up with that?"

"Beats me. I don't know any hairdressers. I go to the barber at the mall."

"Oh yeah, my dad goes there whenever he's in town. Do you have a roommate?"

"No, just a cat."

"Right, you said that," she nodded. "Well, I've put another advertisement in the newspaper, and my friend Rene said she might move in with me, but her boyfriend is a total butthead, and he's always hitting on me. Hey, are you married?"

'Nope, never married."

"That's too bad," she said. "You look like you're almost as old as my dad; he's fifty-two."

Crap. I should have seen that one coming.

"I'll be fifty-two in twelve years," I said, sourly.

"*Really*? Dammit! I've just made an ass of myself, haven't I?" Her face turned bright red. "Please tell me you're not offended. I'm just coming off the week from hell, now that Arnold moved out, plus I'm going to have to knit next month's rent."

I nodded in sympathy for her financial woes.

"Don't sweat it," I said, forcing my mouth into something resembling a smile. "I'm sure you'll find a roommate sooner or later."

I wanted to address Walter's grievance with the gangsta-rap mix from the fifth dimension of hell, but I had to be downtown in thirty minutes. The Greenfield County Sheriff's Department was holding a news conference with an update on the search for Stephen Hodges, a sixteen-year-old who had been missing for three days,

"I'm making applesauce. Want a jar?" Marnie asked. "It's the least I can do, since you were nice enough to deliver my magazine."

"Oh, that isn't necessary," I said, politely. "I just live one floor below, and it's not like I was moving a piano or anything."

Marnie shoved the mason jar into my chest. "I insist," she said. "This is my first attempt at canning, and I'd really appreciate some feedback by someone who isn't a family member. Plus I said you were old. My bad."

I have a phobia about food prepared by strangers—it's part of the whole hermit thing. I imagine a shrink would say I have obsessive-compulsive disorder, and they might be right. You could hand me a black forest cake with cherries picked from the Queen's own private orchards, if it's not wrapped in plastic from the factory or prepared in my own kitchen, I'm not going to eat it.

I glanced at my watch. I'd spent enough time engaged in idle chit-chat with Marnie. Since it was an honest gesture, I decided to accept her gift and use it as a doorstop.

"Thank you for the applesauce," I said, still using my best artificial smile.

"Great!" Marnie chirped. "I'll look forward to your critique. Maybe I can come downstairs sometime, so I can meet Walter."

"Maybe – Crap! I have to get going. My sister is coming over, and I have to clean up my place, or I'll never hear the end of it," I lied.

"Okay, Mr. Conrad. Have a good one and say hi to Walter for me," she said, closing her apartment door.

As I sauntered down the hall, I felt like I'd suddenly become a relic – or worse, Mr. Frederick Graves, my fifth grade teacher who always wore a brown corduroy blazer with the patches sewn into the elbow. He was a veteran of the Second World War and reeked of Aqua Velva and cigarettes, and he'd force you to suffer through an entire Perry Como album during a detention for what he called "acting smart" in class.

I wandered into the front foyer to leave a note for the mailman, thanking him for his happy little prank. As I pulled my notepad out of my breast pocket, it occurred to me that crime fighting was beginning to take its toll on me.

Clairvoyance is not a gift, no matter what *James Van Praagh* has to say about it. I literally cringe whenever he's a guest on *Oprah* or *Dr. Phil*, because celebrity psychics earn millions by convincing innocent people that family members who pass on still watch over us in a kind of spiritual guardianship.

Like that ever happens.

My psychic abilities are a major league pain in the ass, because my brain acts like a satellite dish for graphic images of what is yet to come. As a foreteller, I am the unwitting recipient of the average person's subliminal intent, and I've probed the fractured minds of people whose habits are of a malevolent nature.

It is no easy thing when a macabre canvas of rape, murder and torture pillories your senses every time someone conspires to kill a human being or commit a serious crime. Your brain pounds relentlessly with migraine headaches until you intervene, and your spirit peels away like dried paint on a long-abandoned house. When you're not stopping a crime, you still have bills to pay and groceries to buy. You celebrate your birthday alone while everyone else is in the company of family and friends. Christmas is just another day on the calendar, and you wind up disclosing your fears and frustrations to a fat Siamese cat.

Well, at least I do.

I resolved to pull my head out of my ass, because self-pity is a quality I loathe, especially when it's coming from me. I tore a sheet out of the notepad and scribbled a message for the mailman that was sure to provoke his wrath:

"Dear US Postal Service: I live in Apartment 112, and the only magazine I subscribe to on a regular basis is Fly Fish America.

– Marshall Conrad
P.S. You Got Me. Ha. Ha."

CHAPTER 3

Stella Weinberg is not long for this earth.

She doesn't realize it yet, but I've foreseen her demise, and it will likely occur within the next three years, unless she makes some significant changes to her lifestyle. I first met Stella during a hastily assembled news conference at the Greenfield County Sheriff's Department. Search and rescue teams had scoured every square inch of a wooded area in Crossfield where Stephen Hodges was last seen partying with friends, and I assumed the worst.

The meeting room was teeming with reporters from the local news media, who took up the first three rows. I craned my neck for a place to sit and spotted a metal chair beside an obese woman who sat alone, stuffing her face with cheese doodles.

She flashed me a friendly smile and pointed an orange-stained finger to the empty chair beside her, then motioned for me to come over. I nodded politely, then reluctantly sauntered over and wedged myself between the fat lady and the wall. I'd been sitting for less than ten seconds when she gave me a hard nudge with her elbow.

"They're going to say they found a body," she whispered. Her breath smelled of artificial cheddar and fried cornmeal. "Did you see the sheriff? He's looking pretty grim – spooked, I'd say."

My fist impulse was to get up and watch the news conference from the back of the meeting room, but the look on the sheriff's face suggested that she might be onto something.

She pointed a meaty finger at a middle-aged woman seated beside the podium. "See that lady over there? She's the new coroner. Oh yeah, that kid is dead – why else would she be here, right?"

"You have an insider's knowledge," I whispered. "Are you a reporter?"

She glanced at me through the corner of her eye. "Not likely. Reporters have a nasty habit of ignoring the glaringly obvious," she said, crumpling the plastic cheese doodle bag into ball. "It's obvious the kid is dead. Less obvious is that he's victim number one. I'd say this is the first of many murders that are about to happen in our safe little city."

Her suggestion that Stephen Hodges was the first victim in a yet-to-happen killing spree surprised me. My abilities usually allow me to see violent crimes like murder well in advance, because a perpetrator's willful intent stands out like a warning sign on the highway.

"It's possible that he simply got too drunk and died of something like alcohol poisoning, if he was partying with his friends," I whispered, deciding that I'd listen to her theory.

"Not a chance," she said. "You've heard the old saying about a person's eyes being the window into their soul, right?"

"Yeah."

"Well, trash that idea – it's all in the face. Look at the sheriff. He's practically gray. You'd think he'd be used to seeing dead bodies by now."

She was onto something.

Sheriff Don Neuman is a twenty-five-year veteran of law enforcement, first coming to Greenfield back in 1988 after suddenly resigning from the Homicide Division of the Boston Police Department. I assumed that his reasons for moving to Greenfield had something to do with rumors that he'd experienced a nervous breakdown after a particularly violent murder-suicide. I studied the sheriff closely and noticed that his hands were shaking as he tentatively flipped through a yellow legal pad. Something had rattled him, and if the woman's hypothesis was correct, then it was going to be a short news conference.

"This morning at three-forty-four, search and rescue teams working in conjunction with the Greenfield County Sheriff's Department found a body in a wooded area of Crossfield," the sheriff read aloud. "The area around the body was immediately cordoned off, and the county coroner arrived on scene at approximately four-eighteen."

The woman nudged my arm again. "Never doubt a fat lady in a frock," she whispered.

"The body was removed from the area at seven-forty-five, and an autopsy is scheduled for tomorrow morning," he continued. "We are initiating a homicide investigation in partnership with the county prosecutor's Office. At this time we cannot disclose the identity of the victim until notification of next of kin. We will schedule another news conference when more information becomes available. Thank you."

The reporters started shouting questions at the sheriff as he retreated from the podium with the Coroner, and he motioned for everyone to settle down. "It would be inappropriate for me to disclose further information while the investigation proceeds. We can only report the information contained in the news release," he said, as three sheriff's deputies blocked the doorway leading out of the meeting room.

"Well, that's that," the fat lady said. "By the way, my name is Stella Weinberg. I own The Curiosity Nook over on Shelby Avenue."

"I'm Marshall Conrad," I said, shaking her hand. "I'm a curious onlooker."

"You're a cat lover too, huh?" she said, pointing to the cat hair on my black trousers. "Siamese, it would appear."

"It looks like you're batting a thousand," I said, brushing Walter's hair off my leg. "Your predictions are bang-on, and apparently you're an expert on cat hair. Do you have any more insightful gems to share?"

"No gems today, just a handful of rocks," she said, as she heaved a large woven bag onto her lap.

"Rocks?"

"The curiosity business isn't exactly booming lately," she continued. "I started my shop because I have this habit of finding odds and sods that few people notice as they go about their daily business – that and I'm a pack rat."

I liked her candor.

Stella Weinberg appeared to be the kind of person who, like me, is an outsider – although in her case, the fact that she is five foot two and weighs over two hundred pounds might have something to do with her reclusive lifestyle.

"Things are going to get pretty ugly in town. I can feel it," she said, grimly.

"Okay then, I'll bite. Why is a killer on the loose, and when will he strike again?" I asked.

"Because of *this*." Stella pulled a rock out of her handbag and placed it on her lap. "I've been lugging this bugger around all day. Have a look at it, and tell me what you see."

I picked up the chunk of granite and guessed that it weighed about five pounds.

"It seems rather heavy for something the size of a baseball," I said, gauging its weight with my right hand.

Stella frowned. "Take a gander at what's on the bottom."

I flipped it over and noticed a spiral that looked like it had been stamped into the rock's granite surface with a die.

"I'm no archeologist, but this looks like a symbol of some kind," I said. "Maybe it's a Mi'kmaq artifact."

"If that's a Mi'kmaq symbol, then I'll wear a bikini and give you a private fashion show," she winked.

"Okay then, you found a shape that was etched into a rock by space aliens," I said, trying to get the image of a near-nude Stella Weinberg out of my head. "I don't see how this is related to a dead sixteen year old or murders that may or may not happen in the future."

She gave me a disapproving frown. "Mr. Conrad, I've been a Greenfield resident for over forty-five years," she huffed. "Once upon a time, when I was thin and glamorous, I used to hike the forests and hills all over the county, and I've found everything you can think of – from arrowheads to petrified bear turds. Want to know something else that might surprise you?"

"What's that?"

"I've acquired twenty rocks just like that one in the past three weeks. Each rock is almost identical in size to the one in your hand, and there's a spiral doo-dad carved into each of them. What do you think of that?"

I considered Stella's question carefully before answering. Maybe she'd chanced upon some archeological treasure that had gone unnoticed until now. That seemed to be the logical explanation.

"Don't even think about telling me that it's an archeological relic," she said, reading my mind. "I found each rock in different locations along my bus route."

"Let me get this straight – you're linking *this* with a murder in Crossfield? I'm sorry, but I just don't get it."

Her frown deepened as she scratched the back of her neck. "I'll be frank with you. I'm an overweight woman who rides the bus, and I know that people stare at me," she said, with a hint of resignation.

I nodded sympathetically. "Because I'm a big woman, I don't have the freedom of mobility that most people enjoy. The bus stop is two blocks from my house. I get off the bus and walk one block to my store. When I open my doors at nine-thirty in the morning, my feet are sore, and I'm usually out of breath. Twenty days in a row – twenty rocks in a row. Combine that with the discovery of a murdered sixteen year-old, and you've got yourself a bona-fide mystery."

It might have been a coincidence, but there was a certainty to her voice that gave her theory a lot of credibility. I'd seen all kinds of bizarre patterns of behavior on the part of criminals over the years, and there was no reason to doubt what she was saying.

"Naturally, if you tell the police about this, they'll show you the door," I said. "Maybe you should get in touch with Chesterton College to find out what they think."

Stella nodded . "I'm not sure if it's the spiral symbols or the locations where I found the rocks that has me unsettled."

"Why's that?"

"A spiral is one of the oldest symbols throughout history. You can find them scratched into boulders from thousands of years ago on every continent, and it's pretty much accepted that a spiral is emblematic of resurrection or rebirth. You don't find them on a bench inside a bus shelter or lying in the middle of the sidewalk for you to trip over."

"So you think a killer has taken up residence in Greenfield, and he leaves rocks all over the place like a business card?"

"In a strange way, yes," Stella said. "A lot of effort has gone into preparing that little symbol – it's shiny, like someone buffed it. Whoever did this might be a gemologist or a craftsman. That's my take on it, anyway."

I ran my index finger over the buffed contours of the spiral engraving and ran through the facts. Stephen Hodges was dead, the sheriff looked spooked, and twenty spiral-engraved rocks don't just appear unexpectedly out of thin air.

"Right now we have one dead kid and no confirmation from the police that a murder has occurred." I said with a shrugged. "You run a curiosity shop, and I'm just an average Joe who came to a news conference one afternoon. It's been fun playing Sherlock Holmes with you, but I need to head back home."

Stella grabbed my arm and squeezed.

"Average Joes don't hang out at news conferences, and you're about as average as Chinese food at a doughnut shop," she said with a sly smile.

"Maybe I'm an author, and I'm writing a book about crime in Greenfield County."

She flashed me a skeptical look.

"It's also possible that I'm just a concerned citizen who's been following the story about a missing sixteen-year-old kid. Had you considered that?"

Stella pointed to my hands. "Pretty scuffed up knuckles you've got there, Mr. Conrad. Either your hobby is brawling at the Regis Hotel on Friday nights, or you've got a few mysteries of your own."

"We're just chock-full of mysteries in Greenfield these days, Stella." I said. "Tell you what – if you make any more supernatural discoveries that might have something to do with Stephen Hodges, let's talk about it over coffee."

She shrugged and handed me her business card. "You're right about going to the police – we've got nothing to offer their investigation that would be taken seriously. Who wants to listen to a fat lady talk about her rock collection anyway?"

I nodded as I opened my wallet and inserted her card. "I don't normally accept business cards from people who are stranger than me, but for you, I'll make an exception. I might even buy one of your curiosities if you're nice to me."

She heaved her bulk off the metal folding chair and stood up. "What's this? No card for me?" Stella feigned surprise. "Don't tell me, you're an investigative journalist who suffers from prolonged shyness."

"I appreciate your discretion, Stella, but really, I've got nothing to hide from anyone," I said, sliding my wallet in my back pocket.

She raised a single painted eyebrow. "Nothing to hide, eh? You're a strange bird, and coming from me, that's a compliment."

"Because I don't have a secret decoder ring?" I asked, my voice dripping with sarcasm.

"Seriously," she said. "Have you ever noticed that we don't get a lot of crime here in Greenfield? It's one of the few places where you can walk in a dark alley without the fear of being accosted by some fruitcake."

She was testing me.

In the twenty minutes since she'd started our conversation, I'd learned that Stella Weinberg loved a good mystery and was open to the possibility that a scientific explanation sometimes offers more questions than answers.

"Yup, it's a safe place to live." I said flatly.

"Do you believe in ghosts, Marshall?" she asked, dead serious.

"Nope."

"I thought I saw a ghost about two years ago, and do you want to know something really weird?"

"What's that?"

"Damndest thing I ever saw. It was the middle of the night, and I was pushing my little shopping cart home from the *Shop Stopper Price-Mart*. You know, they have that midnight madness sale every year."

"Yeah, I always go there to stock up on cat food."

"Well, it's only a few blocks from my house, and it was a mild evening, so I cut across Delaney Park, because I like the swans. Have you ever looked at the swans in the moonlight? They're just beautiful."

"No, I hate birds," I said sourly.

"Right. Well, I felt like taking a breather and just admiring the swans as they paddled about in the moonlight. Anyway, I heard a woman scream, and then a loud crack echoed through the park. I damned near had an accident right there on the bench, because I was alone, and I don't exactly run the hundred-yard dash on a regular basis."

I had a sense of where this was going and thought it would be best to end the discussion.

"Stella, I have to leave. It was nice meeting you," I said, trying not to sound paranoid.

"No wait," she blurted out, putting her hand on my chest. "I got up as quickly as I could and pushed my cart back onto the street, because I was scared to death. Then I caught a glimpse of something out of the corner of my eye."

"What was it?" I asked.

"Just a flash of light for a couple of seconds, but it was long enough for me to clearly make out the shape of a man's body, and *Jesus H. Christ*, but wasn't he shooting into the sky like a rocket!"

I blinked at Stella, and said nothing as I considered how to respond.

It was clear that our meeting wasn't just a chance encounter. She'd come up with a theory about Greenfield's first murder in over ten years, and her statement about seeing a mysterious flying man was a deliberate shot across my bow.

"You should write books, because that's a helluva good story," I chuckled, nervously.

"Funny thing though, Marshall, but the next day I read in the paper that a Sheriff's Deputy found a man handcuffed to park gate, and it turns out that this guy tried to rape a woman in the park that same night," she said, assessing my reaction.

"You were probably frightened to death," I said, downplaying her theory. "People have been known to see things when they're terrified."

"Yeah, that's what I thought too," she said. "But I remember a very distinctive feature about the figure I saw darting into the sky."

"Do tell," I said, still sounding sarcastic.

Stella squeezed my hand and leaned in toward my ear.

"*It had glowing eyes*," she whispered.

CHAPTER 4

Dictionaries define evil as morally wrong, wicked and injurious. I've always been struck by how generic that definition sounds.

Some argue that evil exists because man's first wife suckered him into eating that damned forbidden apple, thereby condemning all of humanity, while others insist that man himself creates evil by his nature. Since I wasn't around to view what happened in the Garden of Eden, I believe that uncovering the reasons why evil occurs is largely irrelevant when someone is pointing a gun at your head.

I'm practical that way.

I'd been thinking a lot about my meeting with Stella Weinberg. Her suggestion that Greenfield was about to experience a killing-spree might have been easier to dismiss if she hadn't shown me that spiral-engraved rock. One rock is a coincidence, but more than twenty? I knew there was a connection, but I just couldn't put my finger on it.

Then there was the issue of why I didn't foresee Stephen Hodges' death. Now *that* was unsettling. Though I have unique abilities, there is a random quality to what I foresee. Sometimes a vision is crystal-clear and plays out like a movie trailer; other times they're just fragmented clues, and I'm forced to assemble them like a jigsaw puzzle.

I imagine you probably want to know how I came to possess what you might call "super powers." Surely a guy who can fly can also figure out who is behind the death of a sixteen-year-old kid or the secret meaning of the collection of spiral-engraved rocks at Stella Weinberg's curiosity shop, right? If only it were that simple.

It might be disappointing for you to learn that I didn't morph into a crime fighter at puberty like the *X-Men*, and I am not the result of a wartime experiment to produce a super soldier like *Captain America*. I don't possess super powers. I *borrow* them.

Kind of.

Consider for a moment that more than six billion people occupy our planet, and every single person who has lived or who is yet to be born owns the ability to do harm or good. If just one percent of the world's population engages in criminal behavior, then at any given moment, sixty million people are regular participants in everything from shoplifting to murder. That's a staggering number when you consider ninety-nine percent of the world's population assumes law enforcement will always be there to protect them.

I don't particularly like cops, and I feel that it's important to remember that, as a rule, they more or less enforce laws most of us willingly abide by. Still, you have to feel for them for two reasons: cops are outnumbered by the bad guys, and when cops actually do prevent a crime from happening, say by conducting a sting, civil libertarians scream "entrapment" until they're blue in the face. It makes you question who the real bad guys are, doesn't it?

Willful intent is a powerful force. It eclipses any good that might exist in human beings, and it flows with energy produced by those whose heart's desire is fulfilled by violence and chaos. It creates impetus with every criminal act and transcends cultural, religious and philosophical norms.

Because evil is a supernatural force, some people have the capacity to harness the energy it creates. They might be psychics who aid police in finding a missing person, or artists who depict the classic struggle of good versus evil in everything from painting to literature. I possess the ability to channel the darkness and shape its properties. My body absorbs energy, particularly when I'm in the actual presence of evil. That's when my eyes will glow with white light. If you still don't get it, I'll dumb it down for you: bad guys are a supernatural battery, and I am the Energizer Bunny.

The first time I harnessed the power of willful intent was at a summer bible camp in 1982. I was raised a Baptist, and Pastor James Gregory took it upon himself to ensure children in his congregation understood that while God might forgive our sins, the only way to obtain absolution was to seek the counsel of the good Pastor in the privacy of his cabin on Lake Chebucto.

I'd recently committed the unpardonable offense of being caught by Stanley Ibsen with a worn out copy of *Penthouse*. He then took it upon himself to rat on me. This was after I refused to trade him the magazine for his Mike Bossy autographed hockey puck. When Pastor Gregory found out about my misdeed, he summoned me to his cabin for a discussion about why I would be going straight to hell and how I might avoid that terrible fate.

It was strange that he insisted on meeting me at 11:00 PM, when everyone at camp was sound asleep, but I assumed that my sin was of such a serious nature that God had a right to mete out punishment at a time of his choosing. As I sat on Pastor Gregory's ugly plaid sofa, I listened attentively as he explained the reasons for temptation and how the Devil was always looking for new ways to corrupt children and youth.

"God wants you to know that lust is a dangerous sin, Marshall," he lectured. "Most children your age can be led astray, and it doesn't help that you don't have a father's strict hand to ensure you remain an obedient servant of God's will."

I nodded silently.

"You should have known better," said the Pastor. "You've been a member of our church community all your life, and I've always expected more from you."

"I-I'm s-sorry, Pastor Gregory," I whimpered. "Trevor Jarvis gave the magazine to me on the last day of school because he didn't have the five dollars he owed me."

"I see, someone else is responsible for a sin that you committed – how lucky you seem to be." Pastor Gregory thrust a thick bible onto my lap. "Read Romans six-twenty-three, though you should have it committed to memory by now." He walked over to the front door of his cabin as I leafed through the thin pages of the New Testament. "What does it say, Marshall," asked the Pastor as he flipped the lock.

"The wages of sin is death," I whispered, as I fought the urge to throw up. "But the gift of God is eternal life through Jesus our Lord."

"That's right, Marshall," he said, as he dimmed the Coleman lantern. "While God offers everlasting life through Jesus, the only way to know that God has forgiven you is for you to remember what you did to God on this day."

I sniffled. "O-Okay."

"That magazine contains pictures of whores, and the people who publish it are agents of the darkness," he said, his voice turned hoarse and hollow. "Their purpose is to deceive boys like you with nakedness and sex."

My head started pounding. The dim light inside the room stabbed at my brain, and my stomach rolled with each wave of nausea. "I'm s-sorry – I don't feel very well right now. May I go back to my cabin?" I asked in a weak voice, as I held my stomach.

"No!" the Pastor growled. "You've brought the Devil to the doorstep of my bible camp. I know the depth of your sin, and so does God. If you're feeling sick, Marshall, then it's God's will. Maybe you're sick because the filth associated with what you've done has stained your heart, and you're troubled because you've been found out!"

The room became blurry, and I ground my fists into my eyes. I felt a bead of sweat roll down my back, and I hoped God would accept my apology, because he was seriously kicking my ass for reading that Penthouse magazine.

"The Lord knows what you're doing, and he wants me to remind you never to sin again," whispered the Pastor, in a voice filled with menace. "Get down on your knees as I pray that God forgives you – take my hand, Marshall."

I slowly dropped to my knees and hesitantly offered my hand to Pastor Gregory.

"Holy father, forgive this sinful child for his filthy misdeed. Let your grace guide him to a path of virtue and teach him to shun all temptation. I ask that you give me the wisdom to teach boys like Marshall about the wages of sin. As I take his hand in mine, I pray that you will show him the blessings of a virtuous life through Christ Jesus. Amen."

His grip tightened around my hand. "Keep your eyes closed, Marshall. What I'm about to do will never leave this room, do you understand?"

"Yes, sir," I said, as tears began rolling down my face.

"God punishes boys who look at pictures of whores in filthy magazines," he hissed. "Do you fantasize about fornicating with whores, Marshall? Is that how you honor God?"

"No, sir," I sniveled.

He pressed my hand against his chest. "You'll know that God has forgiven you after tonight, Marshall, won't you?" The pain of my headache raged like a bottled storm as Pastor Gregory slowly lowered my hand below the cold metal of his belt buckle.

"Please, I need to go now, p-please," I sobbed.

"You'll stay here with me until God has forgiven you, Marshall Conrad," he scolded. "Through me, the holy spirit will purge you of this sin"

Pastor Gregory's groin throbbed against the palm of my hand, and I tried to pull away as he placed his other hand on top of my head, pushing me toward his crotch.

I'd always believed Pastor James Gregory was a person who exuded virtue not only through his words, but also through deeds. He started a fund to help the Johanssons rebuild their home after a fire destroyed all their worldly possessions.

He spearheaded a capital campaign to raise money for a new baseball diamond, which they named in his honor.

Yet there was a hint of mystery surrounding his personal life. Pastor Gregory was a fifty-two-year-old bachelor who lived alone in a bungalow next to our church. He never entertained in his home, and his interaction with the community was only a product of his ministry. His moral authority was absolute, and nobody ever thought to question why he'd never married or why he ran a bible camp exclusively for boys.

Maybe they should have.

As the migraine and cramps wracked my body, images of countless boys summoned to a meeting with Pastor Gregory flooded through my mind. I was awash with his thoughts, and I could hear the Pastor's voice inside my head:

"Punish these children for the shame they've brought to God. Compel them to beg the Lord for forgiveness. God has chosen you to act as a vessel for their redemption; make them feel God's power. Pleasure yourself on their bodies and threaten each boy with hellfire and damnation should they tell a soul. These are filthy children, and you want them – you've always wanted them."

At fourteen years old, I was experiencing my first face-to-face encounter with willful intent. I was a witness to the blackness of Pastor Gregory's soul, and it was a stew of perversion and disease that fueled my body with a frenzy to lash out – to make him experience what he'd done to so many other boys before me.

"God will absolve you, Marhsall," he whispered reassuringly. "It's time to seek his forgiveness." He pushed my hand firmly into his groin.

"Like hell it is!" I spat.

My eyes blazed furiously as the dim cabin exploded into brilliant white light. Pastor Gregory screamed as I crushed his testicles into a paste that saturated his trousers, dripping blood down my left arm and onto the carpet. A torrent of energy surged through my veins, and Pastor Gregory writhed in agony as I raised him over my head.

"*S-Satan…*" he blubbered.

"I'm not *Satan,* you pervert!" I snarled. "You wanted to hurt me like you hurt all those other boys, but not tonight – *not ever again.*"

I was too enraged to realize a supernatural phenomenon was occurring inside Pastor James Gregory's cabin that night. This might sound strange, but I distinctly remember feeling no sense of astonishment by the fact that I was holding a man over my head by one hand. It was as if my metamorphosis was a natural result of Pastor Gregory's willful intent to harm me. I simply *became.*

"Help me, God, h-help!" the Pastor cried sheepishly from above my head as I relaxed my iron grip on his crotch.

"Wall," I said, in a monotone voice.

Pastor Gregory wailed as he jettisoned across the room and crashed into a bookcase. His body bounced like a tennis ball and landed on the floor in a heap. He moaned loudly as an old photo album fell out of the bookcase and landed on his face.

"Book," I said, and the photo album sailed into my hands.

Each page of the photo album contained a single Polaroid of a naked boy with each boy's first name neatly written at the bottom of the page with the year he'd snapped the picture. I nearly threw up on the carpet when I discovered a blank page with my name on it.

My assault on Pastor Gregory made enough noise to awaken the camp counselors, and I spotted beams of light bouncing off the branches of the pine trees surrounding the cabin. I quickly ripped the pages out of the photo album and threw them on top of Pastor Gregory so the counselors would find them when they arrived. It was time to make an exit.

"Door," I whispered. The back door of his cabin flew off the hinges and then crashed into a tree. As I stepped outside, I heard the voices of the counselors approaching, and I uttered the one word that would forever change my life.

"*Fly!*"

My body became weightless as an invisible force pushed against my feet, lifting me off the ground. I closed my eyes, and my skin tingled with electricity as I shot into the sky like a bullet. I pressed my hands tightly against the seams of my trousers as the cool midnight air flowed through my hair and whistled past my ears. I was flying. I was actually flying!

I opened my eyes, and I could see the moon's reflection bouncing off the rippling surface of Lake Chebucto as I slowed my ascent. I should have been terrified by whatever supernatural force was responsible for keeping me in the air, but I was overcome by the magnificence and wonder of what was happening to me.

My muscles throbbed with energy as I gazed over the pine forest stretched out like a carpet in all directions, and I could see the headlights of automobiles on the interstate cutting through the darkness. Moonlight painted the water with silver as a family of loons chattered in the distance. A kingfisher dove into the lake with a loud splash, and I listened to the lonely *whoosh* of the wind gently rolling over the treetops below my feet.

The sky is a breathtaking realm of majestic creatures, whose kings are eagles or condors. I had no business trespassing into their domain, yet there I was. I remember feeling that perhaps this was a sin of far greater magnitude than what had led me to my meeting with Pastor Gregory.

He was no longer a secret – I'd made sure of that.

Pastor Gregory would be arrested, and the scandal would capture the headlines for months as his trial proceeded. I'd probably have to testify in court and recount everything in painful detail. He'd be found guilty and sentenced to spend decades in prison for his crimes.

****

But it didn't work out that way.

The now defrocked minister was in protective custody, because his lawyer argued that he was now hated by the inmates of the Greenfield County Jail and might not live long enough to make it to his trial. It was a pointless exercise. Corrections officers found his lifeless body in a pool of his own blood after he hacked his wrists with a plastic knife.

Nobody bothered to investigate how he smuggled the plastic knife back to his cell. Some were enraged that he'd escaped justice, but not me.

I was embarking on a dangerous journey that would reshape my life. I would come face-to-face with willful intent on many occasions as I explored the murky depths of evil men's souls. There was no Uncle Ben to teach me "with great power comes great responsibility" – but God, how I could fly.

CHAPTER 5

Walter the cat has it all figured out.

His life is a stress-free vacation that includes staring out the bedroom window and squawking loudly at birds that land on the windowsill, taking naps in selected locations throughout my apartment and unraveling freshly installed rolls of toilet paper all over the bathroom floor. How he came to live with me is a story I'm sure he wouldn't care for me to share with anyone, because the fact that I bought him for ten dollars at a garage sale might lead you to believe he is a fraud.

It is wrong for anyone to say they own a cat. How can you own something that has the ability to make you do what it wants? I can't say he is a companion because that word implies he lives with me in the capacity of a helpful friend. Walter isn't helpful at all – he helps himself.

I've known many cats in my life, and he is the only one with the ability to open a refrigerator with the goal of seating himself on the bottom shelf and consuming a stick of butter. He enjoys the sound of elbow macaroni falling on the kitchen floor at 3:00 AM, and I've recently installed a set of childproof locks on the cupboard doors so I can get some sleep. He is the feline equivalent of an irresponsible roommate, and his body resembles a stuffed turkey. He refuses to play with his collection of cat toys, and the only time I have ever seen him run is when he races into the kitchen after hearing the hum of my electric can opener. I've received numerous rebukes from the veterinarian about Walter's ballooning girth, so I now suffer the nightly embarrassment of walking my cat around the perimeter of my apartment building in a harness as part of an exercise regime.

I know – what kind of crime fighter complains about his cat? I do seriously need to get a life.

I was in a sour mood as I dragged Walter along the sidewalk outside my apartment. I'd just finished reading a special edition of *The Greenfield Examiner* that featured a full-page spread about the death of Stephen Hodges, and I needed to get some fresh air. The headline proclaimed, "Body Found Lashed to Tree," confirming Stella Weinberg's theory that Stephen Hodges had been murdered, and authorities were refusing to comment on reports from members of the search team that the body was missing its internal organs.

Obviously, a disemboweled body meant this was much more than a random killing. The murderer must have targeted him for some reason, and he would have put a great deal of thought into his method of killing, so why hadn't I foreseen it? I'd glimpsed into many other murders waiting to happen over the past ten years, all of which I'd successfully prevented, and none of them were as graphic or as violent as what had happened to Stephen Hodges.

As we crossed the street and headed back to back to my building, I heard a familiar voice overhead.

"Smile and say cheese!" the voice shouted. I looked up to see Marnie Brindle aiming her cellphone at me.

"Listen, I don't want my picture taken, okay?" I shouted back.

"I like your cat's pink harness," she teased.

"Don't you have anything better to do than snapping pictures of me with your cellphone?"

"Nnnnnnnope."

"Yeah, well stop it. I don't like having my picture taken."

"Jeez, chill out. Hey, I'm coming downstairs – be right there," she said and then disappeared into her apartment.

Lovely.

I was less than thrilled that Marnie Brindle was inviting herself over. I've lived alone all my adult life and the prospect of entertaining guests makes me uneasy, as it implies that some kind of relationship exists between the guest and me. It leads to more visits in the future and statements like, "You should consider getting new drapes for your place – it would brighten everything up." As I opened the sliding door to my living room, I made a mental note to give Marnie Brindle a reality check about bad manners.

"Helloooo, Mister Conraaaad! It's me, Marnie!" Her voice sang out loudly as she knocked on the door, making me pause to consider whether I should actually let her in.

"What?" I grumbled, as I removed Walter's harness and watched him tear into my bedroom.

"Let me in, so we can hang out and listen to your David Cassidy records!" she teased.

"I don't have any David Cassidy records," I groaned.

"That was a joke. Are you going to let me in or not?"

"Fine!" I snapped as I opened the door. "You shouldn't invite yourself over to a stranger's apartment. I could be a freak, for all you know."

"Oooh, scary," said Marnie, making a spooky gesture with her hands. "Well, if you're freaky, then it was worth the trip downstairs, wasn't it?"

"That's not what I meant. Listen, I don't know you from Adam, and I've got a ton of things to do," I grumbled.

"Sure you know me. You've sampled my cooking and survived; that has to account for something," she said as she took off her sandals.

I gave her a disapproving frown. "I'm serious. Haven't you read the newspaper? That kid who went missing in Crossfield was murdered."

"Yes, I heard about it," she said. "I don't think whoever is responsible for what happened to that kid would be warning me that he might be a killer. Are you going to give me the grand tour or what?"

I rolled my eyes. She obviously wasn't taking the hint.

"You're in the front hallway, the kitchen is beside you, and I watch television over there," I sighed, pointing toward my sofa. "It's the same layout as your apartment."

"*You shop at Ikea!*" she chimed, as she strode into my living room and plopped herself on my couch. "I never took you for someone who prefers trendy furniture. Hey, where's Walter?"

"Probably traumatized and hiding in the closet," I snipped, as I sat down on my old vinyl easy chair. "We don't usually have visitors come over, and he's sometimes skittish."

"No visitors, huh? What up with that?"

"Nothing. I just don't have many friends," I said.

"How come?"

"Because I enjoy my own company."

"How come?"

"Because I am a cranky old fart who hates small talk and nosy neighbors."

"I see. Hey, where's your remote?" she asked, ignoring my comment.

"I don't have a remote control for the TV. It broke a couple of years ago, and since my television is only five feet away, I just get up and change the channel," I said.

"What are you, some kind of ludist?" she asked, as she rifled through the pile of clutter on my coffee table.

"The word you are looking for is luddite," I said. "I'm pretty sure they don't own televisions."

"Gotcha. Hey, are you pissed off at me for coming over, because I can go if I'm bugging you," she said, half-smiling. "I just thought it would be cool to hang out for a while, or at least for the next couple of hours."

"Why for the next couple of hours?" I asked with some suspicion.

"Oh, it's nothing I should bother you with," she said, looking nervously through the sliding door at the street. "Hey, I'll go okay?"

"What are you staring at?" I grumbled.

"Nothing."

"I might have long conversations with an overweight cat, Ms. Brindle, but I'm *not* an idiot. Five minutes ago, you were all smiles and chuckles, and now you're staring out my living room window like you're keeping an eye on something. What gives?"

She turned toward me with a look of genuine fear on her face. "I think I have a stalker, that's all."

"Well, you should be reporting it to the police instead of hiding out in my apartment," I lectured impatiently. "What's stopping you from calling them?"

"What's stopping me is that I don't know who it is. I just know I'm being stalked," she said, still glancing over her shoulder and out the window.

"In what way?"

"Just a bunch of dumb emails from a webmail address. You can't trace those, can you?"

"Probably not," I said, realizing something had spooked her. "When you say 'a bunch of dumb emails,' how many are we talking about?"

"Eight," she said as she fidgeted with my broken remote control. "They were sent to my personal email address, and that's what's bugging me, I guess."

This was serious.

Her cheerful manner disappeared, and I immediately felt like a heel for giving her a lecture about visiting strange men's apartments. It was clear she had received a threat of some kind immediately before she started taking pictures of me on her balcony.

"I know you don't really like me, Mr. Conrad," she admitted, her voice barely a whisper. "It's probably kind of weird that I'm sitting here on your couch complaining about a stalker."

"You don't have to call me 'Mr. Conrad,'" I said, sounding sympathetic. "I don't dislike you either. It's just that I live alone, and I don't exactly have many attractive twenty-something, female friends who hang out at my apartment on a regular basis."

She shrugged her shoulders. "Yeah, that's me – *attractive.*"

I kept my mouth shut, because I didn't know how to respond to that statement. There was an awkward silence for about a minute, and then she began to speak.

"You know, I'm not a bimbo," she huffed. "I know that most men think I'm hot, and nearly every guy I meet stares at my boobs instead of looking me in the eye when we have a conversation. I get hit on all the time, even by middle-aged men like you."

"I see."

"I moved to Greenfield to get away from all of that stuff, you know? I mean in Boston, it's practically a way of life," she said with a hint of resignation in her voice. "I figured a smaller place would be easier, I guess."

"Assholes are not exclusive to large cities," I said, trying to sound conciliatory. "Your family lives in Boston? Is that why you wanted to come over to my place?"

"Yes. That and I don't know which of my so-called 'friends' is stalking me," she said. "Hey, you know something?"

"What?"

"You did a nice thing for me the day you delivered my magazine. You could have just left it on top of my mailbox. That's what most people would have done."

"You're welcome," I said.

"You didn't stare at my boobs, either," she joked.

"That would be impolite."

Marnie tried to smile. "I don't take you for someone who worries about what people think of him."

"What makes you say that?"

"Well, from what I've observed, you don't enjoy the company of others."

"Ohhh, from what you've *observed*. Great, now *I* have a stalker."

She frowned. "That's not funny, Marshall, but your comment proves my point."

She was right. I had just put both feet in my mouth – right up to the ankles. "Listen, I'm not good with people," I apologized. "Anyway, the main issue here is finding out what makes you think you've got a stalker."

Marnie sat up and looked around my living room. "Do you have a computer with an internet connection?" she asked.

"In the spare bedroom – follow me."

"Oooh, you're leading me to your bedroom," she teased.

"Shut up," I groaned, as I padded up the hall. "You've got a stalker, remember?"

"If you haven't already noticed, I disguise my fears by the careful use of bad humor." She sat down at my computer and logged into her web-mail account. "I assumed you would have figured that out by now."

"You'll forgive me if I haven't decoded your idiosyncrasies," I said, as I watched the web page load on the screen.

This was the real deal.

She'd received eight consecutive emails over a two week period, each one said "*How do you solve a problem like Marnie?*" in the subject block.

"What are the attachments?" I asked.

"Pictures of me," she said as she clicked on the first email. "This was taken at the bar."

I examined the photo and noticed the date on the bottom right corner matched with the date the email was sent. "Scroll up," I said.

"You see, this is why I'm reluctant to talk to my friends. Everyone I know was at the bar, so it could have been any one of them." Her right hand was shaking as she gripped the mouse. "I'm totally creeped out by the fact the emails are just snapshots. The guy could have been drinking with me one minute and snapping pictures of me the next."

"You look drunk," I said. "You probably wouldn't remember who took it in the first place."

She clicked on the second email, and the picture showed Marnie filling up her Honda Civic at the gas station. "This one must have been taken from inside a car. I can see the window frame."

I nodded. "Yeah, I see that. Listen, I want you to save them to my hard drive so I can have a closer look at them later. Meanwhile, you need to think hard about your interactions with men over the last little while."

"Why?"

"Because stalkers are usually guys who've been rejected by the object of their affection," I said. "You're a very attractive young woman, and it's possible that your stalker is a fella with a broken heart who wants a little payback."

She spun around in my chair. "Great, so it's my fault?" she snapped. "Do you know how many guys I've rejected in the last month? The last six months?"

"Beats me," I said, reminding myself that I hadn't been on a date in more than a decade. "Look, nobody is saying this is your fault. The reality is that we don't know who is stalking you, and you should probably take some steps to protect yourself."

Marnie looked at me pleadingly, her face a mask of fear mixed with confusion. "What kind of steps?"

I clicked off the screen and spun her around in my chair so she was facing me. I didn't want to overstate the likelihood that her stalker was the real deal, and I didn't want her to feel that I was being dismissive of her situation. I dropped to one knee and gave her an empathetic smile.

I reached into my desk drawer and pulled out a key to my apartment along with a small pad of sticky notes. I scribbled out my phone number and handed her the note along with the key. "Here's my number and a key to my place. I want you to program it into your cellphone and your house phone. You can call me anytime."

"Thanks," she said as she began programming my number into her cellphone. "What are you going to do with the pictures I saved on your hard drive, stick them in a Bat-Computer and find the bad guy?"

I tried not to laugh at the irony of her last statement. "I'm going to look at the pictures and see if there's anything you might have missed. It might surprise you to learn that I have a law enforcement background, Marnie."

"Ohhh… you're a cop? I never did ask you what you do for a living."

"Kind of," I said reassuringly.

CHAPTER 6

He planned to use a rigger's knife because it felt like an extension of his hand, and the richly polished steel blade would reflect the woman's eyes when he revealed it to her. He fantasized about the precise moment when the tip of the blade would press against her flesh. A tiny drop of blood would form; her thumping pulse would pound against his palm as she pleaded for her life. She would do anything he demanded at that precise moment. Anything.

For two weeks he'd been obsessing about what he intended to do. Each time he saw her in the office, he'd strike up a friendly conversation, despite her constant criticism of the way he'd been managing his client file. This wasn't a vendetta, he kept reminding himself. She'd always made him feel like less of a man since the day she was promoted into the position he'd coveted for so many years, and he was simply going to remind her that she was vulnerable.

He'd lie in bed and stare at the ceiling, his wife sound asleep beside him. He planned to take what was rightfully his. The woman would disappear for a while, that's all. Killing her was pointless, and besides, if she were alive he could force her to submit to various humiliating acts, for she was a vain woman who valued power more than anything else.

He would take her power away.

He would leave his mark on her body, so she would always remember this day.

She would learn her place.

He'd taken all the necessary precautions because he was a stickler for the smallest detail. He would shower an hour and a half before leaving the house. He'd use a different shampoo, one that she wouldn't recognize because he'd been using the same brand for years. She had always commented that he should get out of the eighties and start using something other than a drugstore two-in-one because it was old school – much like his ideas for managing the company's clients. She was going to regret ever making that remark; he'd make sure of that.

He knew she would be working well into the night, and she'd use the parking lot behind the office because she was too cheap to pay the monthly fee for the secure lot across the street. She would park as close as possible to the back door of the building for safety reasons, and he'd even timed her to find out how long it would take her to start her Rav4. Because it had tinted windows, she would never know he was inside.

He would keep her at knifepoint until they reached the logging road he'd found outside town. It offered excellent concealment, and nobody would hear her scream. He wanted to take his time – she deserved that much. When he was through, he would bind her hands with plastic zip ties he'd bought at the hardware store; they were cheaper than handcuffs, and she wasn't worth the extra expense.

He wouldn't gag her, but he would take her car keys, so that when she eventually escaped, she would have to walk for a mile and a half to the highway for help. The SUV he'd rented was hidden in a ditch next to the logging road, and it was a short five-minute walk from where he'd leave her. He reckoned it would take her at least half a day until someone found her, more than enough time to return the SUV and head back home. His wife wouldn't ask any questions; she would assume he was out of town on business.

It seemed like the perfect plan.

The migraine hit me at 9:30 PM. I was examining the pictures from Marnie Brindle's stalker. It wasn't exactly all that great, because while she was nice to look at, she made me feel old. Then again, she *did* smell good.

So sue me – I'm a dirty old man.

Of course, she *was* scared to death, and now that the police were looking into one murder, I didn't want my upstairs neighbor to become victim number two. Whoever had taken those pictures knew where Marnie lived – the last one showed her on the balcony of her apartment, talking on her cellphone. Since she didn't have any family in town, I felt there was no other alternative than to make my place available until I figured out the identity of the stalker. He would never know she was in my apartment because I usually keep the blinds drawn, and I'd warned her about going near the windows. She would be safe, for now.

I don't wear a costume when I'm taking out the bad guy. My outfit is a black leather jacket, leather pants and motorcycle boots. I don't wear a mask, either. They're tacky. Instead, I pull the hood from my sweatshirt over my head when my eyes start glowing. You're no doubt expecting that I probably take the stairs to the roof of my apartment building and fly to the scene of a crime waiting to happen. If only it were that easy. Unlike your favorite comic book hero, I can't fly to the scene of a crime, because the Energizer Bunny is still sleeping. He usually wakes up when a perpetrator is about to make his move. That's when I can draw on his willful intent and charge my body. I know – that's not terribly glamorous, right? Well, it gets better.

Willful intent acts like a compass, and I am instinctively drawn to the location of a crime waiting to happen, so I will usually drive my Tempo to a secluded spot nearby. I park in a place that offers good cover, and I'll head to the rooftops so I can silently drop down on the perpetrator. The force of gravity on my two-hundred-pound frame usually knocks the guy unconscious, and if everything works out, I'll take away his weapon, cuff him to whatever is convenient, and that's that.

After I've put down a criminal, I might spend the next few hours flying around the city. I can usually prevent a few crimes while I'm at it, but eventually the bunny likes to go back to bed, and he usually won't tell me when he's about to retire for the evening. The downside of this is that I've been known to fall out of the sky into a garbage bin or crash land in a tree more than once. Adding further insult to injury, I'll be forced to take a bus or a cab back to my parked car. Take that, Bruce Wayne – this crime fighter uses public transit!

And the perpetrators?

More often than not, they're discovered by someone a few hours later, and a sheriff's deputy is sent to unlock the handcuffs. Naturally, the police are skeptical about anyone claiming they were attacked by a man in a hood with glowing eyes, so the perpetrator usually winds up getting a psychological assessment. (A part of me muses about just how many more criminals will report being attacked by a guy with glowing eyes before the cops start believing them. You'd think they'd be onto me by now.)

This particular bad guy was cursing to himself as I crouched behind a ventilation shaft approximately two stories above the Rav4. It was clear that he was an amateur as he tried to break into the car with a coat hanger. I heard a loud metallic *snap,* and I half-expected a car alarm to go off, but that didn't happen.

"*Sonofabitch, sonofabitch…*" he whispered as he struggled to slide the hanger in through a slit in the window. I could see the rigger's knife in a black leather sheath attached to his belt, and the red plastic ties stuffed into his back pocket. He wasn't a big man, but he looked sturdy enough – not that it would matter much. I've brought down criminals of every shape and size over the years, so this guy wouldn't be a problem. Normally I would have dropped right on top of him, but I didn't want to damage the roof of the car, so I decided to distract him when I made my move.

I'm a nice guy, that way.

Through the ventilator shaft, I could hear a woman humming a few bars of some top-forty tune, and it echoed through the hallway of the building. Probably his victim leaving her office, but I couldn't be certain. The perpetrator was getting angrier by the second as he fought with the door. I felt the now familiar surge of energy shooting through my veins. There was a loud *click* as the perpetrator's coat hanger finally unlocked the door. The burning sensation in my eyes reminded me to pull the hood over my head. It was time.

"*Hey asshole!*" I shouted, as I threw my legs over the edge of the building and pushed my body off the roof.

"What the…" He choked, as he looked up just in time to see my glowing eyes slice through the darkness of the parking lot. He instinctively vaulted back against the wall of the building as I landed with a hollow thud between the perpetrator and the car.

"*W-Who the hell are y-you?*" he stammered, as he reached for the knife. I slowly raised myself up and cocked my head in amusement as the light from my eyes bounced off the shining steel blade of his knife.

"A little scared, are we?" I whispered, trying to sound as menacing as possible for a bored crimefighter. "Things not working out according to plan?"

In a flash, he lunged at me with the knife and I stepped aside as the blade bounced off the glass of her car, accidentally stabbing the man in the right forearm. He screeched like a cat whose tail was on the wrong side of Grandma's rocking chair as he pulled out the knife and adopted a defensive stance.

"How did you know?" he growled, jabbing the knife toward me.

I gave him an impatient look and folded my arms across my chest.

"This is getting boring," I said, as I spun on my left heel and delivered a roundhouse kick to his face. His head snapped sharply to the left like it was on a hinge, and he dropped like a stone at my feet. I kicked the knife against the back tire of the Rav4 as I grabbed his bleeding right forearm and squeezed.

"Betcha that hurts. You should get that looked at," I said, sarcastically, as I dragged him over to the back door of the building and handcuffed him to the door handle. I could hear the woman's footsteps as she approached the door.

"Who are you?" he whimpered in a defeated voice.

"The guy who kicked your teeth in," I grumbled, as I walked over to pick up the knife and put it on the roof of her car. "Thanks for ruining my night, moron. I missed *Dancing with the Stars* because of you."

My heart froze when I saw the spiral-engraved rock on the ground beside the knife.

CHAPTER 7

The Curiosity Nook is best described as a mausoleum for oddities.

A life-sized Boris Yeltsin cut-out in the window waves hello to prospective customers entering her store, and the first thing you see when you walk in is a magnetic sign in the foyer that reads *If you don't have an open mind, then don't open your wallet*. Once you pass through the foyer, you're greeted by a glamour portrait of Stella that looks like it was done in paint-by-number. The words *Stella Weinberg, Proprietress* are engraved into a brass plate mounted in the bottom of the painting's gilded frame.

"I see that you've been immortalized on canvas there, Stella," I said, with a hint of sauciness in my voice. "How much?"

Stella was organizing the collection of spiral rocks in a display case and hadn't seen me come in. "It's not for sale, Conrad. You can't afford me," she said, as she slid the door closed. "Did you bring it?"

"Sure did."

"Well, let's have a look at it."

I walked over to the display case and handed the rock to Stella. "I found this last night – it has the same spiral marking as the others."

Stella examined the engraving with a magnifying glass. "Where did you find it again?" she asked.

"Oh, some parking lot downtown," I said vaguely.

Stella pulled a china marker out of a cup filled with pens and pencils and wrote "24" on the bottom of the rock, then put it down on top of the display case. She gave me a suspicious look as she took her bifocals off and cleaned them with a small silk cloth. "Parking lot, huh?" she asked, with a deliberate dose of skepticism.

"Yep."

Stella frowned. "All right then, a parking lot it is. Have a look around the store; I'll be right back."

As she disappeared into the backroom, I wandered over to a ten-foot-high bookcase decorated with NASCAR stickers. Each shelf was overflowing with everything from phallic statues to Coca-Cola memorabilia, and I couldn't make up my mind if Stella's curiosity shop was spooky or downright tacky. The walls were plastered with antique photographs in hardwood frames, and the ceiling was a mosaic of 1950s-era travel posters advertising affordable trips to Rio in a comfortable DC-3. I noticed an eerie green glow coming from the radio dial on the ancient Philco that was playing a comedy skit from *The Jack Carson Radio Show*, and I did a double-take when I saw that it wasn't plugged into the wall.

"Nice," I muttered.

"Ya like that?" said Stella from behind her counter. "Genuine haunted radio – it gets them every time."

I peered behind the Philco to find its power source, only to find a brass plate screwed into the floor with the words *made you look* engraved in three-inch font.

"You have a strange sense of humor," I said, dryly.

"That I do," Stella laughed. "So here's the thing, Marshall. I'd like to know if you found that rock in the same parking lot where the cops found a guy handcuffed to a door this morning." She tossed a copy of *The Greenfield Examiner* on top of the counter.

I looked at the front page of the paper. The headline read *Man Charged with Attempted Abduction*, and there was a paragraph-long snippet saying it was the twelfth person found handcuffed by police this year.

"Not sure what you're getting at, Stella."

Stella gave me a stern look and then dropped a large leather scrapbook on top of the newspaper. "Not sure, huh? Have a look inside – maybe it will jog your memory."

I opened the scrapbook to see headlines and articles from *The Greenfield Examiner* dating back to 1995. The first one read *Missing Child Found: Mother Charged*, followed by another story about a teacher who was found mysteriously handcuffed to a dumpster and subsequently charged with attempted rape of a seventeen-year-old student.

"It looks like the Greenfield Sheriff's Department has been doing its job for the past decade," I said, as I flipped through the pages. "How much for the book?"

Stella snatched the scrapbook from the top of the counter. "It's not for sale. Why would you want to buy it from me?"

I gave her a sour look.

"We're not going to talk about those rocks, are we?" I said.

"Eventually. Right now I'm far more interested in where you were last night."

"And?"

"And I'm curious to learn if you know anything about our resident vigilante."

I leaned against the top of the display case and gestured for Stella to come closer. "Shh. I'm an undercover cop," I said, in cryptic tone. "I've spent the last ten years handcuffing bad guys to inanimate objects as a means of positively influencing the public's opinion of the Greenfield Sheriff's Department."

Stella looked unimpressed. "Want to know something?"

"What's that?"

"If you had a secret, it would be safe with me," she whispered. "I'm the most open-minded person you'll ever meet in your life, and I might know some people who could help you find the person who killed Stephen Hodges."

I sighed heavily. "What are you getting at, Stella?"

"I'm suggesting that those headlines in my scrapbook point to something much more interesting than a crazy vigilante," she said. "I make it my business to keep track of anything that can't be explained by conventional means, and I have access to resources that most people would scoff at."

"You're not one of those wacky people who submit bizarre stories to *The Weekly World News*, are you, Stella?" I asked, sarcastically. "You know, 'Werewolf Baby Born in Taxicab' and all of that?"

Stella rolled her eyes. "All right, Marshall, go lock the door and then sit down over there," she said, pointing at a leather lounging chair next to the bookcase. "I have something I want to show you."

Stella once again disappeared into the back of her store as I walked over to the front door and flipped the lock. I was becoming increasingly concerned by her insistence that I had something to do with Greenfield's low crime rate, and it was clear she knew more about me than I liked.

"What's the strangest thing you've ever seen or heard in your life, Marshall?" she shouted from the backroom. "This is important!"

"Why?" I called back.

"Because I don't want you to have a heart attack in my store. It's bad for business!"

I stretched back in the lounging chair and thought of a decent enough lie that Stella would believe.

"I don't know... How about that old Todd Browning movie from the thirties about side-show freaks? That was pretty weird," I said, as Stella returned and heaved a reel-to-reel tape recorder onto the front counter.

"Oh yeah, that's a good one," she said. "I've got three copies of that movie if you want to buy it."

"Thanks, but I'll pass. What's with that old relic?"

"A strange recording I made the other night," said Stella as she fiddled with the volume knob. "You ready?"

"Sure, where's the popcorn?"

"Just shut up and listen," she said, as she hit the play button.

There was a strange hissing as the magnetic tape ran through the heads on the old machine. I could hear the hum of the building's ventilation system and a faint crackle like sparks exploding above a camp fire.

"It sounds like the inside of your store," I said.

"Shh... just listen," she ordered.

The thumping became louder and then took on the familiar sound of hard soled shoes walking on a cement floor. The hissing abruptly ended and then I heard a masculine voice that sounded like it was talking through a hollow tube speaking in what might have been King James English:

"*Thou art immune to their hate, bring forth thy malice. Thou shalt not accept thine guilt. Thy words and thoughts are no bane to thy deeds.*"

She pressed the stop button. "What do ya make of that?" she asked.

I shrugged my shoulders and walked over to the counter. "I don't know, are you in the habit of speaking in a medieval tongue?" I asked. "Where did you record it?"

"Here," she said, eyeballing me. "I fell asleep at my desk, and I heard that voice coming from inside the store, and I was terrified to come out. I mean, how many people talk like that, right?"

"Yeah."

"Well, I didn't want anyone to know I was here, so I just hit the record button."

"Someone broke in? Jeez, Stella, you should have called the cops!"

She rolled her eyes again. "You're not getting it, Marshall – it was after 11:00 PM, and the doors were locked. I was alone."

I gave her a confused look. "So what are you saying – your store is haunted?"

She shrugged. "If only that were the case … well, there isn't much use in continuing to play cat and mouse. You might want to sit down for what I'm about to reveal."

"Fine," I said, as I slumped back down in the leather chair.

She circled the armchair and then stooped over and drew a white circle with a stick of chalk around my feet.

"I've received some information you're going to have some difficulty absorbing," Stella said in a cryptic voice. "Please try to understand that my source of information told me you'd be at the news conference."

"What the *hell* are you talking about, Stella?" I asked, nervously. "You are seriously freaking me out, here."

"Take it easy Marshall," she said, motioning for me to calm down. "I know this is going to sound like you've been set up, but that's simply not the case. There's a reason why I grilled you at that news conference, so don't blow a gasket, all right? I've been following your exploits ever since you went to Pastor Gregory's bible camp."

My blood immediately ran cold.

Nobody outside of the sheriff's office could have known what happened that night when I was fourteen. It was impossible.

"Look, I have to get going – this is just too weird for me," I said, as I got up from the chair.

"*Sit down!*" Her voice boomed through the store, causing the walls to shake. Something shoved me back into the leather chair, and I struggled to get back to my feet. "*I am not your enemy, and you're not the only person in the world with unique abilities!*"

Whatever force pushed me into the chair clamped down tightly across my lap, and my feet immediately felt as if they were immersed in ice. She chanted in a strange form of Latin as she held her hands in front of her chest, her eyes fixed in concentration on my body.

"I'm on your side, Marshall," Stella urged. "Now please, stop struggling and listen to me – I'm trying to help you."

My eyes weren't glowing, and I didn't sense any willful or malicious intent. I dug my hands into the arms of the chair and pushed with all my might, to no avail. Stella invoked a power I'd never before encountered, and she wasn't about to release me until she had a chance to say her piece.

"H-How did you know?" I asked, weakly.

"My familiar told me. Are you going to calm down?" she asked. "We'd both like to offer some explanations, but you've got to have an open mind."

"*Familiar?* What the hell are you talking about?"

She heaved a sigh. "Tsk. I thought you would be more receptive to an alternate view of the world, being that you're a superhero and all."

"I'm not a superhero! I'm a crime-fighter," I snapped. "Tell me right-bloody-now if anyone else knows about me."

She walked over to the chair and put a reassuring hand on my shoulder. "Your secret is safe with me. However, you've developed quite a reputation among the elders."

"*Elders?*" I groaned, in frustration. "*Familiars?* What, are you some kind of a – "

"A witch," Stella cut me off. "Storch, come out here and introduce yourself."

My jaw dropped when Walter jumped up onto the counter. Stupid cat.

CHAPTER 8

"Come now, Marshall, what did you expect?" Stella asked. "You paid ten dollars for a seal-point Siamese cat at a garage sale, for crying out loud."

I was still in shock as I sat in the leather lounging chair staring at Walter. It was my cat, all right, from the large cream-colored paunch that hung down over his rear feet to the small hook in his long black tail. He tilted his head and purred loudly while Stella scratched behind his ears.

"I know this probably comes as a bit of a surprise," she continued. "What are you having problems with... the fact that I'm a witch, or the realization that your cat actually works for a living?"

I opened my mouth to say something and all I could manage was a monotone "uhhhh" as I shook my head in disbelief.

She smiled warmly. "Are you still with us?"

"Context, please." I said, quietly. "I'm not used to stepping through the looking glass, okay?"

"Sure. Walter's real name is *Storch,* and he's been my familiar since he was a kitten. His coming to live with you was a setup, I'll admit that, but it was done with the best of intentions."

"*A setup?*" I groaned. "Listen, I came here today so we could share notes on a bunch of stupid rocks – now you're telling me that you're a witch and my goddamned cat is a spy!"

Walter jumped onto my lap and started rubbing his head against my chest.

"Stop being so melodramatic," she chided. "There's an entire world you haven't been introduced to yet, and it's a hell of a lot more dangerous than kicking the crap out of bad guys in suburban Greenfield."

"Ya think?"

Stella emitted a frustrated sounding grumble. "Look, I know this is a lot to take in, and I will be happy to answer all of your questions, but something is about to happen in this town and it is going to make your experiences with common criminals seem like babysitting by comparison."

She was dead serious.

Ever since I discovered my powers, the question of whether there were other people who might possess similar abilities hadn't really been a priority for me. It seemed logical that other crime fighters might exist, but I never felt compelled to seek them out. I'd never considered the possibility that witchcraft could be anything more than a bunch of menopausal tree-huggers who sell *Party-Lite* Candles or worship unpronounceable goddesses during the harvest, so the fact that Stella Weinberg had just overpowered me with nothing more than a blurry gesture shocked me to the core.

"You're a *Wiccan*?" I asked, as I got up out of the leather chair and put Walter back on the counter.

"*Puh-leaze*. Don't be insulting," she said, in a contemptuous tone. "Wiccans are nothing more than urban wannabes who seek enlightenment to their empty lives by listening to bad folk music and collecting unicorn figurines. They know nothing of pure witchcraft, because in order to become a witch, you must first spend a large part of your life as an apprentice."

"What do you mean?"

"The word *witch* is a designation within my order that is given to an apprentice who has mastered the many thousands of spells and incantations in our archive. The word *craft* implies years of rigorous training and devotion to what is, in fact, the only ancient art left in existence."

"Okay then, what is a witch supposed to be?" I asked, shaking my head.

"Wicca is a path to spiritual empowerment, according to those who associate themselves with that brand of paganism, but they aren't witches," she said. "There are three kinds of witches, and Wiccans aren't among them."

"And those would be?"

"A *Vigil Witch* protects the world from dark magic, and an *Empath Witch* focuses on maintaining order among the elements. I'm a *Sentry Witch* – I maintain the delicate balance between the near and unseen worlds. Mortals like you and me live in the near world, whereas creatures of myth and legend dwell in the unseen world."

"The *unseen world*? Oh jeez…"

She motioned for me to follow her into the back of her store. "By rights, you should have been seconded the moment you discovered your abilities," she said as I followed her through the beaded curtain down a dark hallway. Walter raced past both of us and jumped onto a pile of boxes in the storeroom.

"I don't think I've ever seen that damned cat move so fast in my life," I said.

Stella laughed. "Ha! Don't let Storch's girth confuse you, he's very nimble. Has to be."

"What exactly did you mean by seconded?"

"Pour yourself a cup of coffee, and I will explain," she said, pointing to a small dinette in the corner of her store room.

I tentatively sat down at one end of the table and noticed she had laid out two place settings, as if she'd been expecting company. I reached for the antique percolator and had poured a cup of coffee when I noticed a large leather-bound book entitled *Who's-Who in Thaumaturgy*.

"Thaumaturgy?" I muttered, as I began leafing through the pages, only to find that the entire book was blank.

"You have to be a witch if you want to read what's inside." She sat down beside me. "Security feature."

"Lovely… What the hell is thaumaturgy?" I asked.

"It means 'the working of magic or feats,'" she said, as she ran her index finger over the book's spine. "Okay, now you can have a peek. I'm on page four-hundred-and-sixty-eight."

Amazingly, the entire volume that had been devoid of words less than a minute ago was now filled with handwritten entries in red ink. I quickly thumbed through the book until I found the page that had a woodcut print of Stella's face and the following information:

Castalia Shorent (Stella Weinberg) - Aspecticus Ecclectic Emeritus, 1965

Obligitary and Archivist with specialization in:

Herbology, Wind Whispering, Spirit Summoning, Exorcism, Pure Magick, Observances.

Castalia Shorent distinguished herself during the Troll Ebullition of 1977 after successfully containing eight aberrant tykes and fourteen river trolls from transitioning the near world in violation of the Wellburn Pact of 1233.

Known for her deft application of ancient incantations and vigilant pursuit of rogue spirits, Castalia is third elder of the Lupin Coven in Greenfields on the Pines.

Familiar: Storch of the Maples - 1975

I slowly raised my head only to see a beaming Stella Weinberg, calmly sipping on a steaming mug of coffee. "Pretty cool, eh?" she said.

"Walter is *thirty-six* years old?" I asked in amazement. "Troll ebullition? Wind-whispering? This is nuts!"

She continued smiling. "Oh yeah, trolls are jerks. You can't reason with them at all."

"I need a drink," I groaned.

Stella shook her head and gave me a look that told me she was losing patience, which is kind of surprising, since her revelations of trolls and an unseen world were the kinds of things that get you a lifetime prescription for happy pills.

"Try to keep an open mind, won't you? The unseen world is real, and witches are responsible for ensuring that it remains unseen," she huffed.

"And it should have stayed that way when it comes to yours truly, Stella," I grumbled.

She ignored my comment and continued. "Remember that whole line about not suffering a witch to live? There was a time when we were hunted and burned at the stake – it was also a time when most historians will tell you that legends about vampires, werewolves and faeries were plentiful. Ironic, isn't it?"

"What do you mean?"

"The persecution of witches was a fact of life from the dark ages right through the Renaissance. That's when human beings were overly superstitious, and folklore about faeries, trolls, monsters and general mayhem became common, because witches were too busy hiding from torch-carrying peasants to police the unseen world and guard the near world," she explained. "Those legends are not legends at all – they're established fact."

I gulped my coffee down, ignoring that it burned the roof of my mouth. "You said I should have been seconded – what did you mean by that?"

"Ahh. Good question," she said. "You should have been paired with suitable mentor so you could master your abilities and then use them within The Guild."

"*The Guild?*"

"Yes, it's an ad-hoc body that oversees those few people in the near world who possess meta-physical powers. From what I know of your powers, I would say you're probably a Vanguard."

"Vanguard, huh? Sounds like a brand of luggage."

She rubbed her chin. "You're completely in the dark, aren't you? Your meta-physical qualities were not the result of a long apprenticeship where you learned a trade like witchcraft. You were born with a range of powers, and that makes you unique, even among skilled journeymen like me. Remember when I contained you back there on the leather chair in the store?"

"Yeah?"

"Well, that shouldn't have happened. Your powers are of such magnitude that you could squash me like a bug. You haven't explored the depth of your abilities. Had you been seconded, you would have been paired with another Vanguard, and we wouldn't be having this conversation."

"You mean that I haven't tapped into all of my abilities?" I asked.

"Ha! Not even close," she laughed. "Most meta-physical archetypes own one specific talent. People with super-strength are classified as *Chieftains*. Individuals who can fly or who possess super speed are *Ushers,* and psychics are called *Pathfinders*. Vanguards are unique because they control multiple sets of powers, and from what I can tell, you're probably only using about one third of your potential."

"Jeez," I whispered. "What about my glowing eyes?"

"They're a beacon," said Stella. "Vanguards are fueled by the existence of evil, and their eyes radiate various colors depending on the degree of evil they encounter. Everyone knows that Vanguards are a force with no match in either the near or unseen world, save for perhaps the blackest depths of the netherworld."

"Everyone but me," I said coldly. "So why wasn't I seconded?"

"Beats me." She shrugged. "I'm just a witch. While I know a great deal about the population of the unseen world, I'm not privy to the inner-workings of various sects – not that The Guild is a sect, mind you. It's a regulatory body."

I got up from my chair and began to pace. My mind was swimming with questions, and it was clear that she would be unable to provide all the answers I was looking for.

"Stella," I said quietly. "I don't think I'm a Vanguard. I can only access my powers at night."

"You're a Vanguard, all right," she insisted. "You just haven't figured out how to flip the switch for day work yet."

"Lovely. Please don't tell me I'm expected to fight crime at any hour of the day."

She gave me a confused look. "You're gifted, Marshall. This is supposed to be your life's work. Dear God, it's far more interesting than pushing a broom – that's what you do for a living, isn't it?"

"No," I chided. "I sell crap on *eBay,* and I design websites from my apartment."

"Now that's interesting!" Her eyes lit up. "When you've solved the murders, maybe you can help me sell some of my goods also. Does it pay well?"

"It pays enough," I said. "So where do I find this Guild you mentioned?"

"Good question. Presumably, they will find you. I can ask the elders in my coven, but it might help if I knew precisely what you can and cannot do. It's also important because I'll need you to talk to the rocks in the front of the store."

"Talk to the rocks, huh?"

Stella poured another cup of coffee. "My coven has determined the rocks communicate with one another – we just don't know how to decipher what they're saying yet. That's where you come in."

"Just how am I supposed to do that? I came here today for your input – not the other way around," I said in frustration.

"I'm not entirely sure," she admitted. "Zona Beltane, our most senior elder, said we would need a Vanguard if we wanted to find out the meaning of the stones, and you're the only Vanguard that I know. So, what exactly are you capable of?"

"Oh crap. Lots of things, I suppose. I don't exactly know where to start."

"Well, we know you can fly. How fast can you go?"

"Beats the hell out of me, I've never made a serious attempt at clocking myself. My best ball park estimate would be that I can fly from downtown to my apartment in about a minute or so – that's about four miles."

"Can you teleport?"

"No."

"Can you teleport a person or an object?"

"Not that I'm aware of."

"What's the largest object you've been able to pick up with your bare hands?"

"Hmm... I guess I re-railed a loaded tanker car that was spilling ammonia into a lake."

"No kidding?"

"Yeah. I put my back out, though."

She got up from her chair and walked the length of the storage room. I could see her lips moving as she stood beneath a ceiling fan that was spinning loudly.

"Yes, I can hear what you're saying and no, I don't have a girlfriend." I called out. "Are we done yet?"

"Just about!" she shouted back. "Storch has something he wishes to share with you."

"I don't speak cat," I said as she walked back to the dinette and took her seat.

"That's all right – I'll translate." She picked up Walter and cuddled him in her arms.

"God – he's got your number."

"Nonsense, he's just a tired old man who is deserving of a little affection."

"Why did you pick a cat to be your familiar? Call me crazy, but that's kind of stereotypical, if you ask me."

Stella gently scratched Walter's head. "Because cats are eternally vigilant. Even when they're sound asleep, they're constantly aware of their surroundings. It was Storch who told me the stones in the front of the store are communicating, and he also has seen the face of the person whose voice is on my tape recorder."

"Say again? I thought you said you were alone when that happened."

"To the best of my knowledge, I was. Storch can see what exists beyond the human eye, and he has a warning for both of us."

"What's that?"

"There's been another killing – the police just don't know about it yet."

"You're kidding – where?" I asked, as I threw on my coat.

She placed her hand on Walter's head and closed her eyes.

"He didn't see the location," she said, concentrating. "He caught a glimpse of a dismembered hand poking out of a trash bag in the back of a minivan. There's a set of white coveralls draped over what looks like a couple of other bags."

Panic set in, twisting itself in a knot deep in the pit of my stomach. For the second time in as many weeks, I'd been powerless to stop a killing, which led me to believe that the murders had to be committed by someone with abilities similar to mine.

"Did he see the driver?" I asked, trying to remain calm.

Her eyes squinted as she focused her concentration of what Walter had witnessed. "Nope, but I'm guessing the body was in transit."

"If it's the same guy who killed Stephen Hodges, then he has no intention of hiding the body. That kid was strung up for everyone to see."

"I agree with you" Stella said, as she opened her eyes and scratched behind Walter's ears. "Obviously we can't go to the police with this information, so we're going to have to sit back and see how this plays itself out."

"I can't believe I didn't foresee two murders. Something must be wrong with me." I said, sounding deflated.

"There's nothing wrong with you," she said easily. "Vanguards don't suddenly experience a weakening in their powers unless something of similar power is working against them. It could be a meta-human, but I'm thinking this has something to do with the unseen world and possibly dark magic."

"Why?"

"For starters, the entity that visited my store was communicating with the rocks. You found a rock last night at the parking lot when you stopped that kidnapping, and I'd bet dollars to doughnuts there was a similar rock where they found Stephen Hodges' body."

She was probably right – there was too much happening for this to be coincidental. I walked over to the glass case and examined Stella's collection, as if the rocks themselves would somehow offer a clue as to how I was supposed to communicate with them when my psychic radar was on the fritz.

"I think we should work together and figure this out," I said quietly. "I don't know anything about the supernatural and I'm starting to believe that my ability to foresee violent crimes was jammed on purpose."

Stella placed her hand on my shoulder and nodded. "I need to do some research on the last time something from the Netherworld entered our realm," she said, smiling warmly. "I'm glad you want to work with me, and I promise – no more secrets."

"All right, then," I said, zipping up my coat. "I'm going to go home and get some sleep. I'll call you when I've rested up."

"Take this with you." She handed me a vial containing a clear liquid. "Sprinkle a drop on your doorstep and your windows."

"What is it?"

"A stealth essence – it will protect against anything that might want you out of the picture, if you know what I mean."

"Thanks," I said, as I stuffed the vial in my pocket. "What about Walter? Should I take him home?"

"Not yet," she said, smiling. "He's got some spying to do."

CHAPTER 9

"Where's your cat?" Marnie asked from beneath a plaid blanket on my sofa. "I haven't seen him all day, and I looked everywhere. Oh yeah, I hope you don't mind that I bought you a universal remote control for the TV."

I shrugged as I closed the door to my apartment. "Like I said before, he's probably hiding under the bed or in the closet."

"I already looked there."

"Well, as long as you've entertained yourself by further invading my privacy in your desperate search for my cat," I huffed.

"Entertainment, no; boring, yes – you don't even have any porn hidden on your computer," she chirped.

"Lovely." I mumbled as I lifted a hamper filled with Marnie's neatly folded laundry out of my easy chair. Walter was nowhere to be seen, and I hadn't asked Stella precisely how our cat was able to leave my apartment to conduct his activities as a witch's familiar. "I'm sure he'll come out when he's good and ready."

"Well, I got another email. This time the guy actually wrote something instead of sending me a picture."

"You all right?"

"Just spooked," she said in a distant voice. "I guess that's why I wanted to come down to your apartment."

"You're welcome. What did the email say?"

"Here, you can read it," she said, as she handed me a sheet of paper. "I printed it off for you."

I scanned the header and noticed that he'd changed his email address to a free hosting service I'd never heard of.

"Hey Marnie: I know you but you don't know me. I know you think about me a lot and that your probably scared becuz I sent you all these emailz. It's not something to be scared about cuz I don't know if you like me or not. If you don't like me then that could be bad cuz I think about you since the time we first met and I hope you don't call the cops on me becuz of these emails Im sending you. IF YOU WOULD JUST GIVE ME A CHANCE!"

I glanced at Marnie to get a feel for whether she felt this threat was legitimate or not, then folded the sheet of paper.

"Apart from being functionally illiterate, the last line jumps out at you," I said, as I handed back the note. "Do you know anyone with a fondness for text message lingo?"

She clicked off the TV. "Jeez, that would be every person alive with a smart phone, Marshall."

"Have you recently met anyone new?"

"Nope."

"Any female acquaintances that might be holding a grudge against you? We can't rule them out either."

"Not really," she said. "I mean, all women get pissy with one another – what do you think so far?"

I scratched my chin and was considering telling her that I too was in the dark, when Walter's air splitting meow grabbed our attention.

"There you are!" She jumped from the sofa and swept Walter into her arms. "Where have you been hiding?"

"Yeah, Walter, what have *you* been up to?" I asked, half-thinking that Stella Weinberg might be privy to our conversation.

"God, he's a heavy one." She sat down on the couch while Walter purred loudly.

"Don't remind me," I said flatly. "Also, stop leaving cat treats all over my apartment. He's fat enough as it is."

"Done! So what do you think about the email?" she asked, as she hid a small can of *Pounce* behind a pillow.

"Obviously, your stalker is a guy," I said. "He possesses some degree of technological savvy, because he set up a new email account from an offshore hosting service, which implies that he knows you might be going to the cops. He's probably trying to cover his tracks. His IP address will probably be untraceable, as he's likely hiding behind one of the hundreds of thousands of anonymous IP addresses which are freely available on the Internet."

"Anything else?"

"Yep. I think that you should probably wipe your hard drive, in case he's a hacker or a phreak."

"That it?"

"One more thing. I think we should respond to this email."

Marnie glared at me. "Are you *insane*?"

"Nope," I said, curtly. "If we talk to him, we can learn more about the guy, and he may drop his guard enough for us to find out his identity."

"No. Absolutely not," she snapped. "It's bad enough that I am afraid to be alone in my apartment. The last thing I want to do is give this guy any more information about me."

"Okay, then. You're content to hide out in my apartment until this guy reveals himself, is that it?"

Marnie got up from the couch and walked over to the sliding door. "I don't know what I'm supposed to do," she said quietly, as she peeked out at the street from behind the vertical blinds. "What am I supposed to say? I've never been stalked before. I don't even know if this is some kind of a practical joke."

"Get away from the door!" I ordered.

"I'm just looking, okay? God! I've been holed up in your apartment all day. Let's go out and do something? Anything is better than this."

"Not a good idea."

"Why the hell not? He's not going to do anything if I'm with you," she said in a tone of voice that came within a whisker of whining. "He'll think you're my dad or something."

"Somehow I doubt that. You don't look like my kid."

"Then I'll hold your hand and snuggle up to you." She grinned. "He'll think we're an item. Let's go shopping! I'll buy you a new hoodie – the one in your closet has holes in it."

"That would just be awkward, and I don't think he'd believe that you're seeing a middle-aged man."

She walked back to the sofa and sat down. "Wanna bet? Two of my girlfriends have already slept with their professors, and I've been on three dates with one of mine."

I nodded. "Interesting revelation,"

"What? You're not shocked by the fact that female college students have been known to engage in romantic pursuits with older men, are you?" she asked.

"Not really."

"Good. I don't want you getting all judgmental on me."

"I wouldn't dream of it. Mind you, I think that if I had a daughter in college…"

"Do *not* go there," she warned. "You don't have a daughter, and even if you did, your daughter would know that her dad had been a horny twenty-two-year-old guy once upon a time."

"Point taken."

She scratched Walter's belly as he rolled onto his back and stuck his feet in the air. "I have a question. Why are you single? You're over forty, right? I mean, it's totally cool if you're gay."

"Nope. Not gay."

"So why haven't you married someone? Most men your age have teenage kids by now."

"I guess I just haven't gotten around to it," I said quietly. "As the nature of our relationship can attest, I don't do well with women."

"We have a relationship?" she asked with a cocky smile.

"You know what I mean."

"Here's what I think," she said, still smiling. "You're a deeply private man whose brain works on overdrive and who should probably slow down to enjoy life."

"Uh-huh."

"How long have you lived in this building?"

"I guess about ten years or so."

"Well, I've spent a lot of time in your apartment over the past couple of days, and I've learned a great deal about you."

"Like?"

She stood up and waved her left finger around my apartment.

"There are no pictures of your family," she said. "Actually, you don't have *any* pictures hanging on your walls. You've got three boxes of old *Fly Fish America* magazines in your front closet, but I haven't seen a fishing rod or a tackle box anywhere in your apartment. You don't even have fish in the freezer."

"Anything else?"

"Nobody calls you… ever. Your phone hasn't rung once in the time I've been here. And I looked on your phone bill. There are no long-distance charges."

"I'm cheap," I mumbled.

Marnie plopped back down on the sofa and cradled Walter in her arms. "Where's your family? Don't you ever get lonely?"

I blinked at her and remained silent as I considered whether to answer her questions. I'd forgotten the last time anyone showed even the most remote interest in me, but that kind of disinterest was by my own design. As a rule, I generally dislike most people, and my preference has long been that people should know as little about me as possible. Yet for some reason, I'd let Marnie in. To make matters even more confusing, she appeared to genuinely *like* me. I gave her an uncomfortable smile, and for the first time in years, I dropped my guard.

"My mother passed away when I was nineteen. I am an only child, and I never met my father."

"I'm sorry for your loss," she whispered, sounding like she actually cared.

"No worries."

"Why no girlfriend? Did you get your heart broken? Did the last one cheat on you?"

"No."

"So what happened?"

There was another long pause as the burning sensation I'd not felt for more than a decade began to rise from the pit of my stomach and straight into my chest.

"I was in love, once," I said. "That was a long time ago."

"What happened?"

"Ovarian cancer. She was only twenty-eight."

"I'm so sorry Marshall," she said in a soft voice. "What was her name?"

"Cynthia. She had red hair – just like you."

"Red-heads rock!"

"Yeah, something like that." I said quietly. "Anyway, she was the love of my life, and I think that we only have one person that's meant for each of us in this lifetime, you know?"

"Marshall Conrad, you're not a cranky old man, in spite of how hard you try. You're old-fashioned, and that's rare. It's also kinda sexy."

"Yeah, that's me. I aspire to be sexy in all that I do."

"I have another question."

"Go for it."

"Why do you have so many expired bottles of ibuprofen in your medicine cabinet?"

"Because I get migraines."

"I have another question."

"Geez, are you writing my biography? What now?"

"Where's your motorcycle parked?"

"Huh?"

"Your motorcycle. You've got two matching leather jackets and leather pants in your closet. You've also got two different pairs of motorcycle boots. Harley Davidsons are wicked cool. Let's go for a ride!"

"I don't have a motorcycle. I drive a 1992 Ford Tempo."

"So why do you have two outfits? You're not into bondage or anything like that, are you? I mean, whatever floats your boat, I guess..."

"No, I am not into *bondage*."

"Yeah, but you've got handcuffs dangling from the belt loop on both sets of pants," she said teasingly. "It's totally okay to be kinky. It's almost as sexy as your old fashion morals. Sort of contradicts them, but you know..."

"That's just about enough," I snapped, as I got out of my chair and walked to the front closet and closed the door. "I'm not kinky, I'm not into bondage, and I am not old-fashioned."

"Chill out. I'm just teasing. You know me."

"I have no problem with you hanging out in my apartment, but please respect my privacy," I said, as I slid the closet door to a close. "You don't see me asking questions about your personal life, do you?"

"Ha! You couldn't figure me out if you tried."

"You'd be surprised," I said, as I went back to the living room.

"I would, huh? Prove it."

"Not in the mood."

"No, no – you brought up the fact that you're a mind reader," she said in a sarcastic tone. "Read my mind, oh psychic one. I dare ya!"

"All right, then," I said, curtly. "You're the youngest of three daughters. Your father is a real estate developer and he's worth about five million dollars. Your mother is an attorney for a midsized Boston law firm."

"Big deal. You can get that on the internet."

"You're the only daughter who reached twenty years of age without getting pregnant, or so your parents think." I continued. "But they don't know you had an abortion when you were nineteen, and that your last serious relationship ended when you were hospitalized for what you called a 'nasty car accident.' They believed you broke your nose when your head hit the steering wheel, but hey – what do I know, right? You just didn't tell them that your ex-boyfriend used you as a punching bag."

"Stop, Marshall..."

"You think you're fat, and you've been known to up-chuck your meals as a means of keeping that fabulous figure. You try to befriend those who don't fit into your social circle – much to the chagrin of that same group of friends who label you as doing charity work. You recently befriended a zit-faced junior because you felt sorry for him after your best friend Renee wanted to screw with him by asking him out and then standing him up. That Renee is a nice one, isn't she? You covet her sultry good looks and built-in tan, and you secretly like the fact that her boyfriend hits on you."

"*Stop it, Marshall!*"

There was an awkward silence as she stared at me with a look of shock on her face. "How did you learn all of that about me?"

"Hey, you wanted a clairvoyant – now you've got one." I said with a smirk. "Not a lot of fun, huh?"

"Now I know what you do for a living!" she shouted, as if she'd just invented the light bulb. "You're a psychic for the cops! That is *sooooo* cool!"

"I don't work for the police, and if I were a psychic, I'd have found out the identity of the person who is stalking you by now."

"I've read about this. You're like that guy on TV who talks to dead people."

"Don't get me started on *James Van Praagh*!"

"So do you see dead people?"

"No."

"So what do you do for a living?"

"It doesn't matter."

"Private investigator?"

"Bingo," I lied.

"You're not going to bill me for this whole stalker thing, are you?"

"Nope. Though your family could afford it."

"Yeah, well, I don't need them to know about this. Don't contact them. I mean it."

"All right, then."

"Marshall Conrad, Psychic P.I."

"Shut up."

"Hey, can I be your secretary? I can pretend to be a bimbo."

"No thanks. I work alone," I said.

"So... now what do we do?"

Walter jumped onto the top of my easy chair and began kneading my scalp. "We don't do anything about your stalker, because the ball is in his court. You can still hang out at my place, but stay out of my stuff."

"Done."

"I mean it, Marnie. Stop snooping around."

"I will," she said. "Hey, I forgot to tell you that someone stuck an envelope under your door while I was having a nap on the couch. It's on the kitchen counter."

"You didn't open it, did you?"

"No – but it's an official looking envelope from something called The Guild."

CHAPTER 10

The yellow police tape stretched along the bumpers of thirteen vehicles in the culdesac. Each car or minivan was covered with blue plastic tarp, and four sheriff's deputies blocked the entrance to the crime scene. A large crowd of onlookers and local residents gathered at the barricade as Sheriff Don Neuman gave an impromptu statement for the news media.

"I'll just provide a short update on what we know thus far," Sheriff Neuman said, as he wiped his brow with the sleeve of his tan uniform. "The coroner is on site because of the condition of the crime scene. My office has this morning been in contact with federal authorities who will assist as we conduct the investigation."

"What's under the blue tarps, Sheriff?" asked Bill Sparks, WGBC's crime reporter.

Sheriff Neuman's jaw clenched tightly, and he flashed a contemptuous look at the reporter. "I think it's obvious that we're treating this as a homicide."

"Yeah, we get that – what's under the tarps?"

"I'm sure you can surmise why these vehicles have been covered. Next question."

"Lara Pinter from the Greenfield Examiner. Sheriff, is this murder connected with the murder of Stephen Hodges?"

He threw her a wary glance and said, "At this point, we're treating them as separate homicides."

"Sheriff Neuman," she continued, "has the discovery of thirteen spiral-engraved rocks found in front of each car offered any clues about the motive behind this homicide?"

"We're exploring every lead."

"People are talking about a serial killer. Is there any truth to the rumor that a spiral-engraved stone was found at the Stephen Hodges crime scene?"

"Again, we are exploring every lead. Our forensics team is combing the crime scene, and it would be unwise to speculate on either a suspect or a motive," he said, wiping his brow.

The *Greenfield Examiner* reporter looked unimpressed. "If this isn't a serial killer, then who else could it be? How can you expect Greenfield residents to feel at ease when there have been two murders and there's no suspect?"

"We are looking into every lead, Ms. Pinter," the Sheriff stonewalled.

"Marshall Conrad, curious onlooker!" I shouted. "I have a question!"

Sheriff Neuman searched through the crowd as I pushed myself in front of the reporters. "Go ahead, Mr. Conrad," he said.

"Thanks," I said. "I'm just wondering if anyone from the media knows the slightest thing about serial killers? The reason I'm asking is because I have to assume they know that serial killers are people who've killed on three occasions, or there is often a sexual ingredient to their obsession. What I'd really like to know is if reporters like Lara Pinter can explain the value in reporting that a serial killer resides in friendly neighborhood Greenfield, save for increasing the Examiner's revenue. Seems to me that ain't journalism. What do you think?"

"Mr. Conrad, are you a reporter?" asked Lara Pinter, obviously annoyed that I'd singled her out in front of her colleagues.

"Ms. Pinter, do you get off at the idea of creating a panic all over the city? It's not like I'm trying to tell you how to do your job or anything like that, but isn't it true that you got canned by the Boston Herald for something about plagiarism? I mean, I know that Greenfield is a small city, and you're more than likely chomping at the bit to spearhead a series of stories about two gruesome murders, but I think most people would agree that Geraldo Rivera's best days are behind him, and you don't have a mustache, from what I can tell."

"Are you a reporter?" she demanded.

"Are you a failed journalist?" I snapped back. "I think she's a failed journalist – what does everyone else think? Hey, Bill Sparks, get your damned camera on me. I want your story to be about the crackpot who raised a ruckus at the crime scene. You guys want headlines? I'll take off my clothes and run around here naked, if it will stop you from searching for gory details. Let the sheriff do his job, for crying out loud."

"Right on!" someone shouted from the crowd. "Let them do their job!"

"Exactly," I said, winking at Lara Pinter. She clenched her jaw and discreetly gave me the finger as she scratched her left elbow. "Sheriff Neuman, you don't have anything else to add to this scrum, do you?"

"Nope," he huffed, as he gave me a suspicious look. "We do need to get back to the investigation here, folks, so if the media has any more questions they can direct them to our official spokesperson."

I turned my attention to the crowd of onlookers.

"I'm going to ask all the people who live on this street if they would be so kind as to refuse any reporters' questions," I said. "If you're going to talk to anyone, talk to law enforcement."

The crowd began to disperse as the WGBC news crew began packing up their equipment when Stella Weinberg grabbed my arm and pulled me back to my car. "Just what the hell was that?"

I waved a hand. "You know as well as I do the last thing anyone needs at this point is a full-scale panic. Besides, the only news outlets that will report on my little outburst will be the bloggers."

"You're insane."

"And reporters like Lara Pinter are goddamned predators," I said as I shook my head. "This is America, Stella. The graphic nature of these killings is going to attract the worst kind of journalism, and this city is going to become a circus. Hell, Greenfield will morph into *Nancy Grace* centra,l for shit sake!"

"You're full of beans," she snapped. "You've got other motives."

I nodded. "Yep. Five minutes from now, a couple of sheriff's deputies are going to escort me past this barricade and into Don Neuman's squad car."

"What makes you say that?"

"Because the sheriff probably believes that a serial killer

is on the loose, and he's been trained to recognize the fact that perpetrators like to hang out at crime scenes. Some are even brazen enough to offer their assistance to an investigation."

Her jaw dropped. "You're trying to make yourself a *suspect*?"

"How else am I going to get my foot in the door of this investigation?" I said with a shrug. "Under normal circumstances, I could have prevented this homicide, but the old radar isn't working for some reason, and that has me worried."

"You should be more worried about being indicted for a crime you didn't commit."

"You're probably right," I said, as I watched Sheriff Neuman talking with a burly deputy from inside his squad car. "I think we can probably disclose the location of your rock collection too."

"Don't even think about it," she warned. The look on her face told me that I'd better keep my mouth shut, or she might put some kind of spell on me that would shrivel a part of my anatomy I'm deeply fond of.

"All right then, your secret is safe with me," I said reassuringly. "I have a question, though."

"What?"

"The last time we got together, you said that another murder had occurred. It couldn't have been this one, because I was at your place two days ago, and it's clear that whoever is underneath those blue tarps was alive and well at the time. Care to elaborate?"

Stella gave a heavy sigh as she put on a pair of dark sunglasses. "This probably isn't the best place to discuss my source of information. When you're done with the sheriff, come back to my store, and I will fill you in."

"It sounds to me like you're going to be introducing me to more of this unseen world."

"That's right." She nodded. "It sounds to me like you've accepted that it's real, and it's about time."

"Why?"

"Because you'll have to make some friends if you're going to find the killer," she instructed. "By the way, did you get that letter from The Guild?"

"Yep."

"You're not angry with me, are you? I had to contact them – you need to be seconded if you're going to master your abilities."

"I'm not angry." I watched the burly deputy walk through the barricade in my direction. "I'm to meet someone who goes by the name of 'Ruby.' They didn't tell me when or where I am to meet this person. Do you know who it is?"

"Beats me. If I knew, I'd tell you." She glanced over my shoulder again. "Time for me to make my exit; that deputy is headed this way. Come and see me when you're done talking to the sheriff."

"All right," I said, as I turned around and began walking toward the deputy.

CHAPTER 11

The sheriff's deputy kept a firm hand on my shoulder as he directed me past the police barricade and toward the Chevrolet Impala. The forensics team was setting up portable screens around each of the thirteen cars, and one person dressed in a sterile bodysuit waved a Geiger counter over one of the spiral-engraved rocks that rested in front the car closest to me.

"Pretty gruesome stuff," I said to the burly deputy. "What's with the guy in the radiation suit?"

"Shut up and keep walking," he grumbled, as he gave me a forward push. "The sheriff wants to ask you some questions."

"Okie-dokie then, but aren't you supposed to arrest me or something?"

"Can it, moron."

As we approached the Impala, the rear driver's side door swung open, and I could see Sheriff Don Neuman seated in passenger side of the front seat, talking on the radio. "Climb in," the deputy ordered as he pushed my head inside.

The blue vinyl interior of the car smelled of cigarette smoke, and there were empty coffee cups scattered on the floor. Sheriff Neuman lit a cigarette, slung the radio handset over the steering wheel, and then held his package of Marlboros over the edge of the front seat. "Want one?" he asked politely. "I was on the patch until this morning."

"No, thanks," I said. "I thought Greenfield has a bylaw about smoking in city-owned vehicles."

"That's the least of my worries," the sheriff said, as he took a deep haul on his cigarette. "So tell me, apart from pissing off the Greenfield news media, what interest do you have in my investigation of this homicide?"

"Like I said earlier, I'm a curious onlooker, and it seemed rather unfair that the press was trying to put words in your mouth."

"They'll do that regardless of what I tell them. Your name is Marshall Conrad, is that right?"

"Yes."

"We've checked the residents list for this street, and you don't show up as a local. Either you know something about this homicide or you're purposefully trying to impede an official investigation, and that, my friend, will get you five years behind bars," he warned.

"Do I need a lawyer?"

"Beats me, do you think you need a lawyer?"

"Nope. I haven't done anything illegal the last time I looked."

"I'll be the judge of that."

"You know, I could have just kept my mouth shut during your media scrum."

"So why didn't you?"

"Come on, Sheriff." I said, folding my arms across my chest. "Haven't you ever wanted to say what you really think when some idiot reporter starts asking dumb questions?"

He took another long drag on his cigarette and exhaled through his nostrils. "You live clear across town, according to your motor vehicle records. I'll ask one more time, why are you at this crime scene?"

"I heard about the murder on my radio as I was driving home from the 7-11, and thought I'd buzz by to see what all the commotion was about." I fanned the smoke away from my face.

"You seem to know a little bit about serial killers. We had one in Boston back in the 80s – the creepy sonofabitch liked to hang out at crime scenes and watch us investigate."

"And you're thinking that I might be one of those creepy people, is that it?"

"Something like that." The Sheriff regarded me with obvious suspicion as he flicked his cigarette out the window. "There's always a crowd at a crime scene, but nobody makes a public spectacle of themselves, so that tells me we should probably ask you some questions."

"All right, then."

"Where do you work?" he asked.

"I'm self-employed."

"Doing?"

"Odd jobs – is my employment relevant to your investigation?"

"Just trying to get some background on you, Mr. Conrad. Your name rings a bell, for some reason."

"I can't imagine why," I said calmly. "I'm a person of no importance in the community."

Sheriff Neuman raised his eyebrows. "Tell me about what happened at Lake Chebucto in nineteen eighty-two."

"Why?"

"Because your name was flagged when we did a background check. You were questioned about an assault on a Pastor James Gregory when you were fourteen."

"That's right. The Pastor was a pervert who tried to have his way with me."

"Go on?"

"There's nothing more I can offer." I looked at the twelve gauge shotgun resting in the cradle attached to the car's dashboard.

"You like guns, huh? That's a Winchester Defender – not exactly standard issue for law enforcement, but I am the sheriff, and this is my car."

"I detest firearms. I think that anyone who buys a gun that doesn't hunt game for food is probably compensating for something deeply personal. Anyway, I imagine whoever is responsible for this homicide probably didn't use a gun."

"I'll be the judge of that," said the sheriff. "I'm interested in learning why you know so much about serial killers. Care to explain?"

"Sure," I said, smiling. "I watch A&E."

"Come again?"

"Anyone who watches cable will tell you that America has a love affair with bizarre crimes. A&E devotes about five hours a day or more to programs specifically about serial killers. Don't you ever watch Bill Kurtis?"

"Nope."

"Well you should. It might give you some insight into the killer's motives."

"Go on?"

I looked out the passenger window at the yellow police tape and decided I would start pressing the sheriff for information. "Looks to me like whoever did this wanted to make a very public statement."

"What makes you think that?"

"Come on, Sheriff – yellow police tape? Blue tarps covering up thirteen cars? Men in radiation suits? That's powerful imagery. More powerful than the chopped up body parts those tarps are covering up. People see that on the news, and it probably scares the hell out of them."

"How do you know there are body parts underneath the tarps?"

"You wouldn't be covering up graffiti some wayward teenager spray painted on those cars."

The sheriff looked surprised. "How did you know about the graffiti?"

"I'm not sure I know what you mean."

He lit another cigarette blew the smoke in my face. "There's graffiti on each of those cars, among other things. What do you know about the spirals?"

"The ones on the rocks you found?"

"No, the spirals the killer painted on the hoods of the cars."

"You're kidding, right?" I tried to hide the panic that had just invaded my stomach.

"Not at all," said the sheriff. "Seems kind of interesting to me that someone who knows so much about serial killers would also know there was graffiti at both crime scenes."

"You mean someone spray painted a spiral where Stephen Hodges died?"

"You betcha. Do you know anything about the spiral graffiti that's popping up around town lately?"

"No," I said. "Look, am I being arrested?"

"Let's just say you're a person of interest and leave it at that for now," said the sheriff, as he scribbled some notes in his pad. "You can go, but expect a call from my office in the not-too-distant future, and don't leave town."

"Wait a minute. Don't leave town? Person of interest? Call me crazy, but that would imply you're treating me like a suspect." I tried to conceal my pleasure at having successfully inserted myself in the official investigation.

"We're working on a profile of the killer. Someone from Quantico is flying in this afternoon."

"If you're calling in someone from the Behavioral Science Unit of the FBI, then maybe the rumors about a serial killer are correct."

"Maybe," he said. "We found the first victim a week ago. Do you know anyone who can verify what you've been up to for the past seven days?"

I shrugged. "That's going to take some time, since I work out of my apartment. I don't get out much. Still, I could probably produce a number of transaction records showing that I've been hard at work designing websites."

The sheriff nodded as he scribbled something in his notepad. "Uh-huh, I'll want to see those."

"Sure thing. Are you going to arrest me before I can get them for you?"

"Nope, we're done for now, but we'll be in touch, so don't make any vacation plans just yet."

CHAPTER 12

The cold rain ended as I stepped off the rooftop and into the night sky. My brain was stinging from the vision of what was about to happen on the poorly lit pathway outside the Humanities building at Chesterton College. Receiving two visions the same evening was a rare occurence. The migraine hit me just as the man who'd planned on robbing the liquor store and killing the cashier got out of his car. He shot at me with his 9mm Beretta, and the bullet grazed my right shoulder, leaving a burn mark on my leather jacket.

I didn't intend to punch the guy as hard as I actually did. I think it was an instinctive response – he did try to kill me, after all. I left him bleeding inside the trunk of his Dodge Magnum and took off into the darkness when I caught a glimpse of the German store owner running out the back door with a baseball bat in his hand. I'm certain he saw me, because the last thing I heard as I darted into the air was *"Überraschend!"* which I'm pretty sure means "amazing" in German.

As I soared over the culvert running past the Greenfield Waterworks, it occurred to me the person in my vision might be the same son of a bitch that Sheriff Don Neuman was pursuing, due to the very graphic way he intended to end his intended victim's life.

The six-inch filleting knife he'd been hiding inside his trench coat would be used to carve up her face and remove her eyes. He felt some hesitation about raping her, because he'd always experienced performance problems. Perhaps taking out her eyes would ensure that he would climax – something he'd never accomplished in his life.

He'd kill her slowly, of course. That was the easy part. Then leave her mutilated body on the path, because he wanted the other women who'd rejected him to see what he'd done. He wanted his power back, and this was the only way.

The vision flashed to his face. He was a white man, and his neatly cropped, gelled hair gleamed in the moonlight. He wouldn't hide behind a nylon stocking or a balaclava. This guy wanted his victim to know the identity of her killer, and he intended his face to be the last thing she would ever see.

"Faster!" I growled, as I tightened my fists and willed myself to increase my flight speed. The wind stung my eyes, and I could feel the air currents bump against me as the ground beneath zipped by. I spotted the Humanities Building half a mile away. It was 11:34 PM.

"Shit, I hope I'm not too late," I groaned, as I followed the bend in the pathway leading between a small copse of pine trees. I increased my altitude to get a clearer look at the potential crime scene when I noticed a lone female figure staggering along the pathway about thirty yards from the tree line, where the male was hiding.

"Goddammit, no time, she's gonna see me. Gotta move now!" I growled through my teeth as I dropped into a straight vertical dive directly above the attacker. He jumped out from the copse of trees, and the woman screamed as she raised her arms to shield her face from the knife.

"*Not tonight, asshole!*" I bellowed, as I slammed into his midsection, driving him flat onto the paved surface of the pathway. There was a loud *crunch* as my left shoulder connected with his rib cage. His head bounced off the asphalt. I crushed his right wrist into granules, and the filleting knife fell to the ground with a harmless clang.

The attacker groaned as I grabbed a handful of his trench coat and lifted him off the ground. "Where's the other body, you son of a bitch?" I pulled his face about two inches from my glowing eyes. "Tell me where that other body is, or I'll tear your head off right here and now!"

"Who are you?" he blubbered loudly. "I d-don't know what y-you're t-talking about? Please don't kill me!"

"I'd be doing society a favor. If you want to live longer than the next ten seconds, you'll tell me where you hid the third body."

"I-t-told you I d-don't know anyth…" he whimpered, before he passed into unconsciousness. His body went limp, and he slid out of his trench coat, landing flat on his back.

"Shit," I muttered as I handcuffed him to the sewage grate bordering to the pathway. I checked his pockets for identification and found a crumpled piece of paper. I opened it up to find a hand-drawn spiral on one side. "Goddammit," I whispered, as I turned over the paper to see a wrinkled photograph of Marnie Brindle.

"*Marshall? Is t-that you?*" asked Marnie, her voice shaking. "You saved me…"

I didn't give her a chance to utter another word.

"Fly!" I snarled, and I hurtled into the blackness.

CHAPTER 13

"We've got a problem," I said abruptly, as I locked the front door of The Curiosity Nook. "Lots going on; we need to talk."

Stella stood on a chair, watering a cactus whose shape resembled a crucifix. "Probably do," she said, as she looked at me through the corner of her eye.

"Busy night last night. Someone spotted me."

"I'd seen you once. It stands to reason other people might see you as well."

"No, this is different," I said as I sat down in the leather chair beside to the front counter. "This one knows my name. She's my upstairs neighbor."

Stella stepped down from the chair and pushed it against the wall. "I see. Now you're worried that she'll identify you, is that it? How far away was she?"

"About ten feet."

"I'm going to assume that she required your unique assistance."

"Yeah, it's a long story."

"She's got a hate-on for you?"

"No, no, nothing like that," I said as I slowly massaged my temples. "She had a stalker, and I've been letting her hang out in my apartment until we figured out the creep's identity. I was out on another matter last night, and then my stupid migraine revealed that her stalker was going to kill her outside the Humanities Building at Chesterton College. Anyway, I flew over there as fast as I could, and the guy was just about to slice her face off when I nailed him."

"It looks to me like you're still dressed for battle," said Stella, as she poured a cup of coffee and handed it to me. "Nice costume, by the way."

"It's an outfit," I said, grabbing the mug. "I couldn't go back to my apartment, because I know she'll be knocking on my door as soon as the police are done with her."

"Why?"

"Because I interrogated her stalker about the third body the cops don't know about while I was beating the stuffing out of him. She recognized my voice."

"Did she see your face?"

"No, I had my back to her."

"Is her stalker the killer?

"He was *a* killer – just not the one we're looking for."

"That's too bad," she said, as she knelt down behind the counter and then reappeared with a Buster Brown shoe box in her hands. "It's not the end of the world. You can always deny, deny, deny."

"She identified me. She even said my name."

Stella looked unimpressed. "Big deal – nobody will believe her."

"Really? You don't think the cops are going to be interested in her story when it's corroborated by the guy who tried to kill her?"

"What are the police going to do? Start a task force to search for a superhero with glowing eyes?"

"I am getting too old for this crap," I muttered.

"On the subject of law enforcement, how did your meeting with the sheriff go?"

"That's another kettle of fish," I said. "They've got some expert from the FBI flying down here, and it doesn't take a rocket scientist to figure out that I fit nicely into the killer's profile. Single white male, lives alone, antisocial."

"That was to be expected."

"By the way, that letter from The Guild I received was a bill for my membership dues. Apparently I owe them twenty-three grand, dating back to nineteen-eighty-eight."

"Well, I did tell you they were a regulatory body," she said. "Anyway, the last time we talked, I told you the killer had something to do with the unseen world, remember?"

"Yeah."

"There's someone here to see you." She handed me a pair of sunglasses that looked like they'd come out Elvis Presley's attic. "Put them on."

"Sure, but can you answer a couple of questions first?"

She nodded.

"Did these sunglasses once belong to the king of Rock and Roll? And why do I have to wear them?"

"Yes, they're worth a few thousand dollars, so don't break them," she said, as she grasped to lid of the shoebox with both hands. "You need to wear them so your optic nerves don't melt."

"What's in the box?"

"Someone who dislikes Vanguards, so don't piss her off."

I tentatively slipped the sunglasses over my nose. "This is going to freak me out, isn't it?"

"Probably... Just don't be rude."

"I'll be on my best behavior."

She slowly lifted the lid off the shoebox. A brilliant green light blazed up to the ceiling and shook the room, causing a number of shelved curiosities to fall onto the floor. I heard what sounded like wooden wind chimes clattering away from the center of the shoe box, and the glow produced a mild heat that warmed my face.

"Is he here?" asked a female voice from inside the box.

"Yes, he's here, Ingrid," said Stella.

"Nobody else is there, yes?"

"It's just the three of us," Stella said reassuringly.

"Tell the Vanguard to look inside the box. I must regard his face before I choose whether to disclose what I know."

"I have a name, whoever or whatever you are," I said impatiently.

"Tell the Vanguard that I don't talk to strangers," the voice warned. "Tell him that he'd better mind his attitude, lest he be transformed into a snail. Tell him that I've turned many Vanguards into snails over the past three hundred years, and that snails are quite tasty with garlic and butter."

Stella placed a cautionary hand on my shoulder and squeezed hard. "You're pissing her off, Marshall. Apologize."

"For what?" I huffed. "I don't even know what *she* is!"

"I'm a *Fata*, you moron," said the voice. "Castalia, I'm certain that you said he was rather bright?"

"What's a *Fata*?" I asked the box.

"Spirits bless all of us. Am I to believe that on this creature our collective fate rests? Look inside the box, you idiot; I need to see your face."

"He's a good man, Ingrid, you have my word." Stella gave me a sharp nudge in the rib cage with her elbow. "He's going to apologize for being rude. Aren't you, Marshall?"

I mustered the best polite voice I could think of and adjusted the Elvis sunglasses. "I'm sorry if I've caused you any grief. I'm new at all of this, and I've only recently learned that an unseen world exists."

"Apology accepted, Vanguard. Approach and take heed."

I hunched myself over so I could see inside the shoe box. The green light that had shot up to the ceiling receded into a warm yellow glow as a gentle wisp of warm air caressed my face.

"Oh, you're a handsome one. Castalia, you didn't tell me that he was a cutie."

"Don't say that too often, Ingrid. It will go to his head," Stella laughed.

As I looked inside the box, my jaw dropped at the sight of a tiny child's face with piercing green eyes staring straight up at me. She was dressed in an elegant white gown that somehow produced vaporous white tendrils, which flowed gently around her small body, leading to a pair of wings that resembled those of a dragon fly.

"You're a fairy?" I asked in an astonished voice. "You're beautiful."

"I am indeed a *Fata,* or faerie, as your kind would call us. My name is Ingrid, and I know the being responsible for these unresolved deaths in your world."

"What being?" I asked innocently. "The person I seek is a man, from what I can tell."

"Far from it." She began to walk around the interior of the shoe box. "Reach inside, so I may read your palm."

Stella nudged my ribs again. "That means stick your hand in the box."

"I kind of figured that on my own, Stella. Thanks." I gently put my left hand in the shoe box. Ingrid's tiny wings fluttered in a blur, making the familiar sound of a buzzing insect. She hovered over my palm.

"Good, strong hands," said Ingrid. "Lifeline is straight and true."

"Uh, thanks – I guess."

"There is nothing to be thankful for, Vanguard. Your journey has been difficult, yes?"

"Ummm, I'm not sure that I understand."

Ingrid lowered herself onto my palm and sat on her knees. She placed her tiny hand in the center of my life line and as a mild electrical charge tingled through my body at her touch.

"You're not sure who are you are supposed to be, that much is abundantly clear," said Ingrid in a sympathetic tone. "You miss your mother, yes? She passed suddenly, yes?"

"She's been gone for a long time," I said softly. "I think about her every day. Got a picture of her in my wallet."

Ingrid looked up at my face and smiled warmly. "She watches over you and is proud of what you've become. You honor her with your deeds."

"Thank you."

"You miss your mate. She was taken from you. Very sad."

"Y-yes, she became sick and passed away."

The tiny faerie pursed a thin pair of lips and concentrated.

"You could have chosen to ignore your great gifts," said Ingrid. "Yet you help others despite the pain of your life and the storm inside your mind."

"I guess so. I mean, I don't really like people, you know? Half the time, I tell myself to keep doing what I do because humanity must have some redeeming value. I guess that's what keeps me going."

"Castalia, this mortal owns the strength of character to do what must be done. Has he determined the meaning behind the stones?"

"No Ingrid, not yet," said Stella. "Marshall hasn't tapped into all of his abilities."

"Hmm... A Vanguard who does not know his place? Castalia, am I violating the pact if I emerge from this box? I should like to see the stones for myself."

"It's all right, Ingrid. Marshall and I are grateful that you're here."

"Well and good, then," said Ingrid. "Vanguard... lead me to the stones."

I slowly lifted Ingrid's near-weightless body out of the shoe box and walked over to the glass display case that contained the spiral-engraved rocks. Ingrid sat cross-legged in the center of my palm as I knelt down so she could look at them.

"Is this all of them?" asked Ingrid.

"There are thirteen more of them, from what I can tell," I said. "The rocks are usually found at the scene of a murder, but Stella found these scattered all over town. There's been another killing, but we don't know where the body is."

"Troubling indeed," she whispered.

"It's not just the rocks, though. I mean, the spiral symbol is appearing all over the city," I said. "First it appeared on the rocks, and now it's showing up at crime scenes. Whoever is responsible must be trying to send us a message."

Ingrid nodded. "You must talk to these rocks, Vanguard. It's the only way we'll ever know their meaning."

"I would, but I don't know how," I said.

"Then seek the counsel of your kind. They can teach you."

"I don't know anyone."

"I see," she said, as she rubbed her tiny chin with an equally tiny thumb. "I suggest a period of contemplation with the stones. You must do this immediately."

"Why?"

Ingrid's tiny wings began to vibrate and she flew onto the top of the glass cabinet. "The being you seek is not of your world. That he breached the pact and entered your domain is a troubling mystery, and I suspect it is somehow connected with the murders in your realm."

"You keep calling him a being."

"That's because he doesn't deserve to be called a Púca," she said angrily. "Most Púca's limit themselves to harmless mischief, but not this one. He's destroyed many of my kind and captured their essence – he has many followers."

"A *Púca?*"

"Yes, he is a powerful faerie of sorts. He possesses abilities that are beyond any magic known to exist in the unseen world. His interest in the near world is a question best left for mystics. I dare not speculate."

"So what am I looking for, then?" I asked, frustrated. "Does he look like you?"

"You cannot see him, because you've not become enthralled by his power," said Ingrid. "He is visible only to his host."

"His host? You mean, like demonic possession?"

"He is unlike any demon, and he cannot control a person's soul," she said as she flew back toward the shoebox. "His purpose is fear. It's all that matters to his kind."

"I don't understand," I said in a confused voice.

"Castalia will offer guidance. I must return to my realm and consult with my kind," she said. "I shall contact you both with more information as soon as it is revealed to me."

Ingrid hovered back into the shoebox and looked up at me with a reassuring smile on her face. "You are a powerful Vanguard, and you are noble in spite of what I said earlier. It was pleasant enough to meet you. I will not transform you into a snail."

"Thank you, Ingrid."

Stella closed the lid and slid the shoebox back under the front counter. I took off the Elvis sunglasses and handed them to her.

"Wow." I exhaled, wondering if I was losing my mind. "I've seen some weird stuff, but that tops it all."

"She's pretty cool, you know," she said. "I knew you both would hit it off."

I took off my leather jacket and tossed it over the arm of the chair. "Yeah, I guess so."

"Ingrid liked you. That's surprising, given that she hates Vanguards."

"She did threaten to turn me into a snail," I said, sourly.

"Yes, but she also said you were noble, and I'd have to agree with her."

"Thanks," I said, as I rubbed my temples.

"Feel a bit overwhelmed?" Stella asked.

I yawned. "I just want to go to bed. Listen, can a witch cure a migraine? My head feels like it's going to explode."

"Nope, but I do have an amulet you can wear. Not sure if it will interfere with your ability to foretell."

"Never mind, then – not worth the risk. Look, I'm going to head home."

"Come back tonight and talk to the rocks."

"Wouldn't miss it for the world," I groaned, as I walked out the front door.

CHAPTER 14

There was no point in trying to hide from Marnie Brindle. She had a key to my apartment and would probably be waiting inside to grill me about the previous night.

In the short time since I'd offered to let her hide out at my place, she'd made herself at home to the point of replacing my shampoo with a salon brand and enlightening me with new and efficient ways of folding my laundry. I'd remind her that she was a guest in my home, but then she'd dismiss my comments with a wave of her hand while telling me that her presence was karma.

I had just walked in the door when her voice piped up from her usual spot on my sofa. It was early afternoon, and the curtains were wide open, flooding sunlight into every square inch of my living room.

"Hi, Marshall, what up?"

"Nothing," I grumbled, as I stepped into my bedroom to change into my sweat suit. "Why are the curtains open? Your stalker might see you lying on my couch."

"Ohhh, I don't think that's going to be an issue anymore."

"What?" I shouted, as a stab of throbbing pain shot through my head.

"I said, I don't think that's going to be an issue anymore, Marshall. Not after last night."

"What do you mean by that?" I walked into the living room and closed the curtains.

"Where have you been? I haven't seen you since seven o'clock last night."

"Working."

"I see."

"What isn't going to be an issue anymore?" I went into the kitchen and stuck my head in the refrigerator.

"My stalker," she said. "He's currently handcuffed to a bed at the Greenfield General Hospital."

"You're kidding. Did you finally break down and talk to the police?"

"No."

"Are you going to tell me how he was arrested?"

"I kind of hoped you might be able to tell me," she said, as she sat up on the couch. "Where's your leather jacket?"

"Hanging up in the closet."

"I'm talking about your other leather jacket. You have two, remember?"

"What's with all the questions?" I sat down on my vinyl easy chair.

Marnie curled her knees to her chest and gave me a skeptical look. "First off, I'm not crazy, regardless of whether I was drunk last night, and second, everything I've ever known or believed has been proven false. I think I have a right to grill you."

I continued to play dumb while I thought of a good excuse for my missing leather jacket. "So who is he?"

"A jilted ex-boyfriend named Kyle Peterson. I dumped him before I moved to Greenfield. Haven't even talked to him for over a year, and he was the last person I'd ever expect to be a nut job."

"I figured it would be an ex-boyfriend, if you'll recall."

"Yeah, talk about obsessive," she said. "The police told me he'd been living out of a minivan, and he'd been sending the emails from the public library."

"So you'll be moving back into your apartment, then," I said.

"Sure will. Where's your other leather jacket, Marshall?"

"I forgot it downtown at a friend's store."

"You don't have any friends, remember?"

"Well, she's less of a friend and more of a client," I said. "Her name is Stella Weinberg, and her store is called The Curiosity Nook. It's in the yellow pages. Feel free to call her and confirm the whereabouts of my jacket, if you like."

"No, thanks," she said. "I need you to tell me that I'm not going crazy."

"All right, then. You're the sanest twenty-three year old I know."

"That's *not* what I meant, and you know it."

"Right now, I don't know anything more than I am tired as hell and I'd like to hit the hay for a while." I said, half-yawning. "Look, your stalker is now in police custody, and you can get on with your life."

"You're kidding, right? I mean, how am I supposed to do that after last night?"

"I dunno – maybe talk to a shrink or something. The past week has been traumatic."

"I'm *not* going crazy. I know what I saw last night, and I can't tell anyone, because they would never believe me in a thousand years."

"I didn't say you were going crazy."

She picked up the remote control and hurled it against the wall, smashing it into pieces. *"You were there, Marshall! Why are you acting like this is nothing?"*

"Hey now – try to calm down," I said, in a non-threatening voice. "I don't even know where you were last night, and frankly I'm surprised that you left my apartment. Why don't you tell me everything that happened?"

She glared at me with a look that could bore through masonry. "I went to the pub at Chesterton for a drink, because I was sick of hiding out in your apartment. I had a few too many, and thought it would be best to head over to a friend's dorm. I walked up the path beside the Humanities Building, and this nut jumped out from nowhere. He had a knife, and he was going to stab me. Suddenly, a guy came right out of the sky and flattened my stalker. He beat the living crap out of him and kept asking the guy about a body. His voice sounded just like yours, Marshall! *He came out of the sky!"*

The room fell silent as I considered how to respond. I didn't want to insult her intelligence by dismissing her story as the ranting of a drunken college student. The last thing I wanted to do was give her a reason to believe she was losing her mind.

"Tell me what else happened," I said calmly.

"He had glowing eyes. He was wearing a leather jacket, and he wore a hoodie that covered his face. He handcuffed the guy to a sewer grate, and when I asked him if it was you, he took off into the sky!"

"When you say he took off into the sky, what precisely does that mean?" I asked.

"He could *fly*! He had glowing eyes, and the guy could fly!"

I got up from my chair and walked back to the kitchen. "Would you like a cup of coffee or something? You're pretty upset."

"Damned right I'm upset. I've been scared to death because of a stalker who tried to kill me, and then I was rescued by a freaking superhero!"

"Stop yelling at me. I'm not saying I don't believe you. Would you like a cup of coffee or not?"

"No. Look, I'm sorry. I just know that a flying man saved my life last night. I have a mysterious downstairs neighbor who likes to think of himself as a hermit, owns two leather outfits and right now, one of your jackets is missing, and I am going crazy, and I don't know what to do anymore."

Marnie's eyes filled with tears, and she sobbed into her hands as I came into the living room with a box of Kleenex.

"Here are some tissues," I said, softly. "You're not crazy, okay? The world is filled with unexplainable phenomenon, but a flying man? Come on, they'll start measuring you for a straitjacket if you talk to anyone about this."

"What do you mean by that?" She blew her nose.

"Well, let's assume that superheroes actually do exist." I said, smiling warmly. "This guy saved you last night, and your stalker will soon be serving time, right?"

"Yeah."

"You didn't tell the police, and I'm sure your stalker probably will. That means the police will want to know what really happened last night outside the Humanities Building.

Do you think for one second the cops are going to go public with your revelation? I mean, come on. If you're worried that you're going crazy, do you honestly believe they'd let the press in on a bizarre story like this?"

"What's your point?"

"The point I'm making is that regardless of who or what rescued you, maybe some things are better left unsaid. I mean, if Greenfield has a resident superhero who keeps the city safe, perhaps it's best to keep your knowledge of his existence a secret."

"Why should I? People need to know about what happened to me."

"You think so?" I tried to be the voice of reason. "Let's assume that you have conclusive proof of his existence. Do you want to become a paparazzo's wet dream? Don't you think the press would hound you at every turn? You'd become a national celebrity! You're an attractive young woman, and you could attract a multitude of stalkers who want to become your special friend."

"Oh come on," she said, curtly. "Get off your soapbox."

"I'll get off my soapbox if you'll get your head out of your ass. You're accusing me of being freaking Superman while questioning if you're losing your mind. Do you think the US government would be interested in your story? Is it possible that Homeland Security or the FBI might begin to monitor your every move? Hiding out in my apartment from Kyle Peterson would look like a trip to Disneyland if you went public about this."

She got up from the sofa and stormed to the front door of my apartment. "You know what? A flying man with glowing eyes saved me last night. He sounded a lot like you. He wore a leather jacket like you. Marshall Conrad invited me to stay at his apartment while he helped me uncover the identity of my stalker. Seems pretty fishy to me. Maybe you're not the guy who saved me, but I know what I witnessed, and so help me God, I am going to find out who he is."

"Where are you going?"

"*Away from you.*" She barked as she slammed the door.

CHAPTER 15

The back room of The Curiosity Nook was bathed in a haunting, eerie glow from dozens of candles. Stella Weinberg had placed them in a large circle around a cairn-like pile of spiral-engraved rocks. The freshly swept cement floor was covered with a multitude of white-chalked symbols that radiated in diagonal lines from each of the candles. Twelve small ceramic pots burned something that smelled like jasmine mixed with orange peel and rested at intervals along a bright yellow circle drawn with some kind of sand-like substance.

"This is very creepy," I said, as I sipped a cup of tepid herbal tea. "I hope you're not expecting anything spectacular, Stella, because I still don't have a clue as to how you expect me to talk to the rocks."

"I know," she said plaintively. "I've pulled every conceivable spell I can think of into setting up this room for you. My hope is that one of them will help you figure it out."

"You should have a fire extinguisher handy. There's a lot of stuff burning in this room."

"Oh, those candles won't burn anything; the flames are enchanted."

"Huh?"

She lit a small candle in the center of the dinette and pushed it toward me. "Stick your finger in the flame," she said. "It won't hurt."

I tentatively put my index finger into the flame, and instead of intense pain, a stinging bite of cold raised the hair on my arm and formed goose bumps on my skin.

"It's freezing," I said as waved my hand over the candle. "How did you manage to do that?"

"Mellish Tulip wax – very expensive stuff."

"Geez, you should package it and sell it in your store; you'd make a killing."

"Not a chance, Conrad," said Stella. "It takes a few hundred thousand tulip petal scrapings to create one small candle, and these tulips don't come from Holland."

"Don't tell me – they can only be found in the unseen world."

"Bingo."

"So what are all of the chalk drawings for?"

"Protection," she said. "We don't exactly know who or what you are going to be talking to, and the last thing I need is a class-eight demon entering the near world through the back room of my store. Not that you couldn't take him down, of course – Vanguards are far more powerful than most demons."

"The stuff you're burning in those little ceramic pots, what's it for?"

"Backup plan in case the other protective measures don't work."

"What do you mean?"

"Agents of the darkness dislike anything that smells pleasant." She poured herself a cup of tea. "That's my own special blend of Angelica Root, Bay Leaves and Blessed Thistle. I won an award for that recipe, you know."

"What are the yellow circles around the ceramic pots?"

"Root salt."

"What does it do?"

"Keeps the pots from being overturned by anything that dislikes the smell of what I'm burning."

"Well that makes sense. Did I mention that this is unbelievably creepy?"

"Relax." She took my hand. "You're going to be fine. Trust me."

I looked at the pile of rocks in the center of the circle and noticed they were arranged by size with the largest stones on the bottom and the smallest on top. A white circle had been drawn on the floor about three feet away from the rocks. I assumed Stella would be telling me I'd have to sit there until something happened.

"Okay, Stella, I might as well get this thing over with. What do you want me to do?"

She pointed at the circle in front of the pile of stones. "Sit down in that circle and make something happen, but don't step on any of the chalk symbols, as that would screw up the spells – oh, and take off your shoes. You have to go barefoot."

"I don't have to take off my clothes or anything like that, do I?"

"No, we're conducting a ritual here, not making a porno. Just take off your shoes and tiptoe into the circle."

"All right." I slipped off my shoes and stuffed my socks inside. I looked for a path that would offer as little disruption to the chalk symbols as possible. "I still don't know what you're expecting, but here goes."

I carefully stepped over a symbol that looked like a two-sided fork when a sharp stabbing pain shot up through my feet and into my brain. The air filled with the sharp copper smell of blood, causing bile to rise up into my throat. "Damn, that hurts!" I called out, taking another four steps past a series of inverted triangles until I spotted a clear path to the chalk circle Stella had pointed out.

"Are you all right?" Stella shouted.

"Yeah, just a massive headache, that's all. Do you smell it?"

"Smell what?"

"Blood – I caught a whiff of it as soon as I stepped over the first symbol."

"All I can smell is the stuff in the ceramic pots. Are you sure you're alright?"

"I'm okay. Just going to sit down in the circle."

"Marshall, your eyes are glowing! What's happening?"

"Nothing. I need to concentrate." I sat down inside the circle and crossed my legs.

I looked up at the pile of rocks as a wave of heat washed over my body. The smell of blood burned at my sinuses, and a jolt of nausea churned through my stomach with nearly enough force to make me double over.

"Okay, rocks, say something, because you obviously know what the hell I am!"

Silence.

"I'm a Vanguard, you stupid freaking rocks. Don't piss me off!"

Silence.

"Listen asshole, my eyes only glow when I'm in the presence of evil. Speak your name, or I'll smash these rocks into dust!"

As soon as I closed my mouth, I became weightless.

The flickering, ambient light from Stella's candles disappeared into a vapor, and the cairn dissolved into a mist. I could feel myself drawn through a tunnel so black that even my glowing eyes had little effect. My ears popped as the darkness gradually gave way to a horizon in the distance. I slowly stood up to see a terrifying landscape of burning houses with pillars of smoke towering into a haunting purple sky. The air was filled with the sound of gunshots and screaming voices. A soot-filled breeze clogged my nostrils, and the air tasted like ash and death.

I hovered above the rooftops and stared at a raging firestorm where Greenfield's downtown core used to be. A squadron of fighter jets roared in the distance and dropped a payload of napalm on a crowd of hundreds of people who were shooting and stabbing one another as they stepped over the mutilated bodies of what were probably their neighbors and friends.

I flew over a stand of burning trees and landed in the middle of Delaney Park. The duck pond was black as tar, and dozens of bloated, dead bodies bobbed up and down as a mob of crazed people raced toward me, screaming obscenities.

"Freeze!" I bellowed. The mob ran at me, and I tried to fly upward to avoid them. Their yellow eyes seethed with hatred, and I shielded my face to protect myself from their blows. A flash of terror seized my body as the mob passed through me and headed toward a group of soldiers firing automatic weapons.

"Oh my God," I whispered. "I'm not really here. I must be seeing the future."

It was carnage on a staggering scale. The entire city of Greenfield was burning, and its citizens were hacking one another to pieces with everything from axes and shovels to their bare hands.

A voice that shattered glass and shook the earth boomed in the distance. *"The gate is open, Vanguard. You stand alone!"*

"Who are you?" I called out. "What the hell is this?"

"We feed on the longest day."

Suddenly, a force pushed me back through the black tunnel, and I landed in a heap adjacent to the cairn. My body was drenched in sweat, and my clothes were smoldering.

"Marshall! Jumpin', dyin' Moses, are you all right? You disappeared!" Stella raced toward me with a fire extinguisher in her hands.

"I'm okay," I said in a weak voice. "I think I understand the meaning behind the rocks now."

"What do you mean? What happened?"

"The future. We have until the summer solstice to stop it."

CHAPTER 16

"What happens on the summer solstice?" Stella asked, as she helped me to my feet.

The room was spinning, and I staggered like I was going to pass out.

"All hell is going to break loose," I coughed. My clothes smelled like I'd slept next to a campfire, and the stench of blood clung inside my nostrils as I steadied myself on Stella's shoulder. "That's all I know for sure. I need a drink of water."

"Let's get you into some dry clothes," she said, as she carefully led me away from the makeshift cairn in the center of the floor. "I've seen some amazing feats of magic in my life, but I've never seen a person from the near world vanish into thin air like that. I'd say your attempt at communicating with the rocks was an unqualified success. Not bad for a guy who didn't know what he was doing."

"Yeah, that was first for me." I sat down at the dinette in the corner. "I feel like someone kicked the crap out of me."

She poured a glass of water and slid it across the table. "What's the meaning behind the rocks? What did you see?"

I gulped back the water and handed her the empty glass. My vision was blurry, and my head screamed like a freight train. "Your guess is as good as mine. This is unseen world stuff, and my base of operations is the city of Greenfield."

"Tell me what you witnessed!" she demanded.

"Death." I pulled my socks back onto my feet. "The entire city was on fire. The air reeked of smoke and burning corpses. Mobs of people were stabbing and shooting one another all over town. It was complete anarchy."

"Mobs of people – you mean, like zombies? Jeez, I hope not." Stella flashed a worried look. "I ran into a zombie horde in Littletown, where the Cheevers hold court over the Grassland Peasantry. They're killing machines."

I gave her a confused look for a long moment. "Okay, I don't know what the *hell* you're talking about."

"I'm talking about the living dead," she said.

"Gotcha. Well these weren't zombies, then. Just mobs of people killing each other with everything from machetes to baseball bats." I rubbed my eyes. "A huge, booming voice told me that the gate was open, and I was alone. It said it would feed on the longest day, so I have to assume it was talking about the summer solstice."

"That's less than a week from now," said Stella. "What about the rocks?"

I glanced at the cairn and remembered what Stella told me about spirals when we first met. "You said that spirals are a symbol of rebirth or resurrection, didn't you?"

"Yes, that's a standard belief in many cultures both here and in the unseen world."

"Ingrid said that something called a Púca was responsible for the killings."

"That's right. She also told you that the Púca's host is living among us."

"And that he had many followers," I added. "I'm no expert, but I'd say the spirals are a message aimed squarely at human beings."

"Why?"

"Because the symbol has been found at the scene of two murders, and Sheriff Neuman said that spiral symbols were appearing all over town."

"Right. I get it. You also found a spiral rock when you stopped that abduction, and you found a spiral scribbling on the picture of your neighbor."

"So what makes average people become mass murderers?" I asked. "Ingrid said that fear is the only thing that matters to a Púca – maybe the spirals and the graphic nature of the murders are supposed to scare the living shit out of people."

Stella's face became ashen and she slumped in her chair. "Spirits protect us. This is just like what happened in New France back in 1528."

"New France? What are you talking about?"

"Dammit, I need a copy of *Chroniclus,* and I don't have one," she said. "I'm going to have to talk to Zona Beltane and see if I can borrow hers."

"What's a *Chroniclus*?"

"It's like Hansard for witches. We keep records of any incursions into the near world. If it isn't listed in *Chroniclus*, it never happened."

"What happened in New France?"

Stella bit her thumb. "Trying to remember. Something about Lake Champlain boiling over and mass killings in what is now Burlington, Vermont."

My jaw dropped. "What are you saying? This crap happens *regularly*?"

"I'm not sure," she admitted. "Sentry Witches are gatekeepers, and sometimes certain residents of the unseen world sneak through without our knowledge. It might be for reasons beyond our ability to understand. What I can tell you is that a Púca is a difficult creature to defeat, even for a Vanguard. If we're about to square off with an army of Púcas, well, I don't even want to consider that possibility."

"Why?"

"Because supernatural creatures outnumber near world residents on an almost limitless scale."

I gave her a confused look as I attempted to stand up. My head was throbbing violently, and my legs were still weak. "You're a witch. Can't you just get your coven together and send them back?"

"Do you remember anything about high school biology?" she asked.

"No, I was a lousy student."

"Well, consider that it takes nine months for a human being to come into this world. It takes a further eighteen years until that human grows up, and there's at least a dozen or so years included in the equation devoted to traditional education. I'm over fifty – I spent more than twenty years learning how to master witchcraft."

"So?"

"So everything!" she groaned. "What chance do we have against supernatural creatures that can spawn at the utterance of a spell or incantation?"

I felt sick to my stomach as the gravity of Stella's assertion began to sink in. If the spiral rocks were indeed a mechanism to spawn supernatural beings in the mortal world, then it was a race against time to discover how to prevent my vision from becoming a reality.

"I have to rest," I said weakly. "Can you help me get back to my apartment, please?"

"I'll call a taxi for you. Meanwhile, I am going to consult with the elders."

CHAPTER 17

I've never suffered any major injuries in my crime-fighting career – I guess I'm just lucky that way. I've crashed into trees, fallen off buildings and even experienced ten thousand volts of electricity blasting through my body after lifting a car from under a collapsed power pole, but I suffered no ill effects. You would think that after having foreseen an apocalyptic drama play itself out in the backroom of Stella Weinberg's curiosity shop, something as simple as a migraine would be minor in comparison. Sadly, you'd be mistaken.

After I returned to my apartment, my mind pored through endless vignettes of killings that hadn't yet happened, and my body adjusted to these dark dreams by punishing me with a tsunami of nausea. Normally, I receive one or two visions, but this was off-the-scale psychic carnage. And superpowers or not, I couldn't keep up. As soon as one violent series of images ended, an entirely new set of visions stormed through my brain. My energy was spent, so I stretched out on my couch with a bucket on the floor beside me. I covered my eyes with a sleeping mask, because the smallest beam of light that filtered through the blinds cut into my head like a welder's torch.

Time doesn't exactly fly when you're seized by visions of children shooting their parents or shopping mall security officers smashing little old ladies into pulp with baseball bats. I popped ibuprofen in my mouth like it was candy, and if anyone had seen me lying on the couch, they'd probably have called a coroner. If any good came from the visions, it's that I was fortunate enough to see the face of the person hosting Greenfield's resident psycho immigrant from the unseen world.

He was standing high atop the gazebo in the middle of Delaney Park, surrounded by hundreds of men, women and children chanting in a language that didn't sound like any dialect from the near world. They stood naked, covered from head to foot in blood and gore. Their eyes gazed up in hypnotic fascination at the young, blond-haired man standing high above them. In his hands were two rocks, similar to the ones in Stella's curiosity shop, but this time the spirals blazed in white light, illuminating the gazebo like a stage.

His hollow eyes were black as pitch, and he grinned wildly at the crowd. His yellow, stained teeth contrasted his pale skin, adding to his already sinister appearance. He wasn't naked like those who surrounded the gazebo – he wore white coveralls that were amazingly free of any bloodstains, and his thin blond hair hung limply to his narrow shoulders.

Beside him lay a large, organic mass about the size of a compact car, which oozed a dark brown substance over the roof of the gazebo, dripping into large puddles on the ground. The mass resembled a human organ, its thick veins stretched out from the base to a large opening that opened and closed, emitting a green glow that shot into the sky.

The host grinned madly as he dropped each glowing stone into the orifice, causing it to shake violently. Suddenly the orifice peeled back like a horrific flower. Its fleshy petals flattened themselves on the roof of the gazebo and braced the mass as the green light turned crimson. A claw-like hand emerged through the orifice, its bony fingers stretched out and reaching for the young host. The vision ended with the image of the host pulling a thickly veined arm through the orifice, and I assumed it was attached to the Púca Ingrid had mentioned.

I took the sleeping mask off my face and pulled the wax earplugs out of my skull as I slowly sat up on my couch.

I looked at my watch. Eighteen hours had passed since the vision in Stella Weinberg's backroom. "Holy suffering crap, that was unlike anything I've experienced in my life," I gulped. "Gotta call Stella."

I had just reached for my telephone when someone started pounding at my apartment door.

CHAPTER 18

Rarely does anyone knock at my apartment door. Save for Marnie Brindle inviting herself over, it just never happens. "It's probably some moron selling newspaper subscriptions." I grumbled, deciding I'd ignore whoever wanted my attention.

My stomach rumbled as I shuffled into the kitchen to find something to eat. I poked my head into the refrigerator when the pounding at the door started again.

"Marshall Conrad, you open this door right now!" demanded a female voice that sounded like it belonged at a prayer meeting.

"We don't want any!" I shouted to the door. "Go away."

Undaunted, the voice became shrill, and the door shook violently as whoever was standing outside my apartment became insistent that I let her in. *"Conrad, let me in right now, or I'll break your G-D door down!"*

"Crap," I mumbled, as I looked through the peephole. "I don't see anyone at my door. I don't do practical jokes, Marnie."

"You're testing my patience, Conrad... open this G-D door *right* now! This is your last warning!"

"Dammit," I growled through my teeth as I flipped the dead bolt and quickly swung open the door in an obvious display of dissatisfaction. To my great surprise, Marnie Brindle was not standing outside my apartment. Instead, a little old woman wearing a teal cotton pill overcoat, standing no more than five feet high looked up at me with a serious frown on her face.

"Well, are you going to invite me in?" asked the old woman.

I snorted. "Not bloody likely! My mother always taught me never to invite strangers into my apartment. Harmless looking old biddy or not, I don't know you, but I'd be interested in learning about how you know me."

The old lady scowled. "I don't have the G-D time for this crap, outta my way."

I didn't see her purse coming, but it must have been filled with lead, because when it connected with my midsection, I flew into the wall behind me. My head hit the gyp-rock with a loud crunch, and I slid onto the carpet. "Ow," I said, sheepishly. "Can't breathe – "

The little old lady stood over me and extended a thickly veined and liver-spotted right hand. "You'll live," she said. "Don't say I didn't warn you. You can deduct the damages to your wall from the money you owe The Guild in unpaid dues."

"Pardon me?" I asked, still dazed.

"You got the letter announcing that you'd be meeting me," she said, helping me to my feet with a tug on my arm that almost pulled it out of its socket. "I'm Ruby Thiessen. I've been assigned to you."

"Assigned to me?" I winced as I rubbed my shoulder. "What the heck are you talking about?"

The old lady shoved me aside and strode into my living room, taking a seat on my easy chair. She opened her purse and pulled out a pewter flask. "Want a shot?" she asked.

"No, I don't drink," I said, still dazed.

She unscrewed the cap and held the flask in the air. "A toast, then. To clean living and treating your body like a temple. Whiskey is the Devil's drink, and may the Devil remain scared shitless of me!" She gulped back a huge shot and grimaced as she replaced the cap before putting the flask back into her purse. "Guess you probably have no idea who I am, is that it?" she asked.

"You guessed right." I sat down on my couch. "I've never been assaulted by a senior citizen."

"Fair enough. What do you want to know?"

"You were assigned to me by whom?"

"The Guild," she said. "I'm pretty sure I established this about two minutes ago, when I knocked your sorry ass into the wall."

"I'm not a member of The Guild. I don't even know what it is," I said impatiently. "Look, forget about the damage to my apartment. I feel like death warmed over, so if you could just go back to the Justice League or whatever you call it, I can get on with my day."

Ruby gave me a dirty look and then opened her purse again. "You done flapping your gums?" She pulled out a compact and started applying foundation to her deeply wrinkled face. "I'm not leaving. We've got a lot of work to do."

"What work?" I groaned. "Listen, Mrs. Thiessen, there's a creature from some bizarre mystical realm that I didn't even know existed until a day ago, and he's somehow possessed a local wacko to chop up the good citizens of Greenfield. All hell is going to break loose on the summer solstice if I can't find the guy, and, by the way, why hasn't your so-called Guild done anything about it?"

She flashed me a dirty look as she closed her compact with a loud snap and stuffed it back into her purse. "You're an idiot, did you know that? You also don't know who the hell you're talking to."

"Presumably you're some great sage from The Guild, and you've come here to teach me your mysterious superhero ways," I said. "When you're done here, what do they do? Beam you up to a secret base somewhere?"

"There is no secret base" she said. "I'm staying at the Concord Motor Inn. I'm a member of The Guild, but I'm semi-retired. I'm not here to train you, either. Do I look like G-D *Yoda* to you?"

"So why are you here?"

Ruby stood up from my easy chair and walked over to the living room window. "I'm here because we're stretched pretty thin, Conrad," she said, as she adjusted her silver hair that was tied in a tight bun on the back of her head.

"What do you mean?"

"The Guild is composed of meta-powered beings from all walks of life. There are over two hundred members, and right now; every single one of them is busy with missions ranging from battling international terrorism to keeping a huge asteroid from smashing into the earth and destroying life as we know it."

"And they've yanked you out of retirement so you can work with me?"

She spun around and her thin lips formed a sly smile. "I'm your sidekick, but don't let it go to your head, and don't think I'll be taking any orders from the likes of you," she lectured. "You might be a Vanguard, but I've been a Guild member for over thirty years, and just because I look like a fragile old lady, it doesn't mean I can't mop the floor with you."

"You're a Vanguard, then?" I asked. "Stella said I should have been seconded, whatever that means."

"Pfft – I'm no Vanguard. I work for a living."

"Then what are you?"

"A Chieftain," she said. "I'm also an expert on the supernatural, and the creature with designs on Greenfield is a nasty bit of business."

"The Púca? You know about this thing?"

"Yep. His handle is Grim Geoffrey, and he's pure concentrated evil."

"This is insane." I groaned, getting up from the sofa and going into the kitchen to put on a kettle of water. "Faeries. Púcas. Little old women who carry armored handbags. I didn't ask for any of this, you know."

She followed me into the kitchen and sat down at head of the table. "That you didn't ask for any of this is unimportant, so suck it up. Grim Geoffrey is as real as the unsolved murders in your happy little town, and he's one powerful son of a bitch."

I sat down opposite her and waited for the kettle to boil. "So, Ruby, do you have a superhero name like in the comics?"

"Nope."

"Why not?"

"Because it's dumb." She shook her head. "That and the good citizens of planet earth don't know that meta-humans exist, even though we save their collective asses on a regular basis."

"That's too bad." I grinned. "They should call you *Raging Granny*."

She slammed her fist on the table. "Are you always this kind to senior citizens?" she snapped. "We're not exactly off to a good start, here, and I had so hoped that we'd become the best of friends."

The kettle started whistling, so I walked over to the cupboard and grabbed two coffee mugs. "Want a cup of tea?"

"Nope, I keep my favorite drink in a flask," she said, tapping at her purse. "Do you have any idea what you're up against?"

"Not really," I said, as I poured the water over an orange pekoe tea bag in the bottom of my coffee mug. "I guess this Grim Geoffrey is like a really mean-ass fairy that feeds on fear. The murders were committed by his host. I guess he's a parasite of sorts."

"You're partially right, Conrad." She said. "Grim Geoffrey is a Púca, but he's not a pure breed."

"Come again?"

"He's a hybrid. Part Demon and part Púca."

"So what does that mean?" I fished the tea bag out of my mug with a spoon.

She pursed her lips. "It means that he can take physical form separate of his host, and that his followers are also hybrids."

"Anything else?"

"Yep. You have to kill his host if you want to stop him."

I spun around and stared at her. "Whoa. Wait a minute, little lady. I'm in the business of saving lives, not taking them."

Ruby got up from the chair and walked back to the living room window. "That's what I was afraid you'd say. Actually, that's what The Guild predicted you'd say. That's why they sent me."

"What are you talking about?" I asked.

"If you don't kill the host, we'll have to do this the hard way," she said.

"And that would be?"

"We're going to have to defeat Grim Geoffrey in his own realm."

"Where's that?"

"The Netherworld," she whispered. "In order to do that, we're going to have to locate a portal."

CHAPTER 19

"We're being followed," muttered Ruby, as she peered out the side view mirror of my Tempo. "I understand that you stupidly offered yourself as the prime suspect in the murders. That likely explains the ghost car tailing us since we left your apartment."

I glanced in the rearview mirror to see a gray Crown Victoria with tinted windows about three cars behind us. Out of the corner of my eye, I could see Ruby's frown deepen as she shook her head in an obvious display of disapproval.

"What else was I to do?" I groaned. "It wasn't until you came along that I even knew the name of the killer, and the past week hasn't exactly been pleasant, you know."

"Sounds like a personal problem." She opened her purse and pulled out the flask, then took a big swig and offered it to me.

"Jeezis, put that down, for crying out loud!" I snapped, as I pushed her hand below the dashboard. "The last thing I need right now is a drunk driving charge."

"I take it back – you're not stupid. Just horribly naïve."

"What the hell is *that* supposed to mean?"

Ruby gave me a sour look.

"Think about it for a second. The cops are following you because you're a suspect in two unsolved murders, and you're worrying about being charged with drunk driving?"

I pulled ahead of a city bus and lost sight of the unmarked car. Ruby was right. While I'd intended to learn more about the killer by injecting myself in the official investigation, I hadn't considered the possibility that a supernatural creature was behind the murders. I'd believed this was just a case of finding a serial killer, and been counting on clairvoyance to point me in the right direction.

"Shit." I felt like a complete amateur. "You're right. Everyone is right. Cripes, I wish I was normal."

"Self-pity is G-D embarrassing for both of us," said Ruby. "No point in bemoaning your lot in life. We've got work to do. Pull over into that parking lot."

"Why?"

"Because I want to know who's following the ghost car."

"Are you serious?"

"Yep. White Honda Civic."

"Oh Jeezis," I said under my breath as I pulled into the parking lot next to a 7-11. "That's Marnie Brindle."

"Who's that?" She looked out the rear window of my car. "A cop or something?"

I gripped the steering wheel so hard that my knuckles turned white. "Nope. Just a big pain in the ass."

The ghost car passed us and headed up the boulevard as Marnie's Honda Civic made a hard right turn up an alley. I cut the engine and then heard something hissing from the front left side of my car.

"This day just keeps getting better and better," I grumbled.

"How come?" asked Ruby.

"For starters, I'm getting dumped on by a little old lady with blue hair, who should be vacationing in the Bahamas or sitting on a rocking chair with her knitting. The cops are following me, Marnie Brindle has it in her head that I'm a superhero, and now my car has a flat tire."

"Please tell me you know how to change a tire," she asked, trying not to laugh.

"Yeah, I do." I stared at the steering wheel.

"Well then, get out and change the G-D tire for crying out loud!"

"I can't," I mumbled, my face burning.

"Dear God, why?" Her sly smile had turned into a full-blown grin.

"No jack."

There was silence for about ten seconds, and then she broke into a roaring fit of laughter. "Okay," she said between giggles. "I understand this isn't exactly the Batmobile, but for shit's sake, what kind of crime fighter doesn't have a functional jack?"

"One who is having the worst day he's had in years." I wished I could shrink into my seat.

"Go get your spare out of the trunk and grab a tire iron."

"Why, so you can club me with it?" I muttered. "It's pretty obvious you dislike me for some reason."

"I didn't say that I don't like you." Ruby rolled her eyes. "I said I hate Vanguards. Actually for a novice, you have many redeeming qualities. Go get your spare tire."

"Ruby, we don't have a jack."

"You don't need one," she said as she reached into her purse and pulled out a pair of red leather gloves. "Level-fifty Chieftain, at your service."

I gave her an incredulous look. "Wait a minute; you can't lift up my car. People might see."

"Big deal. If anyone asks, I'll tell them you're my son and you're having chest pains. People always believe that family members can summon Herculean strength when a loved one is in peril. Besides, I'm not going to lift it over my head."

"Fine." I opened the door and headed to the back of my car. Ruby got out and walked over to the front bumper as I rolled the temporary spare to the front of the car and leaned it against the passenger door.

"A screw. I drove over a screw, and it got stuck in the tire," I said, as I pulled the hubcap off with the tire iron and loosened the four lug nuts.

"Coast is clear," said Ruby as she discreetly slid her left hand under the front bumper. "Slap that tire on quickly, in case anyone sees us."

The car creaked loudly as she pulled up on the bumper, raising it about four inches from the pavement. I quickly unscrewed the lug nuts and pulled off the flat tire. "I need new brakes," I muttered.

"Hurry up," said Ruby.

I slid the new tire over the hub and screwed in the lug nuts, then gestured for her to lower the car. She let go, and my car bounced as the tire hit the pavement.

"Thanks." I tightened the lug nuts and replaced the hubcap. "By the way, what's a level-fifty Chieftain?"

She took off her gloves and opened the passenger door. "Someone who is as strong as a Vanguard but less impulsive."

I'd thrown the flat into the trunk and closed the lid when I noticed Marnie's white Honda Civic parked behind a dumpster adjacent to the 7-11. "Sheeeeit," I grumbled as I got back in the car and started the engine.

"What now?" asked Ruby.

"Marnie Brindle is parked over there," I said, pointing at the dumpster. "She probably saw us."

Ruby coughed and then pulled her flask out of her purse. "You going to fill me in on this woman, or shall I go over to her car and smash it into a million pieces?" She took a slug.

"She's my neighbor," I said. "The condensed version is that she had a stalker, and I saved her life. She identified me as I questioned the guy, and when she confronted me, I took off into the sky."

Ruby burst into another roaring fit of laughter. "Is that all?" she asked. "You're a Vanguard. Just hit her with a mind whammy, and she'll forget everything."

"I don't know how to do a mind whammy. I don't know how to do anything, it would appear." I said. "Some nut from the unseen world named Grim Geoffrey is going to tear up everyone in Greenfield, and now I'm told we have to go into the Netherworld, whatever the heck that is."

"Stop your bellyaching – you're a gifted Vanguard, so cut yourself some slack," she said, in about as close to a consoling tone as she could muster. "The Netherworld is a very real place, but it's nothing like what you've been lead to believe."

"What do you mean? No eternal damnation?"

"Not in the traditional sense." She looked out the window at the customers exiting the 7-11. "The residents don't carry pitchforks, and near-world residents who were assholes in life don't go there after they're dead."

"So what is it?"

"If the unseen world has a bad side of town, then the Netherworld would be it. There's no lake of fire or bottomless pit, but there's a lot of brimstone, burning sulphur and a shit pile of powerful demons and other nightmarish creatures."

"I take it you've been there before?"

"A few times," she said. "Right now there is a kind of civil war going on as the various entities duke it out with each other for influence and power. That could be why Grim Geoffrey is moving out and taking his followers with him."

"Moving out?"

Ruby looked at me and her frown returned. "It means that the cost of remaining in the Netherworld isn't worth anything that Geoffrey is prepared to pay when there's a whole world full of free land and about six billion inhabitants to graze on."

"That's it? This isn't a sinister plan at all; this is about friggin real estate!"

"Could be." Ruby took a last shot of Rye from her flask. "Of course, there is a negative side effect, should he succeed."

"What's that?" I asked, as Marnie's car pulled away from the dumpster.

Ruby's face became grim. "You can't have two hells – it upsets the balance of life as we know it."

"And?"

"Let me put it this way." She stuffed the empty flask into her purse. "If he's successful, it means that humanity as we know it will cease to exist, because every spectral entity and his dog will occupy this plane of existence."

CHAPTER 20

The sun was setting as Ruby examined the spiral-engraved rock we'd found lying on the top of the mailbox. "I have to admit, this is new, even for Grim Geoffrey."

"What is?"

"These rocks. This is something entirely different." She tossed it to me, and I added it to the ten other rocks we'd found since changing my tire outside the 7-11. We'd been driving around town for three hours. My stomach growled loudly as my nose caught a whiff of pizza coming from De-Niro's restaurant down the block.

"I take it that we're following the rocks, is that it?" I asked.

"Yes and no," she said, staring at a vacant lot across the street. "I have a hunch the rocks are meant to be like thumbtacks on a map."

"What do you mean?"

"Ever been to a strange place and lost your sense of direction?"

"Yeah, why?"

"Given that you're a man, I know that you would never consider stopping to ask for directions, and it's like that with creatures from the netherworld. They would be lost without the spiral stones offering directions."

I followed her across the street to get a closer look at the vacant lot. The streetlights were out, and the fading sunlight gave the lot a sinister appearance. I'd just crawled through a hole that had been cut in the chain-link fence when my eyes flared into brilliant white light and a pain shot through the center of my brain, causing me to double over.

"Ahh, seeker's light," said Ruby, as she looked at me through the corner of her eye. "You getting a psychic visual on something bad about to happen? If that's the case, I need to put on my gloves."

"No, I'm not seeing anything in my mind." I winced. "Just be on your guard, because my eyes don't flare up of their own accord."

She knelt down behind a pile of discarded refrigerators and slipped on a pair of red leather gloves.

"We have company," she said, gesturing toward the rusted-out hulk of a van. "I hate cats. They always look right at home whether sleeping in a basket or hanging out in a spooky place like this."

I directed my gaze over to where she was pointing and wasn't at all surprised to see Walter sitting on the roof of the rusted-out car.

"Cripes, that's Walter," I whispered. "Jeez, I haven't seen him since yesterday."

"You're acquainted with that fat feline, I take it?"

"Yes, that's my cat," I said, as I rubbed my temples. "Well he's half my cat and half Stella's I guess."

"Who is that?"

"Oh, just a witch I consult with on a regular basis. Walter is her familiar, and he seems to be the only one who knows where the third body is hidden."

Ruby cocked a wrinkled eyebrow. "You lead an interesting life, Marshall," she said quietly. "You sure she hasn't put some spell on you? Because people like us don't normally associate with practitioners of magic."

"Stella Weinberg is a good person. She's an archivist, and she's partially responsible for uncovering the mystery behind the rocks."

"Take it easy," said Ruby, motioning for me to calm down. "We're going to be in need of her assistance if we want to take down Grim Geoffrey."

A cool breeze kicked up the dust in the vacant lot as we turned our attention back to Walter. His unblinking gaze seemed to be fixed on the darkest corner of the lot.

"You're certain of that cat's loyalties, right?" she asked.

"Why?"

Ruby grunted. "It just seems odd that he's living with two people. A familiar can only serve one master, not two."

I shot her an accusatory glare. "What are you getting at?"

"Never mind," she said, dismissing my question with a wave of her hand. "That cat hasn't moved a muscle in the last five minutes. Focus your mind on whatever it is he's staring at, and tell me what you see."

"I don't know how to do that," I said. "Jeez, you make everything sound so freaking easy, and you're forgetting that I'm a novice."

"I don't have the G-D time to be your wet nurse," Ruby said. "Either focus your abilities or get your skinny ass over to that cat and put your hand on him. I G-D guarantee you'll see everything he can see. Now make up your mind!"

"Fine." I grumbled as I closed my eyes and began to concentrate on Walter. In an instant, I could feel Walter's heartbeat throbbing in my temples. My senses became supercharged, and I noticed a sudden drop in the temperature as the wind shifted direction. I opened my eyes and could clearly see the dark corner of the vacant lot that Walter was staring at.

"What do you see?" she asked.

"A leg," I whispered. "It's poking out from a shallow grave, I think."

"Third body. Do you see anything else?"

"No, just the leg. What do we do now?"

"Look for clues and tell The Guild. They'll let the authorities know about the..."

Before Ruby could finish her sentence, the ground shook violently, and the next thing I knew, I was sailing through the air, crash landing upside down against the rusted-out car. I opened my eyes and gasped as I witnessed the size of what had just hit me.

"*You'll die in the dirt, oldsy woman!*" the creature screamed. It nailed Ruby in the chest with what appeared to be a large tree limb. The force of its blow sent her reeling backwards a few feet, but amazingly, Ruby appeared unharmed.

"*The Vanguards can't protects you!*" it howled in a booming baritone voice. It raised the club high in the air directly above Ruby. "*I'll pick my teeths with your bones!*"

"Dennis, how good of you to come!" Ruby shouted, as she picked herself up off the ground. "I figured that an Ogre would be involved in this at some point."

Just then, the beast's giant club slammed downward to smash Ruby into a pulp, but she stopped it with her tiny hands as easily as a left fielder catches a fly ball.

"Dennis, you should know better than to take a swipe at me when I'm sober." Ruby calmly stomped her foot on the ground, causing a concussion wave that staggered the creature and sent him tripping over the pile of abandoned refrigerators. I slowly got to my feet. My shoulder was throbbing from being hammered by the Ogre's club. Ruby walked over to the creature and smashed the giant club into its ribs, which made a sickeningly loud crunching sound that echoed through the lot.

"You can surrender peacefully, Dennis, or I'll sick the Vanguard on you – what'll it be?" Ruby asked.

The Ogre smashed its fists into the ground and bounced back to its feet, but Ruby slammed her hands together causing another shock wave that blasted the empty refrigerators in every direction, stunning the creature. "I'm G-D warning you!" Ruby shouted. "I know your wife, Dennis. Does she know you're involved in this?"

"*Leave her outs this!*" the Ogre screamed, as it made a giant fist and prepared to strike Ruby. I stared at its massive clawed feet that dug into the ground, astonished by its size.

I glanced at a pile of rusted out water heaters, then thrust out my hand and made a snatching motion. One of the water heaters floated into the air and hovered about a foot above the pile. I made a throwing motion and it sailed across the vacant lot, smashing right into the creature's mid-section and sending him careening into another abandoned car.

The Ogre stood up, ripped a door off the car's hinges and prepared to throw it at me. I snatched the water heater off the ground and again sent it smashing into the creature, this time hitting him in the head. The monster fell backward over the rusted out car and landed on his back with his feet in the air.

"Since when do Ogres do the dirty work for hell-spawn?" Ruby shouted. "Your race is far too proud. Did Grim Geoffrey send you?"

The Ogre groaned loudly as it slowly stood up. "I must kill the old woman. You don't understansing," it cried, defeated.

"Are you responsible for the body in that shallow grave over there?" Ruby asked, pointing at the third body.

"N-No," the Ogre sobbed.

"Do you owe Grim Geoffrey anything, Dennis?"

"Y-Yes."

I walked over to Ruby, shaking my head in disbelief. The gray-skinned creature fell to the ground, drew its muscular legs to its chest and wailed uncontrollably.

"You've got to be kidding," I said, in a half-disgusted tone "This smelly hulk of God-knows-what is a freaking crybaby?"

"Shut up, Marshall," Ruby scolded. "An Ogre would never attack a Chieftain and a Vanguard unless he was desperate."

"Fine," I grumbled. "You obviously know what the hell is going on."

The Ogre looked up at Ruby with what I swear were puppy dog eyes. "D-don't telling my wife," it pleaded.

"Are you gambling again?" asked Ruby.

"Y-Yes."

"How much do you owe Grim Geoffrey?"

"Three souls," it sobbed.

"Oh for crying out loud, Dennis, your wife is going to take it out on your ass if she finds out."

It nodded slowly. "I know."

Ruby shook her head, walked over to the creature and helped it to its feet.

"Dennis, you know there are people who can protect you from extortion," Ruby said. "Don't you think your wife deserves a nice quiet cave where you can both live in peace?"

"Y-Yes," it whimpered.

"Did Grim Geoffrey kill the person in this lot?"

The Ogre shrugged. Its thick lips formed a deep frown, adding to its already pathetic appearance. "I made to kill you boths because of the long day," it said.

"The summer solstice?" I asked.

"Yes. The long day makes the fields ripe, and more peoples have to die first."

"Is Geoffrey half-in?" asked Ruby.

"Yes, and he gots a lots of othery types coming for the long day, too. Are you tellsing my wife?"

"I won't, but on one condition. You'll tell me where to find a portal to Grim Geoffrey's realm, and then you head straight home," she insisted.

The Ogre nodded in agreement. "Portals surrounded by the dark magics."

"What the hell does that mean, Dennis?"

"You needs a dark spell before you finds it," he said.

"What's he talking about?" I asked.

"He means that Grim Geoffrey is using dark magic to conceal any portals that lead to his realm," said Ruby.

"So how are we going to find a portal, then?"

Ruby's eyes narrowed, and her face took on the haunted appearance of someone who'd witnessed an act of pure evil. "I'm not sure," she said. "All I can say is that our job just became much more difficult."

I decided against pushing for more information. Ruby was supposed to be the expert on the supernatural, and if we had any hope of finding Grim Geoffrey, it was starting to look like Ruby Thiessen would be the key.

"I goings now, okay? Wife is going to be pretty mad," said the Ogre.

Ruby nodded. "All right, Dennis, go home and stay in your G-D cave, because if Grim Geoffrey finds out about our bargain, you know what will happen."

The Ogre nodded and made a slicing motion at his neck with a hairy finger, and then he looked at me. "You stick to Ruby, Mister Vanguards. She good people."

"Yeah, I'll get right on that," I muttered.

The creature stumbled off into the shadows and bounded into the air with a giant leap, then disappeared into the night. Ruby pulled her pewter flask out of her purse and took a slug.

"Okay, that was a thousand kinds of weird," I said, still wondering if what had just happened was real. "What now?"

Ruby's frown deepened as she stared at the shallow grave in the distance. "We split up," said Ruby. "You consult with your witch friend, and I'll leave an anonymous tip about the body."

"And then?"

"I'm not sure," she said grimly. "Right now I'm just not sure at all."

CHAPTER 21

Stella Weinberg was snoring loudly in the leather armchair next to the front counter, a large, gilt-edged book entitled *Chroniclus* on her lap. The Curiosity Nook was open for business, but Stella was out like a light. Were there any negative ramifications associated with waking a sleeping witch?

"Stella, wake up. We need to talk," I whispered, as I gently nudged her shoulder.

She didn't budge.

I decided to grab the book and read up about the cataclysm that had occurred in Outremont, and as my fingers brushed the cover, a sharp electrical jolt surged up my arm as an iron grip fasten around my wrist.

Stella yawned. "You're lucky that book is set on stun."

"I wanted to have a peek at what you were reading. No harm intended," I said, rubbing my arm.

"You look like you slept in your car," she said, with a stretch.

"Thanks, I've been up to my ears since we last talked, so you'll forgive my haggard appearance."

Stella got up from the chair and walked behind the counter with *Chroniclus* under her arm. She had a worried look on her face.

"What's wrong?" I asked.

"Gee, where do I start?" Stella asked, sarcastically. "You haven't seen Storch, have you? He's been gone since yesterday."

"Funny you should mention that," I mused. "I have concerns about our cat."

"What kinds of concerns?"

I thought about how I should convey my suspicions about Walter's loyalty and immediately felt like an idiot, as the mere fact that I was even contemplating that a cat might be a double agent seemed insane.

"Your face is betraying your feelings, Conrad," she said. "Out with it."

"All right, then," I said, cautiously. "As you know, I don't know a damned thing about your unseen world – "

"Wait a minute," she snapped. "It isn't *my* unseen world. Don't take that tone with me, pal."

"Fine," I muttered. "You'll forgive me if I'm just a tiny bit flustered."

"Why? If you exist with all of your remarkable abilities, it stands to reason that similar beings exist, even those whose area code isn't listed anywhere in this realm."

"Cripes, I'm doing the best I can," I growled.

"*Do better*," Stella shot back.

"Okay, this isn't going well. Let's start over."

"Good plan."

Stella crossed her arms and gave me a stern look as I decided to take a more diplomatic tone.

"Walter – Storch, I saw him last night."

"Go on."

"Have you read today's paper? About the third body?"

"Yes, that's where Storch wound up?"

"That's right – I'd like to know why your familiar hasn't reported to you," I said. "I mean, he should be keeping you informed, shouldn't he? Walter wouldn't be keeping information from you, right?"

She made a huge effort of rolling her eyes as she shook her head in frustration.

"Are you daft?"

I blinked and gave her a confused look. "What do you mean?"

"Look, I am a witch, and you aren't," she exhaled. "I have a familiar, and we're paired for life. That's how it works."

"Yeah, but he's not here, and before last night, I hadn't seen him since – "

"Since you were lying on your couch with a sleeping mask over your face," she said.

"How did you know that?"

"Storch is *my* familiar. I see what he sees – right from his eyes and into my mind. I thought I'd already established this fact."

"So you know about last night?" I asked, half-wondering if she'd seen me in the nude.

"Yes, I know about last night. I know you weren't alone, and I know you ran into some unpleasant company," she said in a businesslike voice.

"Our cat didn't happen to see the killer, did he?"

"Nope. If he did, our cat would be dead, and I would probably be next on the hit list."

I looked at the copy of *Chroniclus* under her arm and decided to inquire if the book contained any clues about what was going to happen in Greenfield.

"You mentioned you had to consult with the elders, and that *Chroniclus* would offer some insight. Any news?"

"We'll get to that," she said, placing the large volume on the countertop. "Why don't we compare notes first. What have you got so far?"

"Well, you obviously saw me on my couch," I said.

"Yeah, what was that all about? You looked like you were on your deathbed."

"Oh, just more crippling visions of bad juju in Greenfield. That and someone from the Guild showed up at my door."

"That's who you were with last night?"

"Yes, Ruby Thiessen. She's a Chieftain."

Stella spun around and glared at me.

"*The* Ruby Thiessen?" she said, sounding less than enthused.

"Yup. Apparently she's been assigned as my sidekick. Do you know her?"

Stella's face darkened and she dug her nails into the countertop. "Sidekick, huh?" she said in a suspicious voice. "I guess she must have really pissed off someone in the Guild."

"She told me they were stretched thin, and she knows everything about Grim Geoffrey."

"Grim Geoffrey!" she gasped. "Jumpin', dyin' Moses, that's our guy!"

Stella started leafing through the pages of *Chroniclus* as I sipped my coffee and waited for her to offer yet another startling revelation about the unseen world. I was troubled by her reaction to news that Ruby Thiessen was on the scene. Clearly, at some point in the past, Stella Weinberg and Ruby Thiessen had known each other, and it was obvious they'd had a falling out. It was only a matter of time until the two met, and I wasn't looking forward to the potential fireworks that would ensue.

"Here it is." She spun the book around for me to get a better look. "This page tells you everything you need to know about him. This is starting to make sense."

"Why?" I scanned the page.

"Grim Geoffrey is a Púca, but he's not your average run-of-the-mill Púca."

"Yeah, Ruby confirmed that to me earlier. She told me she's had a run-in with him in the past."

"Grim Geoffrey has a nasty reputation for consuming the souls of those poor saps who get in his way. Few survive to tell the tale."

"She told me he's a hybrid. Something about being part demon and part Púca," I said, as I examined a morbid woodcut showing faeries impaled on spikes. "Ruby mentioned that his interest in the near world has a lot to do with real estate."

"What do you mean?"

"Something about civil strife in the unseen world – battles for land and followers," I said, carefully scrutinizing Stella's response.

"She's half right."

"Oh?"

"There are many beings in the unseen world who'd love nothing more than to relocate to our realm," she said. "It's one reason witches are still around."

"What about the other part? The civil conflict in the unseen world?"

"It mimics what occurs daily in the near world," she said.

"I'm not following you."

"I don't expect you to understand," she said, closing *Chroniclus*. "The near and unseen worlds are connected through living energy that is responsible for what happens here and there. Both worlds exist in the same physical place, and both experience similar conflagrations."

"So the unseen world has experienced war throughout history?"

"Has there ever been a period in human history when a war wasn't raging somewhere?" she asked.

"I'm not an academic, but I'll say no."

"Why do those conflicts occur?"

"Everything from greed to religion, I guess," I said, still unsure of where she was heading.

"Because the near and unseen worlds share the same physical space, good and evil binds both worlds to similar fates but for different reasons," she continued. "War exists in both realms because war is the supreme manifestation of darkness. The difference, however, is that our realm does not exist in a permanent state of war. It's a way of life in the unseen world."

"You've lost me," I said, shaking my head. "A way of life?"

Stella shrugged. "When you wake up in the morning, do you brush your teeth?"

"Yeah."

"Do most people go to work every day and come home each night?"

"Yeah, why?"

"That's what I mean by it being a way of life," she said. "While war and strife might be obscene to the casual near world observer, it's how things are done in the unseen world."

"What happens when someone from the near world ventures into the unseen world?" I asked. "Ruby said that we have to find a portal to the Netherworld and confront Grim Geoffrey on his home turf."

Stella's eyes darkened and she glared at me. "Oh really," she chortled. "I recommend that you abandon that notion right now."

"Why?"

"First off, you need dark magic to find and then open a portal, and dark magic is completely forbidden. Secondly, assuming that your immortal soul isn't ripped to shreds by a journey through the portal, you'll have to contend with entities I'd rather not even think about."

Her cryptic warning made my skin crawl. "Just what the hell am I supposed to do, then?" I groaned. "Ruby says one thing; you say another. I've got faeries that live in a shoebox telling me that I've got the right stuff. A twelve-foot-tall ogre got his ass handed to him by a little old woman, our cat is missing, and I'd like to know why it's suddenly my job to take this guy down when there are others who could do it."

Stella opened her mouth to say something when we heard a loud crash from the back of the store and a drunken female voice shouting obscenities.

"That wouldn't be..." Stella began.

"Yep," I interrupted, "It's Ruby."

CHAPTER 22

The many years I'd spent living in relative seclusion hadn't prepared me for what might happen when two dominant female personalities clash, particularly if both of them possess superhuman abilities. Stella Weinberg, who I'd initially believed to be a nuisance, had proven herself as a valuable resource since she'd discovered the spiral-engraved rocks scattered throughout town. She'd opened my eyes to the existence of the unseen world and committed herself to helping me prevent Grim Geoffrey from running amok during the summer solstice.

Ruby, on the other hand, while abrasive and annoying, provided helpful insight into my abilities as a Vanguard. She was a battle-hardened veteran whose sarcastic bearing and sharp tongue reminded me that, despite my feelings about the nature of my powers, the task of confronting and eventually defeating Grim Geoffrey was not insurmountable. Where I lacked confidence, Ruby made up for it in sheer determination.

I just hadn't planned on two women with a hate on for each other forming an alliance to deal with threat to Greenfield.

Somehow, I'd have to act as an intermediary in order to get them to work together. Yeah, this was going to be bags of fun.

"What the hell kind of broken-down, G-D firetrap is this place, Conrad?" Ruby shouted from the backroom of Stella's store. "I'm tipped off about this place being of interest to Grim Geoffrey, so I peer through the skylight to take a look, and the G-D roof crumbles beneath my G-D feet!"

Before I could answer, Stella's face flashed with intense anger as she grabbed a small green crystal from underneath the front counter and stormed down the hallway leading to the backroom.

"Oh crap." I groaned and hopped over the counter and raced after Stella. "This is going to be ugly."

"You don't know the half of it," Stella snarled. "Chieftain or not, she has no right to invade my sanctuary."

We emerged through the beaded partition separating the hallway from the back of the store and found Ruby Thiessen brushing broken chunks of roofing tar from her red, pleated skirt. A large cotton duck backpack hung from her shoulders as she stood atop the crumpled storage shelf she'd landed on when she fell through the ceiling.

"You call this dump a sanctuary?" Ruby complained as she stepped over a pile of overturned boxes. "Looks more like a supernatural fire hazard if you ask me."

"Nobody's asking you, Ruby," I warned, trying to keep the peace. "You could have come in through the front door, you know."

"If I had done that, your good friend Ms. Weinberg probably wouldn't have voluntarily disclosed what she's hiding in the back of her store, now would she?" Ruby's eyes narrowed. "Nice little collection of odds and ends you've got here, Castalia. Why don't you tell Marshall why you're holding out on him?"

Stella was apoplectic. "I've had just about enough from you," she growled, as she prepared to throw the green crystal at Ruby.

"I wouldn't toss that at me, Castalia – I'll be forced to shatter it with a clap of my hands, and the energy that would be released is enough to smash the spell you're using to keep that creature in here subdued."

I grabbed Stella's arm just as she was about to throw the crystal at Ruby.

"Wait a minute!" I shouted. "What the heck is she talking about?"

"It's none of your concern," she snapped as she tried to pull away. "Don't listen to her."

Ruby cocked an eyebrow, and her mouth formed a malicious smile. "Why, Ms. Weinberg, you haven't told him, have you?"

"Told me what?" I demanded. "What's she talking about, Stella?"

"Nothing, let go of me." Stella snatched her wrist out of my hand.

"All this time you've been presenting yourself as a wise old sage to our Vanguard friend, and you haven't told him why The Guild monitors all practitioners of magic," Ruby said, flowing with sarcasm. "You probably didn't mention how the future of your order depends on Marshall, did you, Ms. Weinberg?"

"Help me out, here, Stella," I pleaded. "What's she getting at?"

"That's why you sent your G-D cat to live with him, isn't it?" Ruby chided. "Your people wanted to keep a close eye on him, didn't they?"

Stella began shaking, and the temperature in the back room of her store suddenly shot up. Her eyes flashed with rage as Ruby walked to within arm's reach.

"Your people don't have the capacity to understand why Marshall was selected," she hissed. "You're filling his mind with notions of conducting exorcisms, and you haven't the slightest idea what you're up against."

I wedged my way between Stella and Ruby in hope of defusing the situation. I'd already had a sample of what both of them could do. One of them might wind up dead if they came to blows.

"*Enough!*" I shouted. "If what Ruby says is true, then Stella, you've got some explaining to do."

"Damned right she does," Ruby snapped.

"Shut the hell up, Ruby!" I spun around and looked her straight in the eye. "This union of super-powered beings or whatever the hell you call it is also to blame. If your people were so damned concerned about me, you wouldn't have waited until I was forty to seek me out."

"It's not that simple!" she barked.

"I don't give a rat's ass!" I barked back. "Now listen, for better or worse, we're all involved in this dog and pony show. Now I want some answers!"

"There's nothing for either of you here," Stella shouted, her voice shrill. "Both of you, get out of my store!"

"Weinberg, that's a load of crap, and you know it," Ruby said, as she pulled the backpack off her shoulder. "I can prove it, too."

"Get out of my store!" Stella demanded, her voice coming close to shrieking. "There is nothing for you here!"

Ruby opened the flap of the backpack and reached inside. "I grabbed your hairball friend here after Conrad and I had our little meeting with Dennis the Ogre," she said as she pulled out a dazed Walter. "It took me a while to get your G-D cat to spill the beans, and it would appear he's none too crazy about what you're hiding back here."

"*Storch!*" Stella cried. "Nooo!"

"Walter?" I asked, rubbing my eyes in astonishment. "Ruby, if you harmed one hair on that cat's head, I'll…"

"Calm down, both of you," said Ruby. "I have two cats of my own. He's fine."

Walter jumped out of the pack and tore through the beaded curtain toward the front of the store.

"This is nuts," I said. "I was under the impression that witches were the only people who can communicate with a familiar."

"You're right," said Ruby. "Who said I wasn't a witch?"

"Come again?"

"Long story, Conrad. I'm surprised Ms. Weinberg didn't tell you that I used to be a member of her order. How the hell else did you think I knew so much about the unseen world?"

"*You're a heretic!*" Stella spat. "You were booted out of the order because you dabbled in the dark arts. You're a Chieftain because you purposely cast a spell on yourself."

"Yup," said Ruby, with a smile. "A damned good one, too. Your people still trying to figure out how I did it?"

Stella's face turned beet red, and I worried she might have a stroke if she didn't calm down. There was no way I could have known about the mutual hostility between my two closest allies, and it didn't matter. My trust had been betrayed by both of them, and I was angry at myself for dropping my guard.

"Enough already," I said, looking squarely at Stella. "I want to know what the heck Ruby is talking about. I also want to know why a coven of witches sent Walter to keep an eye on me."

"Your mother," she muttered quietly. "She was a witch, Marshall."

"This is going to be good," Ruby laughed. "Where's the popcorn?"

"Shut up, Ruby!" I snarled.

Stella slowly walked over to the dinette in the corner. She heaved her bulk onto the chair at the head of the table and looked up at me with a hollow expression.

"Your mother was a witch, and your father was a Vanguard," she said, quietly. "Her hope was to leave the order and marry him, but it's forbidden to marry outside our kind. When she became pregnant – "

"What happened?" I demanded.

"When she became pregnant with you, your father fell victim to Black Malaise."

"That's a handy revisionist history, Weinberg," Ruby interjected. "Why don't you call it what it is?"

"What's *Black Malaise*?" I asked, as I sat down next to Stella.

"You're a good man," she said, as she took my hand. "You don't want to know any more about this."

"Tell me!"

She slumped in her chair and stared blankly at the place mat in front of her. "It's a death curse," she said, quietly.

"Your father was put to death because he jeopardized the sanctity of the coven."

"*What?* By who?"

"Nobody knows," she said, her voice almost a whisper. "The truth was never to be revealed to you."

"Well, it's all out in the open now," Ruby snapped. "You're leaving out the part about how the covens tried to pin the murder on me, because I used dark magic to gain my powers. That was a G-D convenient way of covering your collective asses, wasn't it?"

I was devastated.

A tidal wave of nausea invaded my stomach as I glowered at Stella. I'd trusted her, because I knew nothing of witchcraft or the unseen world. Stella had falsely represented herself to me, and I felt like an idiot for blindly following her lead. My instincts told me to escape, to flee, to get as far away from Stella and Ruby and the conspiracy that had led me to them in the first place.

But I couldn't.

I needed them.

Greenfield faced an unspeakable evil, and fate had chosen me to stop it.

I turned to Ruby, who had a smug look of satisfaction on her face. "My father was killed by a death curse?"

"Yep," she exhaled. "Black Malaise is the most powerful spell in all of witchcraft. The victim begins hallucinating as the fabric of reality peels away. Their emotions become self-destructive as they obsess over whether they are losing their minds. Slowly, the victim falls into an unmitigated despair, and they usually commit suicide to end their pain."

"Oh my God," I whispered. "My father was a Vanguard, and I inherited his powers."

Ruby nodded. "Orson Conrad was a powerful Vanguard. He saved my bacon on more than one occasion. I warned him against consorting with your mother, but he loved her with an intensity that blinded him to the plot against his life."

"Now I understand why my mother was inconsolable in the years before her death," I whispered.

"I'm so very sorry, Marshall," Stella sobbed. "You were never to learn about what happened."

"Who killed my father?" I asked.

"That's a good question," said Ruby. "It's one of the reasons The Guild assigned me to you."

"Why does the future of Stella's order depend on me?" I asked quietly. "You both know that I haven't scratched the surface of my powers."

Ruby grabbed my face and looked me straight in the eye. "Your powers are off the G-D scale, Conrad. You're a Vanguard, but your mother was a witch, and that makes you one as well. Storch came to live with you so we could keep an eye on your powers. They didn't know which set of abilities would manifest first, and the Guild was unaware that your mother had a baby – that's why you fell off our radar. Word got out about a rogue meta-human in Greenfield, and the Guild put two and two together."

"*Off the scale?*" I asked in astonishment. "I fall out of the sky, for crying out loud!"

"Just as you haven't completely tapped into your Vanguard credentials, Marshall, you haven't even scratched the surface of magic," said Ruby. "A Vanguard who is also a Sorcerer… Well, let's just say it's a deadly combination."

"We need you to defeat Grim Geoffrey," Stella whispered. "It wasn't supposed to happen like this. I planned to teach you everything I know, but the spiral rocks began appearing, and he's preparing to unleash an army on the near world. The only thing that can stop an incursion of this magnitude is someone who is, as Ruby said, 'off the scale.'"

My mother had never spoken of my father, but I knew he'd been a meaningful presence in her life, because she wore her sadness like a comfortable sweater. I never bothered to ask about my father for fear of upsetting her. She once told me I would be called on when the time was right. It never occurred to me until that moment, precisely what she meant.

"I hate to be the bearer of bad news," I said, as I quickly snapped out of it. "Unless either of you have a crash course in witchcraft or a Vanguard boot camp, we're screwed."

Ruby squinted her eyes as she scanned the backroom of The Curiosity Nook while Stella continued to stare at the place mat.

"Where is it, Weinberg?" she asked. "Marshall knows the truth, so you might as well spill the beans."

Without looking, Stella raised her right arm and pointed to an unfinished cabinet on the wall above the percolator. "It's there," she whispered. "Spirits protect our collective souls if you let it out and Marshall can't contain it."

"One way to find out," Ruby said through her teeth as she walked over to the cabinet and prepared to open the unpainted pine door. "It's time to see what you're made of, Conrad."

CHAPTER 23

"Ohhh shiiit!" I wailed as I careened through the air, smashing into the cinderblock wall near the rear entrance. A warm trickle of blood ran down the side if my forehead and into my right eye as I struggled to my feet. Once I opened my eyes, the backroom of Stella's store exploded into a crimson light, bathing the floor with an eerie glow. A putrid breeze that smelled like rotting garbage was blowing out of the pine cabinet, filling the entire room with its horrid stench. I leaped to my feet when something cold and damp brushed against my face and made a dry chuckling sound that echoed throughout the backroom of the store.

I squinted to see what Ruby had unleashed when something crashed into my midsection, sucking the wind from my lungs. I gulped for air as my body lifted off the cement floor and rose to the ceiling. Completely immobilized, I searched the room, only to see Ruby suspended in mid-air by the same force that was holding me in place. Stella was trapped against the wall adjacent to the dinette.

"What the hell is that, Stella?" I shouted. "I can't see anything!"

"I-It's a Grave Demon, Marshall," she cried, "It's toying with us!"

"Where is it?" I shouted.

"Here," it said, in a whisper filled with menace. "You can't see me, but I can see you."

"Show yourself!" I demanded.

"Why should I?" it asked, as if amused by my question. "Surely you know the magic word, human." The invisible force holding me against the ceiling squeezed on my ribs, causing a sickening crunching sound. "*Say the magic word.*"

"I don't know any magic words!" I screamed in pain, struggling to catch my breath.

"This creature is beyond magic!" Ruby shouted. "Grave Demons generate strength when someone is about to die!"

"Your deaths, old hag!" the disembodied voice hissed. "I might start with the Vanguard; he looks so helpless."

She was right – this was about power. In less than ten seconds, whatever Stella had been hiding in the pine cabinet had quickly contained three people with supernatural abilities, and its sights were clearly set on me.

A black mist began pouring out of the pine cabinet and collected in a floating pool that bubbled away as it hovered a few feet above the shop floor. It swirled counter clockwise as a host of contorted faces writhed in agony, appearing and disappearing amid the murky vapor.

"What do you want?" I shouted.

"Souls!" it whispered, this time loud enough for everyone to hear. "Your souls – all souls!"

"You can't have them!" Stella bellowed in pain. "Return to your realm. I command you!"

"Ha-ha-ha-ha-ha!" It cackled wildly. "The fat sow traps me in a box made from enchanted wood and now wishes for me to leave. I've changed my mind – I will start with *you!*"

Slowly the boiling black mist floated toward Stella, who was still wedged against the wall beside the dinette. The myriad of contorted faces shifted into expressions of anger and hatred as she struggled to free herself.

"*Imperio Impedimenta, Imperio Impedimenta!*" she chanted as the mist inched toward her feet.

"Your pathetic incantation is no match for me," the disembodied voice taunted. "It took the power of your entire coven to trap me, and they are nowhere to be seen. You're alone, sow!"

"Hey, asshole," Ruby snarled. "You're tangling with more than one witch, and I know your name, you sonofabitch!"

The black mist stopped inches from Stella's feet and began swirling in a clockwise direction. The angry faces that had been bubbling away suddenly took on a variety of puzzled expressions as they turned their attention toward Ruby.

"Sallos! Leave this place now!" she commanded.

So that's what Stella and Ruby were up to. They were distracting the demon so my powers could charge on the evil surrounding the creature. I clenched my fists, straining against the invisible force holding me against the ceiling and pushed outward. I glanced at Ruby, who winked as a sly smile formed on her wrinkled face.

"I am Sallos and Semyazza, old hag," it laughed, as the black mist that had been floating above the floor drew inward and began to take a physical form. "I am Thammuz, I am Orobas, I am Iblis!"

The putrid stench quickly dissipated and immediately the temperature in the back room of Stella's store dropped like a stone. The sweat on my body began to freeze as frost formed on the various shelving units and spread out across the floor. I continued to press against the force holding me in place as I watched the demon's transformation continue.

"You're full of shit, Sallos," Ruby taunted. "I know Thammuz personally, and he's going to be pissed that you're impersonating him."

"Silence, hag!" the demon screeched, as it stood up and towered over Ruby.

I stared in astonishment at the creature.

It wore a hood and was dressed in a tattered black robe that was torn near the bottom, revealing two emaciated legs with red skin covered in festering boils. It had three toes on each foot, with long black claws that easily dug into the cement floor. Two massive claws stretched out from the ripped sleeves of the trench coat toward Ruby's throat.

This was my chance.

"Sallos!" I shouted, from above. "I want to see your ugly face!"

The demon spun around and looked up at the ceiling. Its face was a mass of puffy red boils that burst, dripping puss down its sharp cheekbones. Two yellow eyes flashed a menacing gaze toward me, and it grinned wildly, revealing a set of razor sharp teeth as white as freshly fallen snow.

I remembered the Latin I'd learned from Mr. Graves back in fifth grade. Stella was still chanting the same Latin incantation, and it became clear to me that she'd been sending me a cue to join in.

"*Subsisto!*" I shouted, in as close to a commanding voice as I could muster.

"Eh?"

The demon looked down at its feet to see the frost that had covered the walls and floor had now frozen its feet in blocks of ice that branched out in all directions.

"*Subsisto!*" My voice flew out of my mouth like an explosive blast, shattering the invisible force that had been holding me against the ceiling. I glided to the floor and stood in front of the demon. Stella and Ruby dropped to their knees and tried to catch their breath.

"You'll die where you stand, Vanguard!" the demon roared as it raised two massive fists above my head.

"*Ab aeterno!*" I growled, as I grabbed the demon's fists and squeezed. "There are no souls for you to collect today, asshole!"

The creature shrieked as the room filled with the loud crunching sound of its bones being crushed. I leaned backward, pulling the demon toward me, and then pivoted on my heels, throwing the creature toward the same cinderblock wall I'd crashed into moments earlier.

Stunned but not defeated, the demon threw back its shoulders as its robe fell to the floor in a heap.

"Your powers cannot defend against the netherworld," it hissed, as a long black tongue emerged from between the razor sharp teeth and licked the puss off its face. "I'll have your soul as a snack."

"Not gonna happen," I snarled, and I threw myself toward the creature in a flash of crimson light. My left shoulder connected squarely with the demon's abdomen, and it crashed once again into the cinderblock wall.

"*Immobulus!*" I shouted, and immediately the demon's hands and feet became encased in ice. It screamed with rage as I looked back at Stella.

"Throw me that crystal, Stella!" I ordered.

"What for?"

"Just give it to me – *now*!"

Stella tossed the crystal toward me, and I snatched it out of the air without looking. I walked up to the demon that was now trapped in a solid block of ice and stood one inch from its disgusting face.

"Y-you're a witch!" it cried out. "This cannot be."

"I'm that and a helluva lot more, you piece of crap," I spat. "See this crystal? I'm going to exorcise your sorry ass!"

"N-No!" it pleaded. "I know the one you seek. I can lead you to him, show you how to defeat him."

"You mean like how you defeated me?" I thrust the green crystal in its face. "Do I look like an idiot to you? Because I'm pretty sure that agents of the darkness are less than trustworthy."

"Marshall, *wait*!" Stella shouted. "Don't destroy it."

I glanced over at Ruby, who nodded in agreement. "She's right, Conrad."

"You see? You see?" it pleaded. "Listen to your friends!"

Stella walked over to me and put a reassuring hand on my shoulder. "If you don't destroy it, Marshall, you can put a lien on its essence."

"Use the crystal," said Ruby. "You can imprison the demon inside and draw on its knowledge and power – like a battery."

"Why not destroy him?" I flashed a threatening stare at the demon. "Ruby said it contains a lot of energy – probably enough to dissolve a scumbag like him."

"It's Sentient Quartz," said Stella.

"What the hell is that?"

"A supernatural sponge," said Ruby. "It absorbs whatever you command, and from the looks of Sallos here, I bet he'd be more than happy to spend eternity inside that rock, rather than have his essence destroyed."

I looked at the demon who nodded in reluctant agreement.

"You know how I can defeat Grim Geoffrey?" I asked without blinking.

"Possibly," it hissed. "I know how you can exorcise him, and I know the location of his host."

"Sounds like a bargain, then. Get your ass in there," I ordered.

Immediately, the block of ice dissolved into a pool of water at my feet as the demon's body transformed once more into a black mist. I thrust the crystal into the center of the mist, which was immediately consumed.

"A pet rock," I laughed as I held the crystal in front of my eyes. "You all right in there, Sallos?"

"Yes," the rock said with a reluctant whisper. "Asshole."

I turned toward Stella and Ruby, who kept a healthy distance from each other.

"Ruby was right," said Stella, exhausted.

"About what?"

"Your powers are off the scale."

CHAPTER 24

"Congratulations, Conrad," said Ruby, as she sat down beside Stella at the small dinette. "You're the proud owner of a talisman. A pretty useful one, too."

I stared at the green crystal containing the essence of the grave demon and tried to make sense of what had just transpired.

"This has been a disturbing afternoon," I muttered as I glanced at Stella. She knew my comment was aimed squarely at her.

"I don't know who killed your father," Stella said quitely, as she fiddled with her teacup. "I know you're angry with me because I wasn't honest with you from the start."

"Thanks for stating the obvious," I said. "It's bad enough we're facing a creature that by all accounts is among the most feared beings in the unseen world. Now I learn that I've inherited an entirely new set of abilities I know less than nothing about. Cripes, I don't even know how to be a Vanguard."

"Taking down a grave demon is no small task," said Ruby, as she reached into her purse and pulled out the small pewter flask. "Seems to me that you rose to the occasion."

"I don't like secrets," I said quietly.

Stella glared at me. "Coming from you, that's laughable. You're the person who's made it a priority to shut himself away from the world."

"Gimme a break." I rolled my eyes.

"Marshall, secrets are necessary for people like us," she lectured. "I understand how everything that's happened up to now feels like a lie, but – "

"Shouldn't it?" I snapped, cutting her off.

Ruby crossed her arms and flashed me a disapproving frown. "You're sulking, Conrad. Not a very attractive quality for someone with your gifts."

"Gifts?" I laughed. "I'd trade them in a minute for something resembling a normal life."

Ruby snorted. "What, and miss out on cool shit like kicking the crap out of bad guys? Seriously, are you telling me that you'd trade away all of your powers to do what? Become a chartered accountant? Get over it. You'd miss soaring above the treetops or bending the laws of physics, and don't tell me you wouldn't."

She was right.

Though I pretty much dislike or mistrust everyone I encounter, I still feel a jolt of self-satisfaction whenever I save a person's life. Even if the person I just saved would never know how close to death they might have come. It's as if I'm shaping the future – for better or worse.

"I don't know how I am supposed to balance a Vanguard's powers with those of a witch. Someone killed the father I never knew, and I'm to just pretend that nothing happened?"

"There isn't time for self-examination, Marshall," said Stella. "We have a lot of work to do."

"Fine," I muttered. "Are there any more bombshells about my past that I should know about?"

Ruby and Stella both shook their heads.

"If this crystal is a talisman, what am I supposed to do with it?"

"Grill Sallos for information," said Ruby. "Oh, and by the way, he owes you big time. He impersonated five other demons, and according to netherworld law, that's akin to staging a coup."

I held the green crystal up to the fluorescent light above the dinette and gave it a little shake. "Hey, demon, are you in awake in there?"

It vibrated in my hand and then glowed brightly. "Where else would I be, moron?" Sallos complained. "You're the one who put me in here."

"Do I have to go into the netherworld in order to destroy Grim Geoffrey?

"Yes and no." The bright glow from the crystal faded, and there was a long pause.

"Your understanding of the netherworld is based on religious beliefs," the demon said. "Your kind speaks of hell as if it's a punishment for the sins you commit in your mortal lives – mostly because humans are colossally naïve."

"What's that supposed to mean?"

The demon gave a dismissive sigh. "Your kind doesn't realize that hell exists right here in the near world. Humanity sows the seeds of pestilence, which yields a crop of pain and incalculable loss. You claim to learn from your mistakes, and you dumb down the penance for your collective sins by invoking the netherworld as punishment for your failings as a race."

"Oh, this guy is a complete jerk," Ruby interrupted. "He's spinning a yarn of pure BS."

"Just can it for a minute, Ruby," I said, as I motioned for her to stop. "I think Sallos might be onto something."

"Well, thank you for your vote of confidence, mortal. That means so much to me," it said, dryly.

Stella shook her head in obvious disagreement. "Limit your discussions with Sallos to simple questions that require a yes or no answer, Marshall. He's still a demon, and he'll do everything he can to deceive you. It's his nature."

"Maybe," I nodded. "Then again, if he's persona-non-grata in his realm, it would seem to me that I own his ass."

"Now we're talking," chimed Ruby. "Lay into him!"

I squeezed the crystal in my right hand just enough to remind the grave demon that I could destroy his essence on a whim.

"You wouldn't purposefully lie to me, Sallos, would you?"

"I'm a demon, you moron. It's what I do," it shot back. "Of course, I am a coward at heart, and my desire for self preservation would naturally ensure full and honest disclosure."

"Then disclose the location of Grim Geoffrey."

"That is impossible," it chuckled. "He is protected by a vast army of followers. Assuming you entered a portal into the netherworld, his minions would destroy you."

"I defeated you, didn't I?"

"That you did, Vanguard, but I am one, and his followers number in the thousands," Sallos warned. "You also forget that your opponent isn't just a demon. He's a Púca. The only way to defeat a malevolent Púca is to destroy the source of its power."

"And that would be?"

"Fear," it said. "You must starve him of the fear he's been spreading throughout your domain."

"Great!" I threw my hands in the air. "This just keeps getting better and better. How the hell do you stop an epidemic of fear in a small city like Greenfield where there are three unsolved murders and spiral symbols showing up all over the place?"

Ruby got up from her chair and began to survey the damage to the back room of The Curiosity Nook. "Weinberg, you're still an archivist, right?" she asked as she kicked at a pile of overturned boxes.

"The best one on the eastern seaboard," Stella said proudly. "Why?"

"Do you have a copy of the Big Black Book?"

"No!" Stella protested loudly. "Absolutely not. It's forbidden."

"We'll just stretch the rules a little bit," said Ruby. "I'm pretty sure your order won't be considering the ethical questions associated with using the Big Black Book if they're all dead, so what's the harm?"

"What are you getting at, Ruby?" I asked.

Stella glowered at Ruby and shook her head. "We mustn't," she lectured. "Dark magic is too great a risk, Ruby Thiessen. You know that neither of us has the power to undo the damage from even one small spell in that book."

Ruby looked unimpressed as she returned to the dinette and took her seat.

"Can we get back to the task at hand? The solstice is drawing near," I said. "The grave demon said fear is the key to beating Grim Geoffrey."

"That's what I'm talking about, Conrad," said Ruby. "The Big Black Book is bound to have something we can use."

"Okay, I'll bite. What's the Big Black Book?"

"An archive filled with powerful spells that individual sorcerers have utilized and improved upon. Sort of like Wikipedia for the dark arts."

"Wait a minute," I said. "Isn't Wikipedia filled with inaccuracies, because many of its authors are frauds and charlatans? Call me crazy, but it might not be a good idea to use unproven methods."

"First off, many of the spells are proven, and the one Stella is concerned with is risky because the people who tried to cast it simply didn't possess the power to bend it to their will," Ruby said. "Now if the person had powers that were off the scale, well..."

"It is morally wrong to cast a spell on an entire population!" Stella interjected. "You're proposing that we use the Big Black Book to transform Greenfield's entire population into zombies."

"I am not," Ruby chided. "The spell I'm thinking of will simply desensitize everyone in town from the dangers associated with mass hysteria. If you've got a better way to stop fear from spreading throughout the community, I'm all ears."

Stella crossed her arms and glared at the ceiling while I considered what Ruby was suggesting. To my knowledge, there had been only three killings, but each victim had been killed in the most graphic way imaginable. Investigators had found numerous spiral-engraved rocks at each crime scene, and lately, the city had been experiencing an outbreak of graffiti as the spiral symbol began appearing all over town. To make matters worse, the news media was publicly speculating on the likelihood of a serial killer being responsible the unsolved murders, and everyone in town was talking about it. If fear was the common denominator, maybe Ruby was onto something.

"Stella, in your vast experience as a witch and an archivist, do you know of any spell we could use that doesn't qualify as dark magic?" I asked.

She shook her head. "There isn't one."

"Is there any way we can find a portal to the netherworld and find Grim Geoffrey before the solstice?"

Stella shook her head. "Not a chance. There simply isn't enough time."

"If we cast this spell, how difficult is it to undo?"

She ran her fingers through her hair and gave me a dead-serious scowl. "Assuming I agree to do this, we'd have to ensure that the spell wears off when people are asleep. That way, they can wake up in the morning oblivious to any possible ill side effects."

"How long could the spell last?"

"Until a counter spell is used."

"Well, that sounds easy enough," I said, with a hint of optimism. "I mean, maybe we could cast the spell, and then it would draw out Grim Geoffrey's host."

Stella shrugged. "That would definitely draw him out. But you don't understand the ramifications of a mass spell and why it's extremely dangerous."

"What do you mean?"

"What if we die?" she asked. "Who'd undo the spell? We'd have an entire city wandering around on some kind of netherworld Prozac, completely desensitized to feelings and emotions that separate humans from drooling zombies. So do the math."

Ruby slammed her fist down on the table, causing the legs to buckle. "Weinberg, there isn't time to discuss the ethical questions when all hell is about to break loose. You're also discounting Conrad's abilities as a Vanguard and a witch," she said. "He kicked the living shit out of a G-D grave demon using elementary school freakin' Latin – he captured its essence and he saved our lives. Cut the guy a little slack."

Stella was about to say something, but Ruby didn't give her a chance.

"Think about it, Weinberg. You do the math. Conrad is powerful. He's never received any formal training, and isn't it just a little bit strange that Grim Geoffrey has chosen Greenfield to launch his lovely assault on the near world right here, right now?"

"I don't think I understand," said Stella.

"Of course you don't. That's one of the reasons we're in this mess," Ruby groaned.

The back room of Stella's store fell silent. Finally, this was all making sense. Grim Geoffrey must have known about me, and that's why he'd chosen Greenfield. The three murders were partly about raising the level of fear in the community, but also to test the waters and determine what kind of threat I presented to his plan.

Stella chewed on her lip. "You're right, Ruby – this is bigger than anything I'd imagined. Marshall has proven himself to be extremely powerful, even with limited knowledge. This is going to get me thrown out of my order, but I don't see that we have a choice."

"Fabulous!" said Ruby, excitedly.

"A word of caution, though. We need to produce an iron-clad plan on how to manage the intangibles, because Grim Geoffrey is extremely clever. He'll throw everything he's got at Marshall."

"That's what I'm afraid of," I said, nervously.

"Don't worry, Conrad. Between Stella and me, there's over a hundred years of combined experience." Ruby said reassuringly. "You've got a grave demon that will help you figure out how to defeat Grim Geoffrey, your cat is a spy, and you, my friend, are a force to be reckoned with."

"So what do we do now?" I asked.

"Stella will get the Big Black Book and collect the ingredients for the spell. The next move is up to Grim Geoffrey."

"Then what?"

Ruby smiled. "Then we take a trip to the dark side."

CHAPTER 25

TV has this nasty habit of giving viewers a distorted take on reality. Shows like *Law and Order* always have a district attorney grilling a murder suspect in a sterile room with the hum of an air conditioner in the background. *CSI* has a hot female forensics investigator forcing a confession out of someone because their DNA was all over a bloody towel found in the suspect's laundry hamper. Stupid TV.

I'd just left The Curiosity Nook and was driving home when I noticed the flashing lights of a police cruiser in my rearview mirror. "Shit," I muttered as I pulled over against the curb. Two sheriff's deputies walked over to my car, so I put on my best fake smile and lowered the power window of the Tempo.

"What seems to be the problem, officer?" I asked. "I wasn't speeding."

He peered inside my car and grunted. "You're Conrad?"

"Yes, what's the problem?"

"Sheriff wants to see you," he said. "You can go voluntarily, or I'll impound this bucket of bolts you call a car. What'll it be?"

I glanced at the second deputy on the other side of my car and considered my options. Obviously the sheriff planned to grill me for more information, and rightly so. I'd injected myself into the investigation at a crime scene, and he was treating me as a suspect. If I refused, I imagined they would somehow obtain a warrant to search my apartment, not that it mattered much. I didn't have any evidence that would link me to the unsolved murders, but I did have a friend named Stella Weinberg, who kept a large collection of spiral-engraved rocks in the back of her store. If the sheriff learned about those, he'd wind up investigating Stella as well.

I decided I'd better comply with the deputy's request.

"Sure thing," I said, stepping out of the Tempo. "Can I drive your squad car?"

"Shut up and get in," said the deputy, as he pushed me into the back seat and slammed the door.

He flipped the cruiser into gear and took off, squealing the tires. We drove in silence for the next ten minutes until we reached the Greenfield Sheriff's Office. I was led inside, past a series of small offices, until we reached a cubicle where a bespectacled man in a grey suit was typing furiously at his laptop.

He said his name was Doctor Robert Duncan, and the badge dangling from his neck emblazoned with the seal of the FBI said that I was probably in a helluva lot of trouble.

"Conrad… nice of you to join us" he asked, without looking up from the computer.

"Thanks," I muttered.

"Got any family in town?"

"Why?"

He spun the laptop around so the screen was facing me and gave me a sly smile.

"Well, for starters, it's because this form requires that I ask if you have any family."

"No, it's just me. Well, Walter is my family, I guess."

"Who's that?"

"My cat. He's a spy, you know."

"What makes you say that? Does he tell you he's a spy?" he asked, dead serious.

"Not the last time I looked," I said, sizing him up. "I mean, he stares out the window all the time, so I accuse him of spying on the neighbors."

"Do you know any of your neighbors?"

"What do you mean – like do I ever go over to the neighbor's for a game of bridge?"

"Nobody plays bridge anymore," he said. "Save for little old ladies who go to church. Does your mother play bridge? Mine still does, and she's seventy-nine."

"My mother passed away a long time ago."

"Sorry to hear that. Tell me about her."

"Why?"

"Just for a bit of background on you, that's all."

"Background as in whether or not she hit me with wire coat hangers or told me she'd cut off my penis if she ever caught me playing with myself in the bathtub?"

Might as well be a smartass.

"Did she?"

"I had a good upbringing; no, I've never been abused; and yes, my penis is still attached," I said, glancing at the badge dangling from his neck. "You introduced yourself as Dr. Duncan. I'm not getting a physical, and you're asking me if I was mommy's special boy. I'm going to roll the dice and say you're a psychologist, and you're profiling me."

He leaned back in his chair and put his hands behind his head. I expected him to fire back at my comment with something clever. Instead, he grinned politely, which gave me the creeps.

"It doesn't work that way, you know," he offered.

"What do you mean?"

"We don't question a suspect and create the profile based on his response. We look at the evidence, the method of killing, similarities to other crimes, not to mention the similarities between suspects. All of this gives us a sketch of killer's behaviors that act as a compass. It's not a precise science by any means, but then you probably already know that, don't you?"

He was good. He knew that I was toying with him to get a response, and he'd called me on it.

"You're right," I admitted. "Actually, Marnie calls me on my bullshit a lot like you just did."

"Who's that?"

"Marnie Brindle," I said calmly. "She's my upstairs neighbor who's been dealing with a lot of personal problems lately. She can read me like a book. I hate it when she does that."

Duncan leaned into the desk and cocked his head. "Tell me about her."

I knew what he was doing.

Duncan was trying to determine if I was capable of having an emotional connection with someone. I imagined he kept a mental checklist of attributes that are common among murderers, and if there were enough answers in the yes column, I'd probably be charged with the killings.

"Well, she's beautiful, you know? I mean, she's twenty years younger than me, and I'll probably go to hell for admitting that I've undressed her with my eyes on more than one occasion, but she's, well, rare."

"Explain – "

"Most people are complete assholes, but there's something special about her," I said, surprising myself. "At first glance, you'd think she's a red-headed bimbo, because she dresses the way most twenty-three year olds dress – you know, sexy and all. She's always gabbing on her cellphone about the most mundane topics that make me feel older than dirt, but she makes homemade applesauce, and she's genuine when she's talking to you. I mean, she makes you feel like she gives a crap."

"How long have you known her?" Duncan asked, as he started making notes in a small blue notepad.

"A few months," I said. "She had a stalker, and I let her hang out in my apartment when she was freaked out. I tried to get her to report it to the police, but she refused. I mean, it would have been easy for her to call the cops, but for some strange reason, I got the feeling that she liked hanging out with me."

"What did you talk about?"

I stared blankly at Duncan for a moment. How was I supposed to explain why I was suddenly concerned about a hot twenty-something neighbor? In the short time I'd known Marnie, she'd been both a source of infuriation and strangely, a confidant. Despite her habit of coming over to my apartment unannounced, a large part of me was grateful for her company. She'd shown a genuine interest in me, despite my best efforts to push her away, and she'd pushed right back – right into my life. Sure, she was twenty years my junior, but the sound of her voice gave me something to look forward to, even if she snooped through my personal belongings or fed Walter too many treats.

And she smelled good. My God, did she smell good.

I'd never held Marnie's hand or gently touched her face, but I wanted to. I wanted to do a lot of things to Marnie that I hadn't done with anyone since Cynthia passed away, and for the first time in more than ten years, I didn't feel guilty about it. I sipped back the rest of the coffee, awash with the sudden realization that I was *very* attracted to Marnie Brindle.

"Conrad," said Duncan, snapping his fingers. "You still with me? I want to know what you and this Brindle woman talked about."

My lips curled into a thin smile, and I blinked at the profiler.

"Everything and nothing at all," I said, grinning now. "The politics of campus life – she goes to Chesterton here in town. Relationships and gossip about her girlfriends' torrid affairs with professors. I tell her that I frown on that kind of thing, and she reminds me that I'm an old fart who needs to get an upgrade."

"Why did you offer her the use of your apartment?" he asked.

"I don't know. I guess it seemed like it was the least I could do, since she wasn't going to the police, and of course, there've been three unsolved murders."

"Sounds like you're very close. Are you involved?"

I tried not to laugh. "What do you mean, like involved in a relationship?"

"Yeah."

"Are you crazy? I'm old enough to be her father," I said, trying to force my feelings for Marnie aside.

"Gotcha. I have a daughter about the same age."

Duncan flipped through his notepad and chewed on his pencil. What would he be asking next? It was obvious he was attempting to build a rapport with me to find out if I had any sociopathic tendencies, and it was becoming clear that my feelings about Marnie Brindle weren't consistent with the profile he'd developed.

"You said you took her in because of the unsolved murders in town. Tell me about them," he asked.

"As in disclose everything I know about the killings, so you can see if they gibe with the investigation, right?"

"Pretty much."

"All right, then. Three mutilated bodies. The first was Stephen Hodges, age sixteen. Not sure about the identity of the second victim, whose body parts they found in that culdesac. The third victim was found in a shallow grave. That's all I know."

Duncan spun the laptop around and pointed to a media player window showing a security video from the news conference after the first murder. Stella Weinberg and I were clearly visible from over the sheriff's shoulder, and I instinctively knew the next question would be about why I went to the news conference. There was about one minute of silence as I studied his face.

"Not gonna budge, huh?" Duncan asked.

"Excuse me?" I asked, innocently.

Duncan looked disappointed that I didn't react to the video.

"In my line of work it's common to see a murderer at a crime scene," he said. "You obviously know that law enforcement generally views this as a behavioral trait among serial killers."

"Yep. I suspect you likely have some video that was impounded at the second crime scene showing me yelling at reporters, right?"

"We do."

"So that big brain of yours is looking at this middle-aged man who probably fits your profile, and you're asking yourself why he'd be trying to get his face on the evening news. You've interviewed me and found that while I don't particularly like people, I still possess the ability to care about Marnie Brindle, and that flies in the face of the killers you've encountered, right?"

"Something like that." His eyes narrowed.

"You're wondering if I know something about the murders the police aren't aware of. Is that it?"

"You tell me."

I continued sizing him up and thought briefly about how knowledge that the killer was a supernatural creature from a realm of immortals would register in his analytical mind. There was no escaping the fact that I couldn't disclose the truth behind the killings, but at least I could try and glean information about what the police knew. It was still possible they were hot on the trail of Grim Geoffrey's host.

"Greenfield has always been a safe place to live, and when that first murder happened, I was horrified," I lied. "I went to the news conference primarily to find out what the papers probably wouldn't print."

"Like what?"

"Both the sheriff and coroner were visibly shaken, and that told me this wasn't just an arbitrary killing," I said. "I wanted to hear the speculative buzz in the meeting room. Call it morbid curiosity."

Duncan flipped open his notepad and started scribbling again. I watched his face closely to see if it would lead me to his next question, and I decided to keep my cards close to my chest.

"Mr. Conrad," he began slowly, "few people take as active interest in a police investigation as you, and frankly, I'm perplexed."

"Why?"

"For starters, suspects generally – "

"So I am a suspect, then," I interrupted.

He flashed an angry look that told me he was frustrated by my responses. I'd gotten to him.

He shifted in his seat, and I could hear his teeth grinding as he reviewed his notes. I was certain that what he'd say next would give me an indication as to whether or not he believed I was the killer.

"Look, asshole, you know something about these murders you haven't told the police," he snapped. "You should know that it's an indictable offense to deliberately impede a murder investigation."

Bingo.

His last sentence was meant as a shot across the bow: Tell me what you're hiding, because if you're not the killer, someone else is going to become a victim.

I resolved to throw him a bone.

"I kind of figured that," I said, dryly. "In the interests of ensuring a speedy resolution to Greenfield's unsolved murders, here's what I know."

He rolled his eyes at my sarcasm and flipped to a fresh page in his notebook.

"The first body was found outside of town, and the violent nature of the murder tells me the killer wants to scare the living shit out of people. I know that you and the sheriff believe those little spiral-engraved rocks you're finding all over the place might be a trail of breadcrumbs, and the killer is toying with you."

"Go on."

"You've noticed an increase in graffiti in town – all large spirals painted in red. I'm thinking you don't have any fingerprints, clothing or hair fibers, tire tracks or bloody footprints from any of the crime scenes. In fact, you have less than nothing in the way of physical evidence, and people are under pressure to get an arrest."

He glared at me.

It was obvious that he was frustrated, and he'd hoped his interview with me would put this case to bed.

"Shut the hell up, Conrad!" he growled. "I don't believe you've been completely honest in disclosing everything you know, but here's the thing. I might be a harmless-looking psychologist who profiles killers for the FBI, but I'm still a federal agent. If I find out you've withheld even the tiniest fragment of evidence or information relating to these murders, I will make it my life's work to ensure that you wind up somebody's girlfriend in prison. Got that?"

"I understand," I said, calmly. "Are we done?"

"Nope," he grumbled. "The sheriff will want to see you."

CHAPTER 26

Imagine my surprise.

After following a dumpy looking deputy down a hallway of bulletin boards plastered with wanted posters, I found myself sitting at a table in a sterile room, just like on *Law and Order*. Duncan was leaning against the two-way glass, where a camera was undoubtedly recording my every move. Sheriff Don Neuman sat across from me with a glare that could bend steel bars. He snuffed a cigarette into an ashtray overflowing with cigarette butts, then reached into his breast pocket for his pack of Marlboros.

"I could have sworn we had a bylaw against smoking in public buildings," I said, deliberately trying to provoke him. "As a taxpayer – "

"Shut the hell up, Conrad," he bellowed, slamming his fist into the table. "You're going to tell me what you know about these murders, right here, right bloody now!"

I glanced at Duncan, who shrugged his shoulders and looked bored to tears. He knew I wasn't about to be intimidated by a belligerent Sheriff when I'd just survived a grilling by an FBI profiler. I played along, again hoping the sheriff would disclose something about their search for a suspect.

"If you're going to take that tone with me, I'll have to insist on legal representation before you ask me another question," I said, oozing with sarcasm.

Neuman reached across the table and grabbed a handful of my shirt collar. "You son of a bitch," he snapped, shaking me. "Three innocent people are dead, and you're gonna lawyer up, is that it?"

I calmly craned my neck over his shoulder and looked straight at the two-way glass.

"You have this on tape, right?" I shouted. "Just making sure you've got a record of the sheriff when he roughed me up."

"Bastard!" Neuman snarled, shoving me and then releasing his grip on my collar.

"He's open to rational conversation Sheriff," Duncan said calmly. "You might want to try that approach."

"Thanks for sharing, Duncan," he snapped back at the profiler. "Conrad, you'd better tell us what you know. Or…"

"Or what?" I asked. "Sheriff, I'm more than willing to share everything I know about these murders, but it's going to be the same thing I told your g-man over there."

Neuman got up from his chair and walked over to Duncan. "Gimme your notebook," he ordered. Duncan took the blue notepad out of his jacket and handed it to the sheriff.

It was then that I felt an electric sensation from the shard of Sentient Quartz in my pocket. Immediately, my senses heightened, and I could feel the cool, damp air circulating from the air-conditioner as goose bumps ran down the center of my back. The rhythmic thumping of Sheriff Neuman's heart vibrated across the floor and into my body. Then a familiar voice shot straight into my head.

The Talisman had something to say.

"*Probe his mind, Vanguard,*" the disembodied voice of the Grave Demon whispered. "*This human is lying to you.*"

"*Can you hear my thoughts?*" I asked, without speaking.

"*Yes. Probe his mind, and you'll find out what he knows about the host. Concentrate.*"

The sheriff had his back to me, so I closed my eyes and forced my mind to blot out any sounds that might distract me as I projected every ounce of my five senses onto his mind. Immediately I could hear an inner dialogue.

"*That son of a bitch isn't the killer, and I haven't a clue who the hell it is,*" the sheriff's voice whispered, almost in desperation. "*The goddamned mayor and that asshole prosecutor are going to string me up by the balls if I don't make an arrest. Frigging politicians and their elections. I hate this shit. I hate this fucking town. Jesus, if the media ever find out about the five other bodies. Stinking homeless people – nobody will miss them.*"

My mind flooded with the mental image of a mass grave filled with the dismembered body parts of five people, tangled together like a horrific jigsaw puzzle. Five pairs of hollow eyes stared at a black sky, begging for justice. Their faces were frozen in horror. They'd seen one another killed, one by one. My nostrils filled with the smell of damp soil and rotting flesh. My stomach churned violently as I tried not to wretch.

Five more bodies. Christ!

I'd been struggling for days to get a read on the killer, and despite all the powers Ruby and Stella said I possessed, something was working against me – but how? I'd prevented a woman's kidnapping at the hands of her nut-job co-worker and saved Marnie from her stalker. My powers worked for them, but why not for these five people?

Rage flowed through my veins like a bubbling torrent that threatened to flood the entire room if I didn't keep myself in check. I focused every ounce of anger with myself, with Grim Geoffrey, with witches and The Guild and asshole cats that live a secret life, straight into the mind of Sheriff Neuman. What I learned next sent a bitter chill straight into my soul.

"*We'll put that head in Conrad's car,*" the sheriff's voice echoed, its menace every bit as threatening as any I'd experienced. "*We'll tell the press we received an anonymous tip, and I will slap the cuffs on that son of a bitch myself. There's no frigging way this asshole isn't the killer. Fuck the lack of evidence.*"

"Conrad, are you fucking listening to me?" Neuman shouted, snapping me out of my trance. He was inches from my face, and I glared at him, barely disguising my hatred and disgust.

"What?" I answered, in a voice filled with venom.

"I said you're goddamned lucky I don't charge you with obstruction of justice," Neuman snapped.

"Yeah, I keep hearing that."

His eyes narrowed, and I knew from the look on his face that he'd love nothing more than to turn off the camera and lay a beating on me.

"We're going to watch your every goddamned move. Got that?" he spat. "You won't be able to take a shit without knowing you're on Candid-fucking-Camera. You hear me?"

I leaned forward so Neuman's face was almost touching mine. "*Loud and clear.*"

CHAPTER 27

Spooks come in many forms.

I'm not talking about CIA spooks, though I suspect they have a file on me by now. No, what I'm talking about are three mischievous creatures that I caught rifling through my refrigerator as I walked through the door to my apartment.

"Freeze!" I shouted.

Three tiny creatures with semi-translucent skin and faces resembling surprised spider monkeys stood amid a pile of half-eaten leftovers, yogurt containers and an empty jug of milk in my kitchen. The contents of my refrigerator were smeared all over their bony fingers. The one closest to me dropped a Tupperware dish with a hollow *thunk*, spilling peas in every direction.

"He's here! He's here!" the three shouted in unison, their high-pitched voices sounding like Alvin and the Chipmunks.

I kept my distance, unsure if they might be a trio of assassins from the unseen world who wanted a snack before killing me. The one closest to the fridge was wearing a burlap loincloth, while the other two wore shirts that hung limply from their emaciated frames. The creature who dropped the Tupperware dish took a tentative step forward.

"You're famous," it said, smiling.

"Oh yes, he's famous, everybody is talking about him!" the other two giggled.

"What the hell are you three... *things?*" I gasped, still unsure if they meant me any harm.

"I'm Skilla," chirped the one wearing the loincloth. "These are my sisters, Skeets and Treeny. We were hungry."

My eyes didn't flood the kitchen with brilliant white light, a sure sign they couldn't be evil. I locked my apartment door and surveyed the damage to the kitchen. The cupboard doors were wide open, and the three had emptied the contents onto the countertop. Broken cups and plates littered the floor. My garbage can was overturned. Strangely, my brand-new Bunn-O-Matic slurped loudly as it finished brewing a fresh pot of coffee. Overlooking the melee from the kitchen table was Walter, who sat on his haunches and casually washed his paws. Apparently, he'd been at the butter dish again.

I kicked through the pile of trash that had once been my kitchen, and the three scurried between my legs into the hallway.

"Son of a... *Cripes*, you wrecked my apartment!" I snarled. "How the hell did you get in here?"

"We followed Storch," the three said in unison. "He's very fat, you know."

"Huh – W-Walter?"

"He passes through walls, very clever for a fat one," said the creature in the loincloth. "We can, too."

That explained how Walter had been getting out of my apartment to conduct surveillance on behalf of Stella Weinberg. Smart cat. I sat down the kitchen table and pointed at the one wearing a loincloth. "Skilla," I said.

It nodded and smiled.

"Why are you here?"

"You tell him, Treeny," whispered the one I assumed was Skeets.

"A-All right," she said, hesitantly.

"Ingrid sent us," Treeny said. "She said you were handsome."

"Oh, he's *very* handsome," chirped Skeets. "For a human."

I rested my head on my arms and looked down at the one called Treeny. It had been an emotionally exhausting day, and the last thing I needed was another mystery from the unseen world. Still, if Ingrid had sent them, then it meant she'd uncovered something about Grim Geoffrey, so it had to be important.

"Ingrid is a faerie," I said. "Just what kinds of creatures are you three? And aren't you breaking the rules by entering the near world?"

"Oh yes, we break rules all the time," said Skilla, smiling. "Gremlins always break the rules."

"I see. Don't you run the risk of facing the wrath of Sentry Witches?"

"Oh yes, of course. But we come into the near world many times a year, and we haven't been caught yet. We're very fast, you know," Treeny said.

"Gremlins, eh?"

The three nodded in unison.

"Not that I'm an authority on mythical beings, but aren't Gremlins supposed to be notorious shit disturbers?" I asked.

The three looked as if I'd just slapped them in the face. Skilla pulled a handkerchief that he'd clearly swiped from the breast pocket of the one and only suit I own, and blew his nose.

"We make mischief," Treeny recoiled, stung by my comment. "Gremlins always make mischief, Mister Vanguard Man."

"I kind of figured that out on my own, from the look of my apartment," I said. "What's all this crap about me being famous?"

Skeets circled her finger through the inside of an empty yogurt container and then sucked off the remnants. "This is quite tasty," she said. "What do you call it?"

"Boysenberry. Look, what's this all about?"

Treeny jumped onto the kitchen table, startling Walter, who took off into my bedroom. She sat down and drew her bony knees to her chest.

"You're famous because you'll defeat the dark one," she said, rocking. "He's not the worst of the dark ones, but with him gone, that's one less soul destroyer to worry about."

"You're famous!" Skilla echoed, picking up the scattered peas off the floor and popping them in his mouth like M&M's.

"Yeah, we already established that," I grumbled, impatiently. "What's the message from Ingrid?"

"Tribulation!" the three chirped, almost in harmony. "Yes, a tribulation. All pacts are invalid, and the Sentry Witches are powerless now."

"Tribulation, what the hell is that? Shit, where's my dictionary?" I said, looking at the overturned bookshelf in my living room.

Skeets disappeared in a flash of light and then reappeared at my feet, holding my dictionary.

"We're very fast," he said, flipping through the pages.

"Gimme that!" I snatched the dictionary from his hand and looked up the word tribulation. The definition sounded ominous.

"Grievous trouble, a period of suffering and a severe trial," I read aloud. "Great! So are you guys telling me that even if I destroy Grim Geoffrey, there's gonna be more of this unseen world crap?"

"Plenty more! Plenty more!" they answered.

"Does Stella know about this?"

"Who's that?" asked Skilla.

"Wait, I mean Castalia. Is she aware of this so-called tribulation?"

The trio nodded.

"All witches know about the tribulation," said Treeny. "They've worked for centuries to prevent it from happening. It's why you have witches, isn't it?"

"Yes, Mister Vanguard, there's been no deception among any of the mystics in the near world," Skeets added, with an authority in her voice that impressed the hell out of me, given that she still looked like a surprised spider monkey. "Their ranks have thinned over the centuries as you humans discarded the old ways. Really, your kind brought this on yourselves."

She had a point. A damned good one.

It made perfect sense that a world relying almost exclusively on science and technology as its *raison d'être* would be blind to the supernatural. Five hundred years ago, the known world was comprised of peasants and nobility. Most people were uneducated and superstitious, and it made sense that the church, for example, didn't exactly go out of its way to stomp out superstition among the peasantry if it reinforced their political power.

I consider myself a reasonably educated man, and ever since the police had found the body of Stephen Hodges, I'd seen things that I believed existed only in fairy tales. For whatever reason, as our civilization became more enlightened, it adopted everthing from the separation of church and state to education for the masses. The shining result is that our collective belief in things that go bump in the night has virtually disappeared. Now the gremlins were telling me that modern civilization was going to be in for a shock, and everyone from scientists to theologians were going to have a hell of a time explaining it all away.

I turned to Skilla, who stood frozen, staring at my bedroom door.

"What the hell?" I said, just as the power went out.

"Do not move," Treeny's terrified voice whispered in the darkness. "It's coming in through the bed chamber window."

"What is?" I snapped.

I'd no sooner finished closing my mouth when my eyes exploded into blue light that filled every blackened corner of my apartment.

"Hello, Vanguard," hissed the cloaked figure standing in the doorway to my bedroom.

Before I had a chance to respond, it was on me.

CHAPTER 28

I'd expected the Big Black Book would no doubt draw out Grim Geoffrey's host – that was a given. What I hadn't bargained on was the possibility that I'd be an assassination target before Ruby and Stella had a chance to cast whatever spell they were dreaming up. The trio of Gremlins who followed Walter into my apartment didn't bother to check if someone or something might possibly have been following them. The proof was standing in my bedroom doorway, and it moved so fast that I didn't get a chance to brace myself against the weight of its body as it charged.

When it connected with my chest, I bounced off the refrigerator and hit the floor so hard that I left an imprint in the linoleum. As I opened my eyes, I tasted the salt and copper flavor of blood, followed by a sharp pain in my mouth. The impact had made me bite off a chunk of my tongue. Strangely, I considered if I should put the piece of flesh in a cup of ice so it could be stitched back on.

Dazed, I looked up at the face of the creature that had pinned me to the floor, only to see a black void inside its hood.

Unable to move my hands or legs, I spat a slimy mixture of saliva and blood into its face. The creature screeched loudly and recoiled enough for me to free my hands.

"Not sure what the hell you are," I panted, spitting blood. A sliver of my tongue bounced off the creature's chest. "Not going to waste any time trying to figure it out."

I put my hands together over my face and pushed hard, hoping to get it off my body, and incredibly, they passed right through its chest. What had been solid flesh less than a second ago was now swirling gray vapor that covered my arms right up to my elbows

The creature clawed at its face, trying to wipe the blood from where its eyes should have been. The weight of its body pressed down on my chest, and I heard a crunching sound as the plywood floorboards began to buckle beneath the linoleum.

"Shiiiit!" I gushed, the air pushing out of my lungs beneath the creature's bulk.

"It's a Minion, Vanguard!" shouted Treeny from somewhere in the darkness. "It has come with only one purpose – to kill you!"

"*Ya think?*" I wheezed.

The creature threw its head back and laughed. "They told me you were powerful," it cackled in a voice that made my skin crawl. "Perhaps I've attacked the wrong Vanguard."

Normally I'd have fired back with a snappy comment, but I instinctively knew that I didn't have a chance to defeat the creature unless I could channel the evil that had sent it to kill me. I shut my eyes and imagined my body as a dam of energy, about to release a torrent onto an unsuspecting village. I clenched my fists and channeled every ounce of evil intent lingering in the creature's soul into a compressed ball of energy, and instantaneously, I could feel a fire blazing deep in my chest.

"*Off!*" I roared, my voice shaking the walls, and causing the few remaining items in my kitchen cupboards to roll off the shelves and onto the floor. Chunks of drywall fell from the ceiling as a powdery white dust filled the air, clogging my nostrils.

The creature sailed through the air, crashing through the sliding door in my living room and into the street. I quickly stood up and noticed the power outage in my apartment had extended to the block around my building.

I had to move quickly.

The sound of combat coming from my apartment would have every person in my building thumping at my door. The last thing I needed was for Marnie Brindle or any of my neighbors to walk into my apartment only to find three Gremlins cowering underneath my kitchen table, or the faceless creature standing in the middle of the street.

I leaped into the sky and rocketed toward a green space about four blocks from my building. I glanced over my shoulder to make sure the creature was following me, and bobbed my head at the last second as a long talon took a swipe at my neck. I spotted the green space about a hundred feet below and dove toward the ground. A cold wind blew against my face, drying the smeared blood around my mouth. The creature was right behind me, swiping wildly, and I stepped to the right in midair to avoid a direct hit.

The force of the minion's descent caused it to crash face-first into a large oak tree, scattering acorns and broken branches in every direction. I hovered a few feet above the ground and called out to the creature.

"Who sent you?" I shouted, filled with rage.

The minion stood up, unfazed by its collision with the oak tree, and brushed itself off.

"The one you seek!" it hissed.

"I can destroy you," I called out, unsure if I was bluffing or not. "Grim Geoffrey must be scared shitless of me if he's sent an assassin to take me out."

The Minion raised its fists in the air and smashed them into the ground, shaking the earth with a force that blasted through my body and shook my fillings. "Maybe I want to kill you for profit, Vanguard," the creature bellowed. "Your head will bring a nice reward!"

I sensed weakness.

The Minion had attacked me in my apartment with little warning, but now it stood thirty feet away, the ferocity of its attack reduced. It was sizing me up, trying to discover my weak points. If the creature believed it could overpower me, it wouldn't be trading barbs.

"Why the sudden hesitation?" I shouted, as I waited for the creature to rush me. "Grim Geoffrey is going to be disappointed with you!"

"You will die!" the Minion roared, and it charged at me with blinding speed. Its fury fueled my body with a surge of energy I'd never experienced, and a rush of power coursed through my veins.

My eyes blazed with scarlet rage, penetrating the black void beneath the Minion's hood. Its twisted face was a mass of open sores that oozed with puss, and dripped onto a set of grinning, razor-sharp teeth. It was no more than five feet in front of me when I clapped my hands together, sending out a stream of crimson light that trapped the creature in a ball of liquid energy.

I pulled the shard of Sentient Quartz out of my pocket and flashed it in front of the Minion's face. "You know what this is, don't you?" I spat.

"N-No! T-Take it away" it pleaded.

"But you wanted my head," I taunted. "What's Grim Geoffrey going to do when he finds that a mere mortal kicked the living crap out of Minion from the netherworld?"

"I am a small taste of what is yet to come, Vanguard," it whispered, suddenly sounding defiant. "You might destroy me, but there are hundreds of thousands who can take my place."

"Not if I destroy the one who sent you," I shot back.

The minion curled back its thin lips and formed a curious smile. Its razor sharp teeth appeared bloodstained as they reflected the crimson light of my eyes. Unsure whether I should destroy the creature, I decided to pump it for information.

"Why does your master wish to enter this realm?" I asked. "Why this place?"

"You already know the answer," it hissed. "That wretched witch knew this when I communicated with the beacons in her dwelling."

"Beacons? You mean the spiral-engraved rocks?"

"Yes."

"Where do the rocks come from? Who is planting the beacons?"

"Someone like you – someone in white. But you already know this; you've foreseen it."

"The host?"

"Host?" the creature laughed, as if amused. "The one in white is no host. It is a *herald*. Its sole purpose is to prepare this realm for the arrival on the longest day."

"Grim Geoffrey?"

"That is what you call him, but he goes by many names."

"Yeah, I get that," I said, frustrated. "He sees me as a threat to his plan, is that it?"

The creature threw back its shoulders and roared with confident laughter. Its voice echoed through the park and sent a chill through my skin.

"If you destroy him, it will not stop the tribulation," it grinned. "Our realm is home to everything from blood spawns to lycanthropes, each with designs on this place. They are watching him. They wait patiently to see how he will fare against the likes of you."

"And what happens if I destroy him?" I asked, masking the panic in my voice.

"Time will tell, Vanguard," the creature's grin widened. "The magic that has protected this realm fades with every passing day. The witches and mystics who enforced the pacts have dwindled, because your kind ignores the lessons of the past, to your collective doom."

I'd heard enough.

The Minion had just assembled the last pieces of the puzzle that told me my inevitable battle with Grim Geoffrey was the start of something more sinister than simply feeding on fear and devouring human souls. This wasn't about real estate, as Ruby had suggested. This was about annihilation.

"You will return to your realm," I said, trying to sound determined. "You will tell Grim Geoffrey that human beings have a few surprises up their sleeves. You can tell him the magic protecting this realm might be weak, but it still exists, and there are those who will try to stop you."

"As you wish, Vanguard, but remember: time is short, and your allies are scattered to the four winds, assuming you have any left at all." It chuckled. "You naïvely believe that Chieftains and Ushers or those meddling Pathfinders have the capacity to destroy my kind? Look around you! You're alone! Those with powers like yours engage in misadventure created by humans, not by those who dwell in my realm. You're fighting countless wars on a multitude of fronts. Your ignorance of the old ways has left your flank wide open, and it is just a matter of time until you're overrun."

"That may be so, but don't believe for one second that humanity will simply roll over and let you destroy us," I shot back. "Humanity might have several failings, but you're forgetting one simple fact about my kind..."

"And that would be?" it said, still smiling.

"We know how to fight dirty."

The creature took a few cautious steps back, as if it were expecting me to attack.

"I will convey your message, Vanguard," it hissed. "Enjoy the few precious days you have left."

I watched as the Minion's body suddenly transformed into a wispy gray vapor. A cold wind appeared out of nowhere, kicking up dust that gathered around its body. A funnel of dirt and spectral energy spun around with blinding speed. An arc of electricity shot through the center of the funnel and crackled loudly as the minion's body disappeared into the ground beneath its feet, leaving a smoldering ring of burned grass.

"Nice exit," I muttered, as I started walking out of the park. "If that thing is just one tenth as powerful as Grim Geoffrey, I'm going to be in a world of hurt."

CHAPTER 29

When I returned to my apartment, Marnie Brindle was stapling a blanket over the sliding glass door in my living room.

"Gee Marshall, you know how to throw a party," she said, suspiciously. "What happened, did a super villain attack you in your sleep?"

I looked around the apartment, hoping the trio of Gremlins had enough sense to clear out when I'd lured the minion away from my building. "I see you still have it in your head that I'm Superman," I said, relieved they were nowhere in sight. "I suppose you're not going to believe this was just a smash and grab, no matter what I tell you."

She stepped over my bookcase and planted herself on the sofa. "That's right," she said, still looking suspicious. "The neighbors were going to call the police, but I talked them out of it."

"Thanks."

"You ready to fess up yet?"

"Come again?" I asked, trying to sound innocent.

"Are you ready to tell me the truth? You know, about taking off into the sky after you rescued me," she said, making a flying motion with her hands.

"You honestly believe that I'm a superhero. That I throw on a pair of tights each night to protect Greenfield from guys who shoot poison gas out of umbrellas, is that it?" I wasn't even trying to hide the sarcasm in my voice.

"Yep."

"Well, you keep on believing that. I am going to bed and will report the break-in to the cops in the morning."

She didn't budge from the sofa. She had a look of determination on her face that told me she was going to grill me about what had just transpired, and she wasn't going to take no for an answer.

"This was no break-in!" she shouted. "I was in my apartment watching Conan when the power went out on the whole block, and isn't it interesting that not one minute after the blackout, all hell broke loose one floor below!"

"Noisy crooks," I said, calmly. "Not sure why they'd choose my place; I have nothing of any value."

"Stop lying to me!"

"Who's lying?" I asked. "If you want to believe I'm a superhero, then go for it. I'm not going to waste my time trying to convince you otherwise."

She gaped at me for a second and then burst out laughing. "I'm going crazy," she giggled maniacally. "I have a secretive downstairs neighbor who says he works in law enforcement, though he's not registered as a private investigator. He's got two leather outfits hanging in his front closet, and the guy who saved me from my stalker was wearing leather. I know I'd had a couple of drinks, but the guy who saved my life had glowing eyes, wore a hoodie, and could fly! Christ, even the stalker could see that. He told the cops."

I motioned for Marnie to calm down, concerned she might blow a gasket and end in the nut house. It was enough that she knew my secret, and though I was tempted to tell her the truth, I worried that stories of Witchcraft, Ogres, Gremlins that raid refrigerators, and thirty-eight year old Siamese cats might push her over the edge.

"All right, let's assume you're right," I said diplomatically, hoping I wouldn't set her off.

"I *am* right!"

"Fine. Since you're right, let's discuss facts. Would it be fair to say that a superhero needs to remain a secret?"

"Yes."

"Would you agree that most people aren't exactly psychologically prepared to know that a man can fly?"

"Yes, of course."

I decided to stretch the truth. If she believed I worked in law enforcement, then maybe she'd believe I knew about Greenfield's elusive superhero.

"Marnie, I want you to remain calm, okay?" I pleaded. "Can you do that for me?"

"*Do I look calm to you?*"

"I know how much you want to believe I'm the guy who rescued you, but I'm not. Now before you start throwing things at me, just hear me out for a second, because I've done some investigating."

"Go on."

"I've researched the strange fact that Greenfield has an unheard of single-digit crime rate. It's been that way for more than ten years," I said. "The Greenfield Examiner has headlines going back as far as nineteen-ninety-three that talk about criminals found handcuffed to everything from bike racks to car bumpers. Naturally that didn't make any sense to me, so I dug a little deeper."

"And?"

"Then I met someone who actually saw a person matching the description of the guy you described at Chesterton that night. Her name is Stella Weinberg; she's an archivist. Anyway, she said that she knew about this superhero guy as far back as ninety-seven and then handed me a police report she'd obtained where a suspect claimed that the guy who'd handcuffed him to the gate at Delaney Park had glowing eyes."

"Great, two other people can corroborate what happened," Marnie huffed. "Did she mention that his voice sounds a lot like yours?"

I scanned her face to see if she was buying what I was selling, but she still looked skeptical.

"Marnie, my fiancée was dying in ninety-seven. The ovarian cancer had spread to her liver, and the Greenfield County Hospital didn't have the facilities to provide the right kind of treatment," I said, immediately feeling like the biggest asshole in the history of the known universe.

"In February of that year, I accompanied her to an Oncologist in Boston, where she underwent chemotherapy for three months. She wound up in a hospice in October. She passed away in December."

"Oh my God," Marnie whispered, the skeptical look on her face dissolving.

"If I was capable of supernatural feats like this so-called superhero, I'd have devoted every ounce of whatever mysterious power I possessed into finding a cure for Cynthia," I said, filled with regret. "I'm not your guy. I know you want to believe that I am, but this is a case of mistaken identity. I'm sorry."

She chewed her bottom lip for about a minute as she pondered what I'd just disclosed. I felt sick to my stomach for using the worst year of my life as an alibi, even if what I told her wasn't entirely untrue.

"I'm so very sorry about what happened to your fiancée," she said, quietly. "You do believe that what happened that night was real, right?"

"Yes. Though I'm starting to wonder where this superhero was hiding when we've got three unsolved murders in town," I muttered.

"Who do you think he is?" she asked.

"Does it really matter?"

"You're damned right it matters," she insisted. "People need to know the truth. Cripes, if a guy with glowing eyes who can fly goes postal one day, I don't want that hanging over my head."

"Gotcha."

"I wonder if he has a name. I mean like Batman?" she asked.

"Why would he need one?" I said. "His existence is a secret, and real life bears no resemblance to what happens in comic books."

She stared blankly at my broken coffee table. It was hard to tell if she believed me; her face was sullen, and she had a distant look in her eyes.

"What happened in your apartment tonight? Tell me the truth."

I sat down on the sofa and took her hand in mine. As I looked into her eyes, I didn't see the brightness and optimism that made me like her so much. Instead, I saw a frightened young woman who'd spent far too much time obsessing over whether she was losing her mind or not.

"Just a break-in," I said. "When you open the papers tomorrow morning, you'll probably find that a number of homes were trashed because of the blackout."

"I guess you're right," she shrugged. "I feel like a shit for freaking out on you."

"Don't sweat it," I said, still searching her eyes. "Want to know something?"

"What?"

"This might sound corny, but I really do like you," I admitted, surprising myself. "Since the day you invited yourself into my apartment, you've given me something to look forward to. I've fretted over you. Worried about you. I've found myself daydreaming, like a school kid. Wondering what you're doing, worrying about your safety."

"Really?"

"I was a missing person until you came into my life. I spent years hiding from the world because I never wanted to hurt again. I guess that makes me weak. Since the night you stormed out of my apartment, I've missed your shining eyes, your insults and your sense of humor. I've just missed you, I guess. It's stupid, I know, but – "

"Shut up," Marnie blurted out, as she threw her arms around me and kissed me. Softly at first, then purposefully – the kind of purpose that curls your toes and leads to clothes being ripped off and spontaneous love-making. Then, without warning, she stopped.

"Marshall Conrad, are you in love with me?" she asked, the sarcastic tone I'd missed so much returning to her voice. "Cuz if you are, I'm thinking my pops would probably invite you over for a beer and a meeting with his Smith and Wesson."

"I-I've been alone for a long time," I whispered. "I j-just _ "

"You *are* in love with me!" she laughed, her grin stretching from ear to ear. "Oh my God, but this is *totally* taboo! What about your morals and all that crap about the general wrongness of university professors who carry on with attractive female students?"

"Umm, can I ask you something," I whispered, inhaling the scent of jasmine in her hair. God, she smelled good. "How did we get from you grilling me about superheroes to a tender moment on my couch?"

"You're not gonna get all moral again, are you?" she said, still preserving her sarcasm. "It would be just like you to ruin a spontaneous emotional connection by going over a checklist of why it's so wrong that I'm in love with you."

"Excuse me?" I asked, my voice cracking like a kid who just hit puberty at sixty miles an hour. "You l-love me?"

"Well, duhhh," she said, kissing my nose as she stood up. "I'm not entirely sure why I love you. You're cranky and miserable all the time, and you've got a mean-ass chip on your shoulder. But I know my heart, and I know beneath that cantankerous shell is a deeply wounded man who's terrified to come into the light."

"Wait a minute," I said, my voice still cracking. "Aren't women who've been rescued by superheroes supposed to fall head over heels in love with them? I mean, that's how it goes in the comic books."

Marnie smiled. "First off, I don't read comic books. Secondly, if I were to fall for a superhero, I think a shrink would tell you that I have a subliminal need to be rescued, which I don't. Besides, I'd have no interest in the guy, if I knew who he was."

"Why?"

"Self-preservation – pure and simple."

"What do you mean?"

"The object of the hero's affection is generally the target of some crazed super villain, geez! That's *Superheroes 101,* for crying out loud!"

"Good point," I laughed, escorting her to the door. "What do we do now?"

"I don't know about you, but I need to get some sleep," she said, still grinning. "I have to work in the morning, and God knows I won't be getting any sleep knowing that my downstairs neighbor is in love with me."

She put her arms around me and squeezed while I tentatively slipped my hands on her hips. "I didn't say that I was in love with you," I whispered. "Well, not yet, anyway. I don't know what this is."

"Shh," she said, placing her index finger on my lips. "Get some sleep, and clean this place up in the morning, because we're having dinner here tomorrow night – I'll bring home some Thai food."

"I have a peanut allergy – I could die," I joked.

"Shut up, you moron." She laughed, walking out the door.

CHAPTER 30

I circled June 21st on my calendar and shook my head.

I was nowhere near finding Grim Geoffrey's host, and my apartment looked like a bomb site. The insurance adjuster who'd visited told me they couldn't process my claim without a police report, and the last thing I wanted was another encounter with Sheriff Don Neuman now that he was planning to frame me for the unsolved killings.

I replaced the sheet Marnie had hung over my broken sliding glass door with some transparent plastic and proceeded to tidy up the mess in my apartment.

The phone rang. It was Marnie calling from work during her break. Apparently she was still in love with me.

"Hey you," she said. I could tell by the sound of her voice that she was smiling. "Get any sleep?"

"A couple of hours. Look, I think we should hold off on dinner tonight," I said.

"Relationship remorse already? It's only been about twelve hours since I kissed you," she teased.

"Umm, yeah – about that. Look, I like you; you know that."

"And I like you. What's the problem?"

"No problem, I just – oh crap, I don't know what I am supposed to say here."

I could hear a tapping sound on her end of the line, and I imagined she was clicking her fingernails on a desktop. It had been so long since I'd been involved with anyone, let alone a woman twenty years my junior. I knew that if I were her father, I'd put a hit on the dirty old man who'd been trying to get my kid into bed, and I'd probably have his balls hanging from my rearview mirror.

"You're going through that checklist of reasons why we shouldn't see where this goes, aren't you?" she asked, still sounding upbeat. "God, you're so damned predictable."

"Sorry about that," I mumbled.

"It's not like we're getting married. Why don't you just stop thinking so much and simply follow your heart?"

I didn't know what to say.

I'd completely shut myself away from the world after Cynthia died, and even during our three years together, I wasn't exactly a genius when it came to matters of the heart. Still, when Marnie was around, I felt half-human again. I was free to drop my guard and let her see the real me, the guy I'd forgotten about beneath ten years of taking out my anger on as many bad guys as I could find.

Then there was the issue of Marnie's safety.

She was right about becoming the target of something that wanted me dead. If a cloaked Minion from the unseen world was powerful enough to attack me without my radar kicking in, then any number of bad things could happen to her. Hell, every bad thing and its dog was destined to happen during the summer solstice if I didn't stop Grim Geoffrey. As much as I cared for Marnie, there were bigger fish to fry.

"Let's just take it slowly," I said, trying not to raise her alarm bells. "Very, very slowly."

About ten seconds passed in silence, and I readied myself for another lecture about my old-fashioned values.

"I can do slow," she said, in an equally serious tone. "I mean, this is uncharted waters for me, too. You're not the only one who's trying to make sense of their feelings. Tell you what, I threw the ball into your court, it's yours to do with as you please. The next move is up to you."

"Really?" I tried to conceal the relief in my voice.

"Yep. I've got exams coming up, and I'm going to be buried in textbooks for the next six weeks anyway. Oh, and there's that whole thing about finding the guy who saved my life."

"You really should let that go," I warned.

"Maybe I will. Who knows?" she said. "I'm actually starting to believe that he's skipped town, so my search might just be a big fat waste of time."

"What makes you say that?" I asked, surprised by her assertion.

"There's something weird happening in Greenfield these days. Lots of bizarre stuff happening."

"Such as?"

"Outside of three unsolved murders and everyone talking about a serial killer, there's a whack of graffiti popping up all over the place – big red spirals everywhere. I have a friend who is studying geology, they're examining a bunch of rocks that have spiral engravings on them. It's just nuts."

A sinking feeling nailed me right in the stomach and a wave of nausea rushed over me. I became dizzy and broke out in a cold sweat.

"Y-You've seen them too, huh?" I asked.

"Yep. Hey, I believe you about the break-in at your apartment last night," she said. "You were right about there being a bunch of vandalism in our neighborhood during the blackout."

"Oh yeah? I haven't read the paper yet."

"Forget the paper. When I walked out to my car this morning, someone had smashed my windshield, and there was a big red spiral painted on the hood."

My blood immediately ran cold.

"Marnie, I want you to stay with me tonight. Got that?"

"Umm, I thought you wanted to take things slow?" she asked, sounding confused. "What gives?"

"A break-in at my place, your car gets vandalized. Spiral graffiti. You're right about strange things happening in town. If they hit our place last night, they might not be done yet, so let's just call this an added measure of security."

"Sure, Marshall. Whatever you want. I'll meet you in your apartment around six. Sound like a plan?"

"I'll see you then," I said and hung up the phone.

CHAPTER 31

I am the world's worst handyman.

Unlike most guys, I don't become breathless at the thought of winning a shopping spree at Home Depot. I've never darkened the doors of a hardware store in my entire life. I'd always maintained that if something can't be repaired with either duct tape or a combination screwdriver, then it's time to call a repairman.

Given that I have no repair skills, I knew it might be difficult to slap together some improvised security measures on my car now that Sheriff Don Neuman intended to frame me for eight murders.

And believe it or not, it was surprisingly easy.

I simply unscrewed all four interior door panels and disconnected the wires leading to the power window motors as well as the power locks. I also removed the door lock knobs to prevent him from using a jig to enter my car. Finally, I injected super glue in the window frames so he couldn't force the windows open. If the sheriff intended to plant a severed head in my car, he'd have to smash the glass or force open the trunk to do it.

I was in an unusually upbeat mood for a guy up to his ears in preventing a supernatural holocaust. Maybe it was the kiss Marnie had given me in my apartment the previous night, or that I'd successfully duked it out with two mythical creatures, I wasn't sure. My ribs were sore, and it hurt like hell to breathe, but the power that had flowed through my body during combat was intoxicating.

Stella once said a Vanguard's powers are unmatched by nearly everything in the unseen world. I replayed my battle with the Minion, remembering that it crashed through my sliding door after I'd summoned a torrent of energy from the evil surrounding the creature. I'd shaped the energy into a powerful weapon through sheer force of will, conjuring a mental picture of what I wanted the weapon to look like and how I wanted it to function. Perhaps my powers *were* off the scale, as Ruby had suggested. Maybe the combination of powers associated with my being a Vanguard and a Sorcerer would give me an edge in defeating Grim Geoffrey.

Since nobody had taken the time to instruct me in how to be either a Vanguard or a witch, it made sense to tinker with my abilities. I hopped into my Tempo and headed up the Interstate, hoping to find a secluded spot where nobody would see me experimenting. I drove for about three quarters of an hour, past rolling farmland stretched as far as the eye could see in both directions from the highway. I drove another ten minutes and pulled into an abandoned road overgrown with weeds and debris. My car sputtered along for three miles while I kept my eyes open for any signs of human activity. The road led through a stand of pine trees, and I parked my car alongside a large boulder, ensuring it couldn't be seen from the road.

I got out of my car and surveyed the area.

It looked secluded enough. I listened for any signs of life. Only the sound of the wind whistling through the pine boughs and the occasional bird chattering away in the distance. I walked through another stand of trees and came to an open space alongside a small creek, filled with the spring runoff. This was as good a place as any.

I already possessed the ability to fly, but until then, all of my powers had only worked at night, the result of channeling the energy from willful intent of a perpetrator I might be attempting to take down. Stella had told me I wasn't hardwired yet for daytime work, and nobody had ever explained whether a Vanguard's powers are naturally occurring – I'd always assumed that willful intent was the source. I decided to start with flight, thinking I'd be an old hand at it by now.

I was mistaken.

"Fly!" I shouted, and nothing happened. Feeling like an idiot, I closed my eyes and concentrated, focusing all of my thoughts and feelings on the smallest point of contact between the ground and my feet. I imagined an invisible force pushing upward, similar to how opposing magnetic fields act against each other. Suddenly, my feet left the ground, and I gently hovered upward.

If I broke my concentration, would I fall? I immediately thought of Marnie's kiss, and landed flat on my ass.

"Okay, I guess I'd better not lose my concentration. I'll try it again."

This time I kept my eyes opened. I conjured the image of opposing magnetic fields and once again lifted off the ground.

"H-Holy s-shit," I said. "Let's see how high I can go."

I looked up at the clouds and picked one as a target. Then I imagined my body as a rocket. There was a muffled boom as I shot straight up into the sky, hurtling toward my target like a guided missile. It was the fastest I'd ever flown, and instead of a cold wind blowing against my face, air friction scraped against my skin like sandpaper. My body buffeted against air pockets that felt like someone was kicking me in the ribs. I slowed my ascent to a hover and looked down at the patchwork quilt of the earth below my feet.

Interestingly, I didn't feel a surge of energy in my eyes. I resolved that "seeker's light" had nothing to do with a willful display of a specific power and that it was an instinctive response to the presence of evil. There was no evil at ten thousand feet in the air, so I pivoted my body toward the earth and flew downward, this time at a controlled speed.

I landed a few feet away from my car, pleased as punch. "All right, that's one down. How many more to go?"

I looked around and spotted another boulder larger than the one beside the Tempo. I could probably lift it over my head under normal circumstances, so I walked over and leaned into it with my shoulder to see if it would move. I gritted my teeth and pushed as hard as I could, but the boulder didn't budge.

"Now what?" I said, scratching my chin. I wasn't about to wrap my arms around it and blow out my back, so I leaned into the boulder again, this time imagining it was light as a feather. I dug my heels into the ground and pushed, focusing my energy on the point of contact between my shoulder and the rock. Amazingly, the boulder moved in the direction I was shoving, plowing the earth at its base.

I swung myself around and placed both hands on the front of the boulder and pushed harder, this time using my legs. The boulder rolled on its side, exposing a soil encrusted surface alive with insects. I wiped the dirt off my hands, proud of my achievement, then decided to lift the boulder over my head and throw it.

I searched the surface of the boulder for a crack or depression that would help me keep a good grip in preparation for the lift. I dug my fingers into the rock and bent with my knees so I wouldn't injure my back. With a huge groan, I pulled upward while straightening my legs. I'd just swung the boulder up over my head when a voice called out from beside my car.

"Remember to let go of the boulder when you throw it!" Ruby shouted.

Startled by Ruby's sudden appearance, I staggered backward and tripped on some deadwood. The weight of the boulder was immediately on me and I instinctively remembered the ball of energy I'd used to throw the Minion off my chest back at my apartment. "Off!" I shouted, and the boulder sailed in a horizontal trajectory, smashing through trees and eventually landing about a hundred yards away. An automobile-sized furrow of crushed trees and plowed earth lay in the boulder's wake.

"Ruby!" I barked. "You scared the shit out of me – I could have been crushed!"

Ruby hopped on the hood of the Tempo and casually took a shot of whisky from her pewter flask. "Relax," she said, calmly. "I wouldn't have let that happen."

I stomped over to my car, my blood boiling. "You've got a lot of nerve trying something like that," I snarled.

"Stop your pissing and moaning, Conrad." she said sourly.

If I was angry before, I was mad as hell now.

I'd purposely driven for over an hour so I could be alone, and somehow, Ruby had found me. She'd probably been watching me experiment with my powers and instead of offering some advice, she'd treated me like a source of personal entertainment. I'd had more than enough of Ruby's bad attitude since the day she showed up at my apartment. It was time to push back.

I thrust out my right hand like a medieval battering ram and fired a blast of energy that sent Ruby careening off the hood of the Tempo, crashing into a pile of rotting timber. She quickly got to her feet and stuck out her chin defiantly. Her eyes narrowed with black anger, and she drove her gloved hands together like a jackhammer, blasting a concussion wave toward me.

I stretched out my other hand and trapped the energy into powerful ball of compressed force, then I hurled it back at her. "Oh sheeeeit!" she wailed, as the energy bomb hit the ground and exploded, blasting the deadwood in all directions while she catapulted through the air. She landed flat on her back and stared at the sky with stunned look on her face.

"Truce," she coughed. "I had that coming."

I was still incensed as I reached out and helped Ruby to her feet. Suddenly, her small hands fastened around my wrist and she pivoted on her heels, swinging me around and around like a hammer thrower at the Olympics.

Okay, so she was strong.

When she let go, I jettisoned through the air until she was little more than a dot on the horizon. I remembered how I summoned the ability to fly and slowed my ascent until I had enough control to fly back toward her.

"Never drop your guard!" she shouted. "Not even for me!"

"Truce, then," I said, landing at her feet.

"Truce," said Ruby, grinning.

CHAPTER 32

It was a rare moment of comraderie.

As we sat on the hood of the Tempo, it occurred to me that while everything about Ruby rubbed me the wrong way, there had to be a reason why she was annoying as hell – I just couldn't put my finger on it. She was a twig of a woman, but she'd lived a long life, and every wrinkle on her face told a story of broken bones and smashed teeth. I speculated on what kinds of creatures she'd fought against over the years. As a retired member of The Guild, she'd probably seen her share of cataclysms. That probably explained why she handled stress better than me.

And she was clever.

You don't live as long as Ruby without having a few tricks up your sleeve, and I imagined that she'd learned her lessons the hard way – through trial and error and perseverance. It was Ruby who'd told me to use the shard of Sentient Quartz on the Grave Demon. She'd also forced Stella into a corner when she challenged her to find a way to defeat Grim Geoffrey without resorting to dark magic. Stella had reluctantly agreed, realizing that she'd wind up kicked out of her coven for doing it.

Ruby Thiessen was a paradox. Her diminutive stature concealed an indomitable spirit, and in the short time I'd known her, she'd taught me the importance of brushing yourself off and soldiering on.

Today she seemed distant.

I'd just finished giving her an update on my grilling at the sheriff's office, the trio of Gremlins and my battle with the Minion. Under normal circumstances, she'd have torn a strip off me for battling the Minion in my apartment and nearly blowing my cover, but not today. She just sat on the car and stared off in the distance. I told how I was finally able to draw on my powers, hoping my enthusiasm would snap her out of it. Instead, she nodded silently, taking it all in.

"How did you get out here, anyway?" I asked. "I took precautions so that I'd be alone."

"I'm still a witch," she said. "I cast a veil so you wouldn't see me, and I was in the backseat the entire time."

"Ah, that makes sense," I nodded. "You're a huge pain in the ass, you know."

"Yep."

I put a reassuring hand on her shoulder to show my concern. "Is everything all right?" I asked.

She glanced at my hand and then at my face, then back to my hand again. "You planning on moving that any time soon?"

"Sorry," I said, taking my hand off her shoulder.

"When all this Grim Geoffrey shit is over," said Ruby, as she handed me her pewter flask, "I'll set up a formal training plan for you."

I took a swig and grimaced. "I thought you weren't going to be my wet nurse," I said.

"Changed my mind."

"How come?"

"Politics," she huffed. "The Guild disagrees with our alliance."

"You mean working with me and Stella?"

She nodded. "Yep. But they don't understand the degree of danger facing the near world, and said they'd revoke my membership, since it's forbidden for Guild members to work with anyone from the covens. Pompous assholes."

"So what happened?"

Ruby glanced at me, and her lips curled up into a malicious smile. "I gave back the gold watch and told them to stuff it."

I was surprised, but not shocked.

Stella said Ruby was thrown out of her coven for using dark magic; now the Guild was cutting her loose because of their suspicion toward witches. Clearly my father must have been an important person for a schism to develop between the two orders charged with protecting mankind.

I wasn't surprised that she'd told The Guild precisely where to go. In a way, I was proud of her for taking a stand, because it was something I would do. This was politics at its worst – ignore a threat in the name of party solidarity.

I tried to think of something conciliatory or noble that might help Ruby feel better, but nothing came. "I'm sorry, Ruby," I said. "It will be their loss."

She hopped off the hood of the Tempo and stretched. "No matter," she said. "The Guild has never really bought into the supernatural."

"I hope you realize that I have no intention of ever joining The Guild," I said, dead serious. "I detest political bullshit."

"No worries," she said. "Of course, you know they're going to come down hard on you if you don't join up. They see you as some kind of sacred cow because of what happened to your father."

"Mooooo."

Her smile broadened, and then she started laughing hysterically.

"Oh yeah, they're going to love you to death, Conrad," she snickered. "Speaking of politics, how's that old psychic radar working?"

"Still on the fritz," I grumbled. "I was going to try a couple of experiments, but then you showed up and picked a fight with me. Why do you ask?"

"Big news," she said. "Congressman Byron Aldrich has a summer home at Crystal Beach. His wife was up there cleaning the place out, and she's been missing since last night."

I swallowed and pushed back a feeling of mad panic that grabbed my stomach and squeezed. "You're kidding – don't they have Secret Service Agents or something like that?"

"Nope. Secret Service protects the President. Congressmen and their families have private security."

"How the hell did the guy get past her security detail, then?"

"That's a damned good question." Ruby nodded. "According to the latest newscast, they didn't even realize she was gone until they noticed that she hadn't checked in with them for over three hours."

"Cripes, this is huge," I said, stunned.

"You might want to get that radar working again," Ruby said, poking me in the head. "Like now."

"Why?"

"Because I saw an aerial shot of the house when I was watching the news." She frowned. "Someone painted a big red spiral on the roof."

CHAPTER 33

I wasn't about to waste any time complaining about why I hadn't foreseen Marilyn Aldrich's kidnapping. I'd done more than enough of that over the past few days, and it no longer mattered. The important thing was to figure out how to get my psychic radar working again, because for all I knew, the Congressman's wife was already dead, and it would be a matter of time before someone found her mutilated corpse.

If she were still alive, it meant I finally had a chance to confront Grim Geoffrey's host, but then what? Ruby told me I'd have to kill the host if I wanted to prevent the cataclysm from happening during the summer solstice, and I'd refused. That's why we'd been searching for a portal into Grim Geoffrey's realm. If we could defeat him on his home turf, there would be no incursion into the near world.

We'd been unsuccessful so far.

Dennis the Ogre had alluded that dark magic was responsible for our inability to find a portal. Now, with less than a handful of days to go before the summer solstice, Grim

Geoffrey had raised the stakes. But why Marilyn Aldrich? Why a congressman's wife?

Byron Aldrich had won reelection thanks in large part to his wife's popularity as a media personality. I didn't vote for the guy, because Republicans have always given me the willies, but if I were going to vote Republican, it would be because of Marilyn Aldrich.

Before entering public life, she'd been the host of *Greenfield Morning*, a lighthearted news and information program on KGRB. Each day, she'd greet viewers with a cheerful *"Wakie wakie, Greenfield, the sun is shining, and breakfast is on the table,"* endearing her to a generation of Greenfield residents. The show had been canceled when KGRB became a Fox affiliate, and she then hosted a popular talk show called *Greenfield Magazine*, featuring local guests, who'd talk about everything from the world's best chili recipes to the art of fly tying, my personal favorite. Five years ago, she received a Citizen of the Year award from the Greenfield Chamber of Commerce, and then she published the *Jasper Frogginton* series of best-selling children's books. Marilyn Aldrich was, in a word, beloved. I shuddered at how the fear in Greenfield would reach epidemic proportions if she wound up becoming murder victim number nine.

I hopped in my car and headed back to town so I could watch the news and find out if there were any leads in the search for Marilyn Aldrich. Ruby sat silently in the passenger seat staring at each passing power pole, lost in thought.

"Are you sure you're okay, Ruby?" I asked, concerned by her glum demeanor.

She forced a smile and nodded. "I'm fine. I just feel like the chickens are coming home to roost, somehow."

"Because you got kicked out of the coven and the Guild?"

"That's part of it," she said, exhaling. "I've lost a helluva lot in my life, mostly because of my bad attitude."

"You were pretty nasty to me, and I haven't dumped you," I said, jokingly. "Actually, for a miserable old woman, you're not half bad."

Ruby rolled her eyes. "I'm old, all right," she said. "How's the radar working?"

"Nothing yet."

"I'm distracting you. When we get back to town, drop me off at The Curiosity Nook. I need to talk with Stella. Maybe we can conjure up a counter spell that will help you get a bead on Marilyn Aldrich."

"Will do – shit!" I said, glancing at my watch.

"What's wrong?"

"I have a date in thirty minutes that I suddenly have no interest in attending. I should be out there searching for her."

Ruby put her hand on my knee and gave it a friendly tap. "Go on your date. There's nothing we can do about finding her right now."

"I guess so," I said, softly.

"Is she pretty?"

"She's beautiful," I said, suddenly feeling warm all over. "Her name is Marnie."

"Your upstairs neighbor?" Ruby asked. "That sounds awfully convenient."

"She's a lot younger than me, but darn it, she's gotten under my skin."

"Follow your heart," said Ruby, putting a reassuring hand on my knee. "If it's real, the age difference won't matter one little bit."

We drove in silence until we passed the "Welcome to Greenfield" sign at the entrance to town. I turned down Shelby Avenue and drove past Delaney Park until I saw the waving Boris Yeltsin sign in the window of The Curiosity Nook.

"Looks like my stop," said Ruby, as she opened the passenger door. "If you get a fix on Marilyn Aldrich and she's still alive, you call Stella and me. I don't want you going after Grim Geoffrey's host without some backup. It could be a trap, for all we know."

"Will do." I nodded.

Ruby snickered."You're the most uptight forty-year-old man I've ever met. Have fun on your date, and for shit's sake, have some sex."

She slammed the door before I could fire off a snappy comeback, so I pulled back onto Shelby Avenue and headed back to my apartment. I turned on the radio in hopes of hearing an update on the search for Marilyn Aldrich, and I wasn't disappointed. Every station on the dial was covering her disappearance, and reporters were now openly questioning the ability of the Greenfield Sheriff's Department to find her, not to mention Sheriff Neuman's competence.

"If they only knew the truth," I muttered, as I pulled into my parking space and turned off the Tempo.

I stepped out of the car and locked the door with my key, then headed into my building. When I opened my apartment door, Marnie Brindle was sitting at the kitchen table with an assortment of take-out boxes and a huge grin on her face.

"You're right on time," she said, checking her watch. "I'm impressed."

"Thanks." I hung up my coat.

"What have you been up to?"

"Looking for Marilyn Aldrich," I said, sitting down at the table.

"Jeez, that's right," said Marnie. "That's the biggest thing that's ever hit this town. The sheriff's office is swarming with reporters. Even the big networks are covering this."

"Yeah, it's big news."

"Any leads?"

"You mean other than the giant red spiral on the roof of her place out at Crystal Beach?"

Marnie filled my plate with a steaming helping of Pad Thai and coconut rice. "You saw that on the news too, huh?" she asked, handing it to me.

"That I did," I said, as I stuffed a forkful of rice in my mouth. "No leads, though."

"This looks like a job for Greenfield Super-Duper Guy," she said. "I wonder if he's out there looking for her."

I shrugged. "Yeah, maybe."

Then it hit me.

A high-order detonation of corrosive pain blasted its way straight into the middle of my brain, and I doubled over in my chair.

"*Jesus Christ!*" I screamed through my teeth.

Then another blast of pain spread out from my temples to the back of my head. I clutched at my stomach as a hurricane of nausea shot through my stomach, knocking me to the floor.

"Marshall!" Marnie scrambled to her knees and threw her arms around me. "Oh my God, Marshall, what's wrong?"

My mind flooded with a crystal-clear image of Marilyn Aldrich, bound and gagged. Her eyes were giant white O's as the image of a large meat cleaver danced in front of her face, its blue steel gleaming in the light of a kerosene lantern.

Her face was bruised, and her nose looked broken as she struggled to free herself.

The man in white coveralls leaned in and kissed her forehead, his stringy blond hair brushing her face, leaving a trail of slime on her skin.

He was ready to end her. He had to end her.

She was the last one before his master would come.

His master would reward him for his loyalty; he'd been promised so much, and he'd willingly given of himself because his master made everything happen.

Amazing feats.

Like knowing that God had selected him for this one task.

He'd been reading the papers for so many years, searching the headlines for anything that would confirm the end-times were at hand – and the end-times needed the hand of God to usher in the final judgment.

He danced around the barn, kicking up dust and straw as he sang about the hand of God. His hands. His pale, white hands. God wanted the last one to end inside a stable, but the only place he could find that was secluded enough to carry out God's will was the abandoned barn with the checkerboard roof on his family's property. His family was gone now. All gone. It was early still. He'd come back to the barn before midnight – he always ended them before midnight, just as his master wanted. For he was a loyal servant, a favored prophet who would prepare this spoiled earth for God's arrival.

And it would be good.

Marnie helped me to my easy chair, and I collapsed in a heap. The migraine continued to stab at my head like an ice pick on a reciprocating saw as I glanced at my watch. It was 6:47 PM, and I'd been out for half an hour.

"I thought you were having a heart attack." Marnie's eyes brimmed with tears.

"I'm okay," I said, weakly. "I get brutal migraines, and you just witnessed one. Can we do a rain check?"

"That was no migraine, Marshall Conrad!" she scowled. "We should take you to the hospital and get you checked out, just to be safe."

"I'll be fine! I just need to go to bed." I snapped.

Marnie recoiled from my outburst, and I didn't have time to feel like an abusive asshole; I had to find a barn with a checkerboard roof and rescue Marilyn Aldrich.

"I-I'll stay with you then, okay?" she pleaded.

"It's fine, Marnie, I'll be all right. Just go home."

"I should stay here with you," she insisted, sounding slightly angry. "You told me you wanted me to stay with you overnight!"

"*Leave me the hell alone and get out of my apartment!*" I roared, certain I'd forever destroyed whatever affection might exist between Marnie and me.

She shoved me into the chair and flashed a contemptuous glare straight at me. "You know what? You sound just like the guy who saved me when he was screaming at my stalker."

"Just leave, will you?" I groaned.

"Oh, I'm leaving. I'll be seeing you around – you just won't know I'm there!" she shouted, as she stormed out of my apartment.

CHAPTER 34

I had no idea how my psychic radar miraculously reappeared, but I wasn't going to waste any time speculating. The migraine that rolled into my brain like an avalanche showed Marilyn Aldrich was still alive, but I'd have to move fast if she had any hope of surviving the night.

The image of a barn with a checkerboard roof filled my head as I changed out of my street clothes and pulled my kangaroo shirt over my head. I'd have to take to the skies and conduct an aerial reconnaissance to find the barn, but I couldn't just walk out into my parking lot and leap into the air. Marnie Brindle had made it abundantly clear she would be watching me, confirming that she still believed I was Greenfield's elusive superhero.

As I zipped up my leather jacket, it occurred to me that before the night was over, my secret would be out. There was no escaping that in order to rescue Marilyn Aldrich, I'd have to battle Grim Geoffrey's host. Short of somehow luring him away from the barn, I was unable to plot a strategy that would guarantee her safety while simultaneously ensuring she wouldn't see me.

I ran out to the parking lot and hopped in my car. It was 7:04 PM, and I had a little over four and a half hours to find Marilyn Aldrich.

I turned the key, and the Tempo sputtered to life. I slipped it into reverse, squealing the tires as I backed up and then tore out of my parking lot as fast as the four-cylinder engine would carry me. I had to get out of town and find a secluded place where I could park my car and then take to the skies without being noticed. But first I headed to The Curiosity Nook to grab Ruby and Stella. When I arrived, the doors were locked and Boris Yeltsin wasn't waving from his familiar spot in the front window.

"Crap," I muttered. "No time to look for them."

I scribbled a note on a piece of scrap paper from the pocket of my leather pants and stuck it in the door jam, hoping they'd find it when they returned. The note read:

"Radar working. Gone to collect M.A. Barn with checkerboard roof.

Host is on-site, not sure if it's a trap. M.A. severely beaten and will need medical attention, look for me at hospital. If you haven't heard from me by 12:30 AM, assume the worst."

I jumped back in the Tempo and headed up Shelby Avenue, then turned onto the

Interstate and headed north. I drove for another ten minutes, looking for a dirt road or a fireguard – anything that would allow me to get off the highway and out of plain view. I took Exit 12 and headed west on State Highway 6 for another mile and half, until I spotted a fireguard that led from the highway into a thick stand of Spruce trees. It would have to do. I glanced at my watch. 7:44 PM.

I pulled my car off the highway and drove up the cut line until I couldn't see the highway through my rearview mirror. The Tempo's engine strained against the mud earth, kicking up huge clumps of muck that sprayed out from both sides of my front tires. I got out of the car and looked around to ensure I was alone, then pulled the hood of my kangaroo shirt over my head. 7:53 PM.

I stretched out my arms and then pushed off the ground with every ounce of energy in my body. I slowly hovered above the trees and then started scanning the area, hoping to find the barn. Nothing.

I floated higher and winced as the setting sun blinded my eyes, amplifying the stabbing pain of the migraine. I squinted, so I could get a better view of my surroundings, but there were no buildings anywhere in sight. The best thing to do would be to fly at a high altitude in a zigzag pattern over a large area. Maybe that would lead me to the barn with the checkerboard roof.

I spotted a series of rolling hills in the distance and used them as a navigational aid, scanning the ground as I went. The forest gave way to newly planted crops of corn and canola, and I spotted numerous barns, but none of them had checkerboard roofs. I considered heading toward Crystal Beach on a hunch that I might be able to hone into his location if I focused on his willful intent, and then it came to me.

I shouldn't have been searching for a checkerboard roof, instead, I should be combing the ground for signs where nature had reclaimed the earth from the constant plowing of farm equipment or from the grazing of livestock. That meant trees and brush should be growing where spring crops would normally be in full blossom.

I continued zigzagging until I spotted a tract of land in the distance that wasn't consistent with the topography surrounding it. I leaned into the air currents and clenched my fists, increasing my speed until I spotted a set of tire tracks that cut across a field of overgrown weeds before disappearing into a depression in the ground. As I flew higher, I spotted numerous rusted-out farm implements scattered as far as the eye could see. Waist-high weeds bobbed and weaved in unison in the damp evening breeze, while a small group of sheep bedded down for the night. The low ground eventually gave way to what once might have been a bald hill, which was now carpeted with scrub and bramble. I noticed a rotting wind pump bent at a forty-five-degree angle that pointed to another depression in the ground, and then, jutting out from between two hills, there it was: the checkerboard roof.

I immediately stopped in midair and hovered about five-hundred yards from the barn. The left side had collapsed and the roof sagged in the center, as if a large anvil had been dropped from the sky directly above. A set of tire tracks circled the barn, but there was no truck or car in sight. I listened closely for the sound of an engine or human voices but heard nothing. A faint light glowed dimly through a hole in the roof. Someone was inside.

I'd expected my eyes to explode into brilliant white light, but nothing happened. If Seeker's Light was indeed a sure sign of the presence of evil, then Grim Geoffrey's host wasn't on site, and that meant Marilyn Aldrich was alone. I lowered myself onto the roof of the barn and landed softly, hoping it wouldn't give way. It didn't. I crawled to the hole in the roof and peered inside, hoping to catch a glimpse of Mrs. Aldrich, but she was nowhere to be seen.

I flew to the ground and then walked the entire perimeter of the barn, just to be certain the man in white coveralls wasn't hiding somewhere. Then it occurred to me that a barn probably has a million and one possible hiding places, so I should hustle my butt inside and find Marilyn Aldrich. I found a side entrance. The weathered door hung loosely from rotting hinges and banged against the wall with each small gust of wind.

I stepped inside, and my nostrils filled with the smell of rotting straw and mold. The dirt floor had long been overtaken by a carpet of moss that stretched out to the middle of the barn, where the roof had given way. I noticed a small tree growing in a massive heap of soil and composted bales of hay, and there was a rusted-out John Deere tractor by the main entrance, covered with decades of grime.

"Hello?" I called out. "Mrs. Aldrich, are you in here?" The sound of my voice echoed across the beamed ceiling, and a barn owl fluttered its wings, scaring the crap out of me. Then I heard a scuffling sound coming from the loft.

"Mrs. Aldrich, are you in here?" I called out again, as I walked toward the glowing light, which I assumed was from the kerosene lantern in my vision. I snuck over a ladder and carefully began climbing, ready at any moment for an attack.

As my head poked over the ledge, the scuffling sound became constant as a muffled voice cried out from beside a pile of rotting hay bales. I glanced over and spotted Marilyn Aldrich, dressed in a pair of jeans and a sweater. Her bound hands hung stiffly from a rusted hoist hook, stretching her arms to their full extension. Blood dripped from her torn wrists and down her forearms, staining the sleeves of her white sweater. Her legs were bound in two places, at the thighs and at the ankles, and her mouth was gagged with another piece of rope that cut into her face. Dried blood collected at the corner of her mouth, and her face was a mass of bruises. She'd been beaten. Severely.

I didn't waste any time.

I ran over and untied the knot behind her head while she flopped around, trying to fight me. It fell to the ground as she turned her head and stared at me, her eyes filled with terror.

"H-Have y-you come to kill me?" she asked, her voice dry and hoarse.

"Nope," I whispered, as I untied the rope around her legs. "Stop struggling, we're getting the hell out of here."

"W-Who are you?" she whispered.

"Shh. Where's the man in white?"

"H-How did you find me?" she asked. "H-how did you know about him?"

"Mrs. Aldrich, there isn't time," I said, untying the knot above her head. Her arms dropped to the floor like a stone. "Is he nearby?"

"N-No," she said weakly. "He went away. He said he was coming back to purify my body."

"I hate to ask this, but has he?"

"N-No, he didn't rape me. Who are you?"

"It doesn't matter," I said, helping her to her feet. "Can you walk?"

She took a tentative step forward, and her knees buckled. I caught her and slung her left arm over my shoulder. "Try it now," I said.

Mrs. Aldrich limped forward, leaning heavily against me. Her right leg was dragging, and it was clear she was in no shape to hoof it out of the barn.

"I'm going to have to carry you," I said. "Put your arms around my neck."

"Why are you wearing a hood?" she asked, her voice almost a whisper. "Who are you?"

"We can talk about it on your TV show sometime," I said, trying to sound optimistic. "Put your arms around my neck, Mrs. Aldrich."

"I-I can't move my left arm," she winced, as she fell to her knees. "Shooting pain."

All the color left her face, and she broke out in a cold sweat. I ran my hand over her left arm to check for any broken bones, but it was intact.

"T-trouble breathing," she coughed. "Pain in my jaw."

"Mrs. Aldrich, do you have a heart condition?" I asked, as I carried her to the door of the loft.

"I have diabetes and high blood pressure. I haven't had my medication since before he took me."

"We need to get you to the hospital," I said, kicking open the door. Darkness covered every square inch of the land surrounding the barn, and I couldn't get my bearings. She needed medical attention, but my car was miles away, and there wasn't time to escape the barn on foot.

"Mrs. Aldrich, close your eyes." I tried to sound reassuring. "Bury your head into my chest, and for and God's sake, do not look down."

"W-Why?" she asked.

"Because the shit is about to hit the fan," I said, stepping out the door of the loft.

CHAPTER 35

My eyes blazed furiously, cutting into the blackness as I climbed higher and higher into the sky. Marilyn Aldrich was screaming like a teenage girl in a slasher movie, and I winced as she dug her one good hand through my jacket and clutched a handful of my chest hair for dear life.

"Mrs. Aldrich, you're not helping!" Air pockets slammed into our bodies like rogue waves crashing against the shoreline. "Calm down. Just calm the hell down!"

"What are you? What the hell are you?" she howled, as she stared at me with a look of unmitigated horror on her face. "Oh my God, you have a hood! You're the grim reaper!"

"Mrs. Aldrich, you're not dead yet, but you will be if you don't calm down!" I shouted, through the wind.

"This is a hallucination," she wailed, as she buried her head into my shoulder. "I'm still in the barn – I have to be!"

I slowed my flight speed; between the air pockets and Marilyn Aldrich clawing at my chest, it was becoming increasingly difficult to navigate in the darkness.

"In a few minutes, you're going to be in a hospital room, and they're going to pump you full of stuff to keep your heart going," I said. "Tomorrow morning you're going to wake up, and the first thing you'll see is the smiling face of your husband."

"B-But what are you?" she asked, her voice muffled by my leather jacket.

"Do you believe in angels?" I asked.

"I think so."

"Then maybe I'm an angel – how does that sound?"

"You're not an angel – you smell like Aqua Velva," she cried. "Angels don't smell like cheap aftershave!"

"This one does." I said, as I spotted the lights of Greenfield in the distance. "Are you experiencing any chest pains or shortness of breath?"

"Y-Yes, are we almost there?"

"A few more minutes," I said. "You're a popular woman. The entire national news media has been covering your disappearance."

"They're vultures, and they try to put words in my husband's mouth. Did you vote for him? He's an excellent congressman."

I shook my head. "How did the man in white kidnap you?"

"I don't remember," she said. "He was supposed to be a painter – we were renovating the summerhouse. I was showing him how I wanted everything done, and the next thing I knew, I was strung up in that barn."

"Did he give you any information that could help me find him?" I asked, increasing my altitude to avoid detection when we entered the city.

"N-No," she said, weakly. "He beat me severely and told me that he was a prophet. He said I was the ninth sacrifice, and that God would reward me in heaven. Then he kissed me and disappeared."

It was just like in my vision. Grim Geoffrey must have somehow tantalized the man in white with a promise that would appeal to him on a spiritual level. He must be some kind of end-times evangelical nut job. I made a mental note to grab Ruby after I dropped Mrs. Aldrich off at the hospital.

I spotted the giant blue *H* of the Greenfield County Hospital glowing brightly in the darkness. I increased my altitude so I was directly over the roof and decided to drop Marilyn Aldrich off in a safe place and then run into the waiting room claiming that a suicidal patient was on the roof. It wasn't pretty, but it was the only idea I could think of that would ensure Mrs. Aldrich received medical treatment while reducing the likelihood that someone might see me floating in the air.

"I'm going to get someone to come up here and help you, Mrs. Alrdich." I said. The glow from my eyes revealed the severity of the injuries to her face. "There's going to be a shit-storm of media coverage now that you're safe, and I'd be grateful if you revealed as little information as possible about what happened tonight."

"I-I'll do my best, Mister…?"

"Just call me Vanguard," I said. "Everyone else does."

As I slowly hovered above a large ventilation shaft, I noticed a flash out of the corner of my eye. I didn't think anything of it and assumed it was just a strobe light from an ambulance. I gently laid Mrs. Aldrich alongside the ventilation shaft and gave her a last once-over to make sure she was all right.

"Good luck," I whispered, smothering the glow from my eyes.

She didn't answer me, and that was just fine. I had to get down to the main floor and alert the medical staff.

I raced across the roof, ducking behind exhaust vents so I wouldn't be seen until I spotted a ladder that led down to the east wing of the hospital. Friction from the metal burned my hands as I slid down to another roof, about two stories above the service entrance. From the darkest corner of the roof, I peeked down over the edge to see if the coast was clear. I spotted a large garbage bin in the corner against the building and dropped down behind it, twisting my ankle in the process.

I found myself in an alleyway about a hundred yards from the emergency entrance, so I pulled down my hood and hobbled as quickly as possible up the alley and toward the Emergency entrance. The automatic doors slid open, and I ran inside.

"*There's someone on the roof!*" I shrieked like a madman. Everyone in the waiting room looked up, startled. "Someone call security, there's a lady on the roof, and I think she's going to jump! Hurry!"

"Where?" asked a nurse who was taking information from a woman in a neck brace.

"On the roof!" I shouted. "She's going to jump if someone doesn't get up there right now."

I must have been convincing, because within seconds, two nurses were on the phone and another got on the PA system and called for security.

I tore out the sliding door and ran through the staff parking lot and off the hospital property. I kept glancing over my shoulder, hoping nobody was following me. The Greenfield County Hospital was about to become famous, and I had no desire to hang around for the media circus that would ensue.

I kept on running for another twelve blocks until I saw Shelby Avenue. The Curiosity Nook was only three blocks away. Satisfied that I'd avoided detection at the hospital, I started walking, so I could catch my breath. I glanced at my watch. 9:25 PM – more than enough time for me to grab Ruby and head back to the barn for a confrontation with Grim Geoffrey's host.

It took another five minutes for me to get to Stella's store. "Thank God," I breathed, as I saw the lights were on. I walked into the alcove and banged on the glass door. "Stella! Ruby!" I shouted. "It's Marshall, let me in!"

The lights suddenly switched off, and Stella appeared at the door with a huge scowl on her face. The door opened, and she grabbed me by my collar, pulling me inside.

"What the hell have you done?" she shouted. "Ruby is having a meltdown, and you, my friend, have just become the front-page headline of every newspaper in the country!"

"W-What are you talking about," I panted, still trying to catch my breath.

"I just printed this off the *Drudge Report* website," she snapped, handing me a sheet of paper. "Marshall Conrad, you've just been outed."

CHAPTER 36

My jaw dropped. It was me, all right. In all my unnatural splendor.

I stood in the doorway of The Curiosity Nook, trying desperately to find a word that would describe the firestorm of shock that seized my body as I stared at the sheet of paper Stella'd handed to me. I opened my mouth to speak, and all I could manage was a sound that curiously resembled a squeak.

Beneath the big black words *Drudge Report* was the grainy image of a man with glowing white eyes floating high above the Greenfield County Hospital. He was carrying a woman.

An important woman.

A woman whose kidnapping had already made national news and who would soon be answering police and reporters' questions about the way in which she'd been rescued.

"Marnie Brindle," I gasped, unsure how she she'd known that I'd be at the hospital. Then I remembered the note I slid in the door jam of Stella's store before I went searching for Marilyn Aldrich.

She must have followed me in her car and snatched the note after I headed out of town. It was a harmless note, or so I thought. A note that directed Stella and Ruby to look for me at the Greenfield County Hospital. A note that gave a conspiracy-minded twenty-three-year-old woman who'd been obsessing about a superhero her best chance to prove she wasn't going crazy.

Stella grabbed my collar and dragged me down the hallway to her office. A small color TV sat atop a filing cabinet with the sound cranked to full volume. A live image of the Greenfield County Hospital shared the screen with the picture from Drudge's website, as the words *BREAKING NEWS: MYSTERIOUS RESCUE OF CONGRESSMAN'S WIFE* rolled across the bottom.

"If you're just tuning in," a bearded and bespectacled reporter in somber voice said, "an incredible story is unfolding at this hour in the small city of Greenfield, New Hampshire. Sources say Marilyn Aldrich, the wife of Republican Congressman Byron Aldrich, is receiving medical treatment at the hospital you're seeing in the foreground. Mrs. Aldrich, you'll remember, has been the subject of a state-wide search after she was abducted from the family cottage at Crystal Beach last Sunday. The *Drudge Report*, an independent, web-based news service, posted the startling picture on the right side of your screen to their website approximately fifteen minutes ago. We can't confirm whether the image is genuine. However, this much we do know: Local police have confirmed that Marilyn Aldrich is under the care of physicians, and are investigating her sudden reappearance. Hang on – I'm getting something. I'm on the phone with Lara Pinter, a reporter with The Greenfield Examiner. Lara, can you hear me?"

"Charles," she said. Her voice was as clear as the day she'd given me the finger at the second crime scene. "We're trying to stitch together information as it comes in, but here's what we've learned so far. Witnesses inside the Greenfield County Hospital report that at around ten after nine tonight, a man raced into the hospital shouting that someone was going to jump from the roof. Security was dispatched to investigate and found Marilyn Aldrich, who'd been missing since Sunday night. I've talked with a security guard who requested that his name be withheld, and he told me that Mrs. Aldrich was not – I repeat, was not – trying to commit suicide, and that she was in need of medical attention. The man told me that Mrs. Aldrich kept on repeating that she'd been held captive in a barn on the outskirts of town and that a mysterious man she calls 'Vanguard,' a man with glowing eyes no less, snuck into the barn, freed her and then carried her to the hospital. When he asked how she wound up on the roof, Mrs. Aldrich is reported as saying, 'He flew me here. He carried me in his arms and flew me here, like Superman.'"

"What do you know about the picture on the Drudge website?"

"About as much as you know, Charles," said Lara Pinter. "The picture arrived in the form of an anonymous email, and it appeared on the *Drudge Report* within minutes of Mrs. Aldrich being admitted to the hospital."

I switched off the TV. I'd heard enough.

Ruby sat in a big office chair, with a mickey of scotch in her hand, and glared at me, her face as sour and crotchety as ever.

"Have you lost your G-D mind, Conrad?" she barked. "Do you even have the tiniest inkling of what you've just done?"

I stared at my feet, unable to answer.

"I'll G-D tell you what you've done. You've just guaranteed that Grim Goeffrey has a national G-D audience, you idiot!"

"I tried to reach you both," I said, knowing Ruby was right. "I came down here to grab you and Stella, but the store was closed, and I had to find Marilyn Aldrich. He was going to kill her, for crying out loud!"

"I should crush your spine for being so utterly reckless," Ruby snapped. "Cripes, Conrad, the Guild is going to want you dead because of this!"

Stella sat down on the small leather sofa beside her desk and motioned for Ruby to calm down. "Let's just hear Marshall's side of the story before we pass judgment," she said, looking up at me. "What happened?"

I folded the picture of me floating over the Greenfield Hospital and stuffed it into my breast pocket. I closed my eyes for a moment and gathered my thoughts, then drew in a slow breath as I prepared to give a detailed account of the last two hours.

"I was on a date with Marnie Brindle in my apartment," I said, slowly. "She's the woman I rescued at Chesteron College, and she's had it in her mind that I am some kind of superhero. You both know that my ability to foretell hasn't been working properly. Anyway, as we were eating, a vision came to me."

"What was the vision?" Stella blinked.

I drew another deep breath as I slid down the wall and sat on my haunches. "I saw Marilyn Aldrich inside a barn. It had a checkerboard roof. I also saw Grim Geoffrey's host – the man in white coveralls. Marilyn was bound, gagged and severely beaten. The guy said his master told him to kill her just before midnight. That's when I came to."

"What time was that?" Stella asked.

"Around a quarter to seven," I said. "Marnie insisted that I go to the hospital, and we had a huge fight. I screamed at her and told her to get out of my apartment, because she'd started on about my being a superhero. When she left, I changed into my outfit and ran outside to my car. I came here and left a note in the doorjam, which clearly you didn't receive, because Marnie must have followed me here and grabbed the note."

"How did you find the barn?"

"I drove out of town and hid my car in a cut line, then flew around until I spotted the barn. I made every effort to ensure I wasn't followed."

"Not G-D good enough, apparently." Ruby took a swig of scotch. "Did you take down the guy in white?"

"No, he wasn't there."

"Son of a bitch!" Ruby growled, and she threw her bottle against the wall, shattering it. "This was a G-D setup the whole time! He planned this, knowing you would rescue her, and it would get huge media coverage. Talk about a helluva way to spread fear."

"It was not a setup," I snapped. "Listen Ruby, you don't know a goddamned thing about how I foretell crimes. He was going to kill her, for Christ sake! I had to get out there and save her."

Stella heaved a huge sigh and once again motioned for both of us to calm down. "I think you're both right," she said. "I think he was counting on what the shock value a dead Marilyn Aldrich might do to Greenfield. Believe it or not, her rescue might have a positive effect."

"In what way?" I asked.

"Distraction," said Stella. "News that a flying man saved Mrs. Aldrich is going to distract everyone from the unsolved killings."

"That's possible," Ruby said, chewing her lip. "Conrad, you'd better get your ass back to that cut line and grab your car, because if they find it, they'll probably pin her kidnapping on you."

"You're right," I said. "But I can't just step out back and fly there. Everybody and his dog is going to be searching the skies for a flying man. Besides, there's still time to get back to the barn and take down Grim Geoffrey's host."

"There's no point in going back to the barn. He'd already know that Mrs. Aldrich was rescued," Stella said. "You need to get your car, but you can't go out dressed like that. They know what you were wearing when you ran into the hospital."

"Well, I can't go back to my apartment."

Stella stood up from the couch and gave a wry smile. "You're forgetting that you're inside Stella Weinberg's world famous Curiosity Nook. I've got something you can wear that won't arise any suspicion if you're pulled over. Give me five minutes, and I'll be right back."

Stella waddled down the hallway. I turned my attention to Ruby, who wore a frown on her face that could shatter glass.

"Were you serious about the Guild wanting me dead?" I asked. "I thought they were supposed to be noble superheroes that go around saving the world."

Ruby nodded. "I wouldn't lie to you, Conrad; they take matters of secrecy to insane levels, that bunch."

I snorted. "Well, they can take a number; I've already experienced one assassination attempt."

Ruby stretched her legs out and plopped her feet on top of the desk. "I said they'll want you dead; I didn't say they would actually kill you."

"How come?"

"You're more valuable alive, that's how come. If anything, you should expect a visit from Ephraim, now that I've been kicked out. They wouldn't want me spilling the beans about all of their internal politics and spoiling their shot at recruiting someone with your powers."

"I see. And who is this Ephraim?"

"He's the head of the Guild," she said, blowing her nose. "He's a Vanguard as well."

I unzipped my leather jacket and folded it over my arm. Clearly the Guild experienced the kinds of political games that define most organized groups. I'd pick Ruby's brain for more information when I returned with my car, as Stella was walking up the hall carrying a garment bag.

"I've always thought your leather outfit looked like you stole it from the costume rack of Elvis Presley's comeback tour." Stella grinned, handing me the garment bag. "The Smithsonian has never forgiven me for not donating it to their collection."

I hooked the hanger on the doorknob and carefully pulled down the zipper, hoping not to damage whatever was inside. The garment bag fell to the floor, revealing a fire engine red tank top with the letters U.S.A. emblazoned in an arc across the chest. Underneath was a pair of blue shorts with a drawstring.

"I suddenly have a craving for Wheaties," I said, examining the tank top. "This wouldn't be?"

Stella smiled. "Yep, it's the same shorts and tank top Bruce Jenner wore when he won the decathlon at the seventy-six Olympics. The shirt still has his sweat on it.""

I pulled the shirt off the hangar and held it over my chest, checking to see if it would fit. "I'm not going to ask how you acquired it," I said, wrinkling my nose at its musty odor.

"Let's just say that Mr. Jenner owed me a favor back in seventy-seven, and he was short on cash at the time."

"Gotcha. Where can I change?"

Stella pointed her arm out the door of her office. "Bathroom is down the hall and to the left."

I wandered down the hall and into the bathroom, thinking that if I ever were to don a costume, it would probably be just a tank top and sweat pants. I put on the tank top and then slid the shorts up over my legs when I realized that I didn't have any footwear other than my motorcycle boots. I looked down at my bare feet, shrugged, and stuck them in my boots.

"Stella," I shouted. "I think I should wear something over my face – just in case some idiot with a telephoto lens takes my picture while I'm flying!" Within seconds, there was a knock at the bathroom door. I opened it a crack, and Stella handed me a green balaclava with the words *Ski Vermont* embroidered into the wool. I pulled the balaclava over my head and glanced at myself in the bathroom mirror.

I groaned and rolled my eyes. "I look like an idiot."

I grabbed my car keys from my pants pocket and emerged from the bathroom, preparing myself for hoots of laughter and ridicule from Ruby. When I walked in the office, Ruby eyeballed me from head to foot, and simply shook her head.

"You have ugly knees," she said, not even trying to conceal the tinge of sarcasm in her voice. "Oh, and the boots are a nice touch."

I rolled my eyes and looked at Stella. "Your turn."

"We can laugh at how stupid you look when you get back here with your car," she said, leading me to the back door. "There's a big trash bin outside. If you step behind it, nobody will see you take off."

"Check."

"Drink this." Stella handed me a Dixie cup filled to the rim with a clear oily liquid that had little gold flecks floating on the top.

"What is it?" I asked, thinking it was a potion of some kind.

"Uzo Gold," she said. "You're probably going to freeze your ass off up there."

I gulped it back, grimacing as it went down my throat. "Thanks," I said, unlocking the door and stepping outside.

"I'll keep an eye out and tell you when the coast is clear," said Stella, as I stepped behind the Dumpster.

I looked up in the sky to make sure there were no helicopters hovering nearby. The coast was clear. "Say the word," I whispered.

"Go!" said Stella, and I pushed against the pavement, rocketing into the air.

I felt a cold rush of wind against my bare feet and realized that my takeoff had blown my boots off. There was no time to go back and get them, so I aimed my body toward the Interstate and began to scan the ground for my car.

CHAPTER 37

There were no tire tracks or footprints other than the ones I'd left when I'd driven the Tempo up the cut line, so I landed beside the front door and hopped in. I started the engine but kept the lights off as I did a U-turn and drove back down the cut line, dodging overturned logs and large rocks until I saw Highway 9.

Mud caked my feet all the way up past my ankles, and I shivered as I tromped on the accelerator and bumped my way back onto the highway. It was deserted, save for a family of mule deer that grazed along the median. Startled, they looked up and then leaped into the brush, with the grace of, well, mule deer, I suppose.

I shivered. My skin was still ice-cold from the flight, so I cranked up the heat, flicked on the headlights and turned on the stereo for an update.

I pressed the auto scan button and listened. The stereo flipped through random channels, searching for a strong enough signal. Unsurprisingly, every single radio station I heard was talking about Mrs. Aldrich's rescue and the picture that appeared on the *Drudge Report*. It finally settled on a good signal from AM 620, Greenfield's "all news, all the time" station. Dave Valenzuela, their morning phone-in host, was reporting live outside the hospital, describing the scene.

"Mark this date on your calendar folks," he shouted. "May third is the date when Greenfield became the most talked-about place in America."

"Lovely," I muttered, as I switched on my wipers. A damp mist descended over the highway, coating the Tempo's windshield with a film of drizzle.

"I have a prepared statement from Representative Byron Aldrich, which I'll now read," said Valenzuela. "The past thirty-six hours have been the most harrowing and painful of my life. I am happy to report that my wife is out of the woods, and I'd ask everyone to respect our privacy during this difficult time. The circumstances surrounding her rescue are, in a word, miraculous. I have no reason to disbelieve the terrifying story of my wife's ordeal, even if the events of this evening are too astounding to believe. I'm just a humble and God-fearing public servant, but my faith tells me that God had a hand in saving my wife, and I'm not about to question His will. It is my sincere hope that whoever or whatever is responsible for delivering Marilyn safely to the loving arms of her husband and children knows that I and my family are eternally grateful. My wife said he was an angel, but I say he's a hero. Thank you, whoever you are."

I switched off the radio.

"I save his wife, and the guy invokes the supreme-being," I grumbled.

I pulled off Highway 9 and headed up the Interstate. This time there was traffic, just not the regular volume you'd expect, since most people were at home, watching the news. I imagined Greenfield residents were peeled to their TVs or chatting up a storm online, and I made a mental note to check out Americanconspiracies.net, half-thinking that Marnie might have posted more pictures.

I wasn't angry with Marnie.

I didn't feel betrayed or used, either. In the short time I'd known the woman, I'd learned that while her values didn't entirely match mine, she was still an honest person. She hadn't sent that snapshot to the *Drudge Report* for profit or fame; she did it for her sanity. She needed to do it. She needed other people to see what she had seen and experience her shock and dismay at questioning their sanity, too.

I decided that when the time was right, I'd explain my reasons for keeping her in the dark. I still had feelings for her. Strong feelings. I just hoped my outburst that evening hadn't scared her off for good.

I passed the "Welcome to Greenfield" sign and took the Shelby Avenue exit. The streets were empty, save for the occasional alley cat prowling around. I drove past Delaney Park and noticed a large group of people standing near the gazebo, staring up at the heavens. A handful of them carried binoculars, and one person had a large telescope mounted on a tripod aimed towards the Greenfield County Hospital.

"At least they're not talking about the murders," I muttered, as I spotted The Curiosity Nook about two blocks away. "Maybe Stella was right about this being a distraction."

I stopped my car in its usual spot and hopped out. Stella was standing in the alcove, holding the door open, and Ruby was nowhere in sight.

"Welcome back," she said. "Did anyone see you?"

I shook my head. "I doubt it. Hey, have you seen my boots?"

Stella gestured with her thumb. "They're in the office… the damned things fell on my head when you took off."

She locked the door behind me as I headed to the backroom.

"I need to lie down for a while," I said. "Do you have a cot?"

"It's already set up in the back. Ruby went to her hotel room, and I'm going to do some research. Go get some sleep."

"Will do," I said, yawning. "It's been a helluva day."

"That it has, Marshall," Stella said, smiling. "Get as much rest as you can, because tomorrow you'll need it."

"Why's that?"

"You're getting a crash-course in magic, starting first thing in the morning."

CHAPTER 38

"Get up, Conrad, we've got a busy day ahead," said Ruby, kicking at my cot.

I slowly opened my eyes, blinked at Ruby, and then dropped my head back on the pillow. "What time is it?" I asked in a lucid voice.

"Quarter to ten," she said, handing me a steaming mug of coffee. "I had to run the gauntlet to get here this morning, so get your lazy ass out of bed."

I swung my legs over the edge of the cot and took a sip of coffee. On the chair beside me was a folded set of clean clothes and a new pair of tennis shoes. Ruby tapped her foot and frowned at me disapprovingly.

"What?" I muttered.

"You owe me forty dollars for the sneakers," she said, presenting me with the receipt.

"Right. Do you take credit cards?"

Ruby shook her head and walked up the hallway to the front of the store while I got dressed. I gulped back a huge swig of coffee and staggered to the bathroom. The TV blared from Stella's office while I freshened up.

"All eyes are on Greenfield this morning after the stunning rescue of Marilyn Aldrich by what appears to be a flying man. That's right folks, you heard correctly, a flying man."

"Lovely," I grumbled, splashing water on my face.

"Police are baffled by how Mrs. Aldrich wound up on the roof of the Greenfield County Hospital. However, they confirm that investigators found the barn where she'd been held captive. Meanwhile, federal authorities are collecting evidence from the family cottage at Crystal Beach where she was last seen. When asked if he could explain how someone could have painted a large red spiral on the roof of the cottage without being detected by security, Greenfield County Sheriff Don Neuman declined to comment. The fantastic events of the last twelve hours come on the heels of a series of unsolved murders in the small New Hampshire city. Authorities are looking into an outbreak of vandalism as hundreds of spirals similar to the one found on the roof of the Aldrich family cottage have appeared all over town, prompting an investigation by the Office of Homeland Security."

I emerged from the bathroom feeling half-human and headed to the front of the store as Stella and Ruby looked over the Big Black Book. Walter was sound asleep in the leather armchair next to the front counter and a big *Closed* sign hung in the front window beside Boris Yeltsin.

"Good morning," I said, yawning.

Stella looked up and smiled. "Good Morning, Mr. Conrad. How are you feeling?"

"Like crap." I shrugged. "What's the good word?"

Ruby closed the Big Black Book and looked at me through her bifocals. "You mean apart from the fact that every news outlet in the country has a reporter covering what you did last night?"

"You're not going to berate me again," I said, sourly. "Because if you are, I'm going to stick my fingers in my ears and start chanting *la-la-la-la*."

"Will you two stop?" Stella pleaded. "There's nothing we can do about the news coverage. Marshall is just going to have to lay low for a while until this blows over."

"Fat chance," Ruby sneered. "The kooks are coming to town."

"What are you talking about?" I asked.

"Supermarket tabloids, Conrad," she said. "*The National Monitor* is offering a one-million dollar reward for conclusive proof that what happened last night wasn't a hoax. Even the Sci-Fi Network is in on the act."

"What do you mean?"

"They've preempted their regular programming for a superhero movie marathon, and during the breaks, they've assembled a panel of geeks and pseudo-scientists to help viewers 'come to terms' with the knowledge that a man can fly."

Stella frowned, pressing her lips together. "I hadn't foreseen that," she said. "The news coverage will certainly distract everyone from Grim Geoffrey's plan, but I hadn't factored in The Roswell Effect."

"Roswell?" I asked. "As in New Mexico?"

Stella nodded. "It's the planetary nerve center for UFO watchers. Ever since that crash back in forty-eight, the city has become a symbol for anyone who believes in government coverups and unnatural phenomenon. Hell, its number one industry is tourism, and you can't walk anywhere in that town without bumping into people wearing 'ET Phone Home' t-shirts – even the Chamber of Commerce sponsors an annual UFO festival."

I tilted my head. "So we should plan on an invasion of geeks and freaks, is that it?"

Ruby waved her hand in the air. "Don't forget the lure of a million bucks," she said. "For that kind of money, I'm almost tempted to club you over the head and drag your sorry ass to *The National Monitor* in person."

Money. It brings out the worst in people.

I'd scraped a living by selling crap on eBay and designing websites. It wasn't much, but it paid my bills. A one-million-dollar reward was sure to attract throngs of people to Greenfield. If everyone was distracted by the discovery of a superhero and the quest for a huge financial windfall, it would decrease the level of fear that Grim Geoffrey needed to hatch his plan. That meant only one thing: he'd have to do something spectacular that would grab everyone's attention while simultaneously scaring the living hell out of them.

"Witchcraft," I said, changing the subject. "We're doing a crash course today, right?"

Stella nodded. "Yes, we are. I'm going to talk about pure magic, and Ruby here will fill you in on dark magic. It's going to come at you fast and furious, so we'll head to the back room and get started."

I stuffed my hands in my pockets and followed the pair down the hallway and into the back room. We walked over to the dinette, and Stella motioned for me to sit down. Ruby went to the office and dragged back a flip board, then handed a red magic marker to Stella.

"I feel like I'm back in high school," I joked. "Is there an exam after this?"

Ruby shot me a dirty look. "Yeah, Conrad, it's what will happen during the summer solstice. You'll know you passed if you live through the night."

"Point taken," I said, trying to sound apologetic.

Stella popped the cap of her magic marker and drew a large circle in the middle of the flip board. "This circle represents living energy," she began. "It is neither good nor evil, it simply exists. It surrounds both the near and unseen worlds and is responsible for preserving the life force of those who occupy both realms. It is neither conscious nor unconscious."

"What does that mean?" I asked.

"It means that living energy is neither self-aware, nor is it unaware at the same time," said Ruby. "It is not a conscious body or a blind force that simply exists for the sake of existing."

This was way over my head, and all I could think of was a mental image of Luke Skywalker sticking his hand out and summoning his light saber while he dangled upside down in a snow cave as the drooling Wampa snow beast approached.

"You mean, like The Force?" I asked, immediately feeling like a complete idiot.

Stella gave a huge frown. "No, Marshall, this isn't like Star Wars," she continued. "Try to think of living energy as an enormous stew of supernatural energy. It occupies our bodies, for example, acting as a catalyst for our thoughts and emotions. Living energy is the spark of life at the precise moment of conception. When we die, the living energy that dwells inside all of us leaves our bodies and returns to the source."

She drew a series of smaller circles around the large circle in the middle of the flip board. "Living energy acts similar to how you can draw power from evil intent, but with one qualification. Just as evil intent is a supernatural battery that fuels your body, evil exists because of living energy, and that's where magic comes in."

"Living energy can be shaped to serve a purpose," said Ruby, pointing at the smaller circles. "Witchcraft is the influencing of events, objects, people and physical phenomena by mystical, paranormal or supernatural means. It refers to the practices employed by a person possessing a combination of skill and conscious focus to wield this influence. Spells are simply a complex variety of tools that help the individual strengthen their focus."

"Like a compass, then?" I asked. "Spells direct a practitioner's capacity to influence living energy?"

"Pretty much," Stella nodded, as she pulled a small glass sphere out of her frock and placed it on the table. "Marshall, I want you to levitate this orb."

"Sure thing," I said, beginning to concentrate. I imagined the orb lifting off the surface of the table and invoked the feeling of lifting a box off the floor. I closed my eyes tightly, increasing my focus, and drew on the energy in my body to make it move. But nothing happened.

"It's not moving," I said, rubbing my temples.

"That's because Ruby put an immobilizing spell on it."

Ruby grinned.

Stella pulled another glass orb out of her frock and placed it a few inches from the first one.

"This time, I want you to focus all of your energy on the levitating the first orb. When you've done this, you'll want to channel that energy into the second orb."

I stared at the second orb and then closed my eyes. I imagined the first orb lifting off the ground, and I directed the mental image onto the second orb.

"Open your eyes, Conrad," said Ruby. "Keep concentrating on the second orb."

I looked at the second orb and noticed the enchanted orb floating above the table. "Wow," I said, as the floating glass ball fell to the floor and shattered.

Stella clapped her hands and smiled warmly. "Well done; you've just passed your first lesson."

"I don't get it," I muttered. "What happened?"

Ruby took the second orb off the table and flipped it in the air, snatching it with her left hand. "What you succeeded in doing, Conrad, was a counter spell. The only difference is that you didn't use an incantation or a potion. Instead, you used your mind."

"Try to think of the second orb as a crude representation of a spell recipe," Stella added. "Your goal was to levitate the first orb, but you needed the second orb to get the first one in the air."

"So a spell is like a ratchet wrench," I said. "If I want to remove a bolt, I need to use the right socket. I can't just remove the bolt through sheer force of will."

"Bingo," said Ruby. "You channeled living energy to levitate the first orb by focusing on the second one. Don't get me wrong, as a Vanguard, you could have levitated the first orb if it didn't already have a spell on it. This experiment allowed you to draw on your pedigree as a witch to shape living energy."

"So what you're saying is that if my mom hadn't been a witch, I wouldn't have been able to break the spell on the first orb."

"That's right," Stella said. "Now you understand at a basic level, how to channel living energy for the purpose of magic. What we're going to do next is employ this basic function of sorcery to find a portal to the netherworld."

"Whoa, now!" I said. "Don't you think that's somewhat beyond my scope of understanding?"

"Under normal circumstances, I'd say yes. But the summer solstice is staring us straight in the face, and we have to begin preparing the spell," said Stella.

"So what am I supposed to do in the meantime? I can't go back to my apartment," I said.

"You can stay at my place," Stella said. "You might as well stay there too, Ruby. It's probably best if we all stick together right now."

"Is it protected by strong enough spells?" Ruby asked. "We don't want some nasty-ass Minion trashing your place, too."

Stella smiled. "Like Fort Knox,"

"Fair enough," I said. "I'll take Ruby to her motel so she can check out. Got an address for me?"

Stella grabbed a piece of scrap paper from the counter top and scribbled the directions to her house. "Here you go," she said, handing me the address.

"Got a key?"

"I'm a witch, Marshall; my house doesn't have a mechanical lock. You need an incantation."

"Ah, what was I thinking?" I asked. "Care to share it with me?"

Stella's face turned beet red.

"Just put your hand over the doorknob, click your heels three times and say 'there's no place like home,'" she said.

I glanced at Ruby, who had a huge smirk on her face.

"You're kidding, right?" I asked. "Do I have to wear ruby slippers that come in my size too?"

Stella rolled her eyes and shook her head. "Very funny, Marshall. Take Ruby to get her things, and for crying out loud, don't touch anything in my house."

CHAPTER 39

Ruby and I had just pulled out of the Super-8 parking lot when we spotted our first kook.

He was dressed in a vintage 1966 Batman costume, complete with a yellow plastic utility belt, and he walked along the sidewalk as if his costume was something he wore every day.

"Looks like some people are taking the news about Greenfield's mysterious flying man a bit too seriously," I said.

"What did you expect?" Ruby grumbled. "America is a nation that embraces the cult of celebrity, and you, my friend, are the star *du jour*."

I drove in silence, pondering what Ruby had just told me.

Now that my secret was out, did it mean I'd have to retire? I tried to imagine what my life would be like minus the heroics. It was difficult. I'd been carrying out a near-nightly vigil for over ten years, shutting myself off from the rest of the world, partly to keep a low profile, but mostly because the world I saw disgusted me. My mother once told me it didn't matter how much paint you splash on a dilapidated house. If the foundation is rotting and the windows are broken, it's still a dilapidated house. That's how I looked at the world; Greenfield was just my little corner of it.

"How do you do it, Ruby?" I asked.

"What are you talking about?"

"Saving people – defending them," I said. "The world is a shit hole, from what I've seen, and you've been a member of The Guild for over thirty years. How do you reconcile protecting a world that's rotten to the core?"

She glanced at me through the corner of her eye and gave a small shrug of her shoulders. "It's not all rotten," Ruby said. "Sure, you've got your drug peddlers and organized crime, but they're small potatoes. Hell, half the time, they're killing one another off."

"That's what I mean," I said. "Crime is everywhere. Murder and rape destroy people's lives, and for what? Our best efforts don't stem the flow of corruption and vice."

"The world is supposed to be a good place to live, but that doesn't mean it's one hundred percent perfect, one hundred percent of the time."

"So how do you do it?" I asked.

"I try to make it better," she said, forcing a smile. "Not for noble reasons or anything like that. I mean, I'm a realist. All of humanity has a dark side, but that doesn't mean humanity isn't worth saving. Besides, I can lift a tank without breaking a sweat. Do you have any idea how bored with a factory job you'd be, knowing that you can bench-press ten tons?"

"Maybe," I said.

"Know what I think?" she asked.

"What?"

"I think losing your fiancée nearly destroyed you. I think this line about the dark side of humanity is just a cover for a whole helluva lot of pain you've bottled up inside. If you had some love in your life, you'd probably be less cynical."

"Maybe."

We drove for another few minutes until we found Stella's house. I pulled up to the curb and rubbed my eyes, because it was a sight to behold.

A white picket fence poked out from a huge garden of wild flowers, alive with birds and insects. An archway rose over a wrought-iron gate, which opened onto a path of flat granite stones leading to a small porch with dozens of wind chimes hanging from the beams. A virtual symphony of harmonic tones filled the air with each small gust of wind as Ruby and I stood at the front door.

"I bet she's popular with the neighbors," I said, looking around.

"Why? Because her house doesn't have a manicured lawn or neatly clipped hedges?"

"I guess so."

"Can your criticism and open the door. I have sore feet, and I want to have a nap."

"You do it," I said. "I'll feel stupid as hell."

"Sounds like a personal problem," Ruby grumbled. "Click your damned heels together, or I'll throw you through the G-D window."

I put my hand on the doorknob and exhaled, as I glimpsed at Ruby through the corner of my eye. Her mouth had formed into an amused grin – she was enjoying this.

"There's no place like home," I said, sourly, as I clicked the heels of my sneakers together, making a thumping sound.

The door made a loud snapping sound and I turned the knob, opening the door.

As we stepped inside and took off our shoes, I smiled at the quaintness of Stella's house. I'd been expecting to see a bunch of symbols similar to the ones scrawled on the floor of The Curiosity Nook the night I talked to the rocks. Instead, the main floor consisted of a small hallway that went straight through the middle of the house. To my left was a tiny kitchen, complete with copper pans that hung from hooks above an apartment-sized stove and small refrigerator. To my right was a living room with a widescreen TV, a sofa and a worn La-Z-Boy recliner that tilted slightly to the right. Tribal tapestries covered the walls that lead to the second floor, along with a number of old photographs in hardwood frames. At the top of the stairs were two small bedrooms. One had bookshelves on three of the four walls, and I assumed this was Stella's room.

I stepped into the bathroom and reached for the light switch but found none. Instead, there was a small oak table with an enormous oval candle that smelled like rose petals. I walked into the other bedroom, searching for a light switch and again, found none.

"This place is spooky," I said. "There isn't a lamp or a light switch anywhere on the second floor."

"She doesn't need them," said Ruby who was making herself at home on Stella's bed.

"How come?"

"She's a Sentry Witch. Enchanted candles act as an alarm bell, should anything decide to enter our realm."

"Well, that makes sense," I said, leaning in the doorway. "You comfortable?"

"Yep."

"She's going to kick you out of her bedroom when she gets home, you know."

"Yep."

"Ruby, is there any part of your personality that isn't a shit disturber?"

"Not in my nature," she said.

I sat down on the edge of the bed, and Ruby gave me a dirty look. "You're not planning to put the moves on me, are you? That would be awkward."

"Shut up, Ruby," I groaned. "I have questions."

"Oh God, what do you want to know now?" She rolled her eyes.

"I want to know why you dabbled in dark magic."

Ruby flashed me an angry look and shook her head. "Next topic, please."

"I don't think so. Out with it."

She sat up on the bed and reached for her purse, pulling out her pewter flask. She unscrewed the cap and took a larger than normal swig, then gave me a disapproving frown.

"Because plain old nicey-nice magic bored the hell out of me," she said. "That, and there was a man."

"Go on."

"Franklin Kirkpatrick Howard was his name," she said, a fond smile on her face. "He curled my toes."

I leaned in and listened attentively. This was the first time Ruby had ever gotten personal with me.

Her smile widened. "He was the original bad boy, a defrocked sorcerer – punted out of his order for screwing around with the Big Black Book. We'd been carrying on for a few years, against the wishes of my coven, of course. He wasn't a bad man, mind you. His interest in dark magic had more to do with increasing his knowledge, rather than a malicious plan or anything like that, and I loved him. God, I did love him so."

"What happened?"

"He summoned a demon one night, or so he thought. Damned thing pulled him into the netherworld, wanted him as a trophy. I fought like a woman possessed. Used every spell I could think of to free Franklin, but it didn't work. The Demon was too G-D powerful. It could have pulled me in too, but I wasn't the one who had sent for him."

Her eyes grew dark, and her face took on a solemn look.

"I had to get him out of there, you see," she said, in a haunted voice. "Because I loved him."

"What happened next?" I asked, softly.

"I used the Big Black Book and called on a black sprite – they're the netherworld equivalent of the mafia. He told me the creature that took Franklin was none other than Grim Geoffrey, and that I'd have to challenge him to a battle if I wanted to free Franklin. He said I didn't have a ghost of a chance of winning if I relied exclusively on pure magic, but if I possessed the strength of a Chieftain, I could defeat Grim Geoffrey and save Franklin. This came at a price, of course, but I was young and blinded by love. He'd give me the spell that would turn me into a Chieftain in exchange for my delivering Grim Geoffrey's head on a platter. So, I made the deal. I transformed myself into a Chieftain using a black spell, and I fought Grim Geoffrey, but it was too late. He killed Franklin during our battle, and my coven yanked me out of the netherworld before I could destroy Grim Geoffrey."

"Holy shit," I said.

"You know the rest of the story," said Ruby, as she took another swig from the flask. "The reason I said the chickens were coming home to roost is because Grim Geoffrey is back, and I'm not exactly a young woman anymore."

I fell into a shocked silence for a minute or so. She slid her pewter flask back into her purse and let out a depressing sigh.

"That's a helluva story," I said quietly.

"That it is," she said, exhaling. "I have to confess something, though..."

"What's that?"

"The Guild intended to send a Vanguard to work with you, but I convinced them that I should go."

I spun my head around and stared at Ruby, stung by her admission.

"W-What?"

She slumped her shoulders and twiddled her thumbs as she stared at the floor.

"Marshall, I am just as nasty a piece of work as Grim Geoffrey. As far as The Guild was concerned, two people had died at the hands of a serial killer, and there was a rogue Vanguard who might be the son of Orson Conrad. But I knew the truth. I'd seen those same symbols decades ago. They surrounded Grim Geoffrey's domain."

"You're kidding."

"I found you because I'd been spying on Stella Weinberg. I knew that the covens had entrusted Stella to keep an eye on you, and when the killings began, I realized Grim Geoffrey needed you out of the picture. I figured a novice like you wouldn't stand a chance against him, but with our combined abilities, we could destroy him. I know that I can never bring

Franklin back, but this is my one shot at finally making things right."

She slid away from me, as if she was expecting me to explode. Emotions welled up inside me as I tried to make sense of what she'd revealed. I wasn't angry, and I didn't feel betrayed. Too much had happened in a short span of time for me to lose faith in her. She'd made a dark bargain to save someone she loved, and that was a selfless act. The irony was that it had led to losing not only the man she loved, but her place in the covens and her membership in The Guild. Her interest in Grim Geoffrey wasn't an act of vengeance. This was about a lonely old woman who'd lost everything that mattered in life, and maybe by helping me, she'd atone for her mistakes and prove to herself that her life meant something.

I put a reassuring hand on her shoulder and smiled.

"I thought I had to learn everything the hard way," I said, reassuringly. "You're quite a woman, Ruby Thiessen. Don't let anyone tell you any different."

"You're not angry?" she asked in a surprised voice.

"Not one bit," I said. "The Solstice is in three days, and I can't think of anyone I'd rather have fighting at my side."

She smiled warmly, and for a second, I thought tears might well up in her eyes.

"You know we're probably going to wind up dead, don't you?" she asked.

"Probably," I said. "Then again, that's par for the course when you're saving the world, isn't it?"

She gave me a mischievous look and smiled. "Yep, par for the course."

CHAPTER 40

It's human nature to make peace with your loved ones and to tie up loose ends at the end of life. Psychologists call this the acceptance stage of dying. I didn't have any family, and I had few loose ends in my life, but the events of the last twenty-four hours told me I should probably leave a record of events leading up to my confrontation with Grim Geoffrey.

Stella arrived home from The Curiosity Nook carrying an armful of newspapers and magazines. Ruby was upstairs having a nap as I stretched out on the sofa, reading a thick volume called *Magic Words and Phrases – A Guide for the Novice Sorcerer*.

"It's a damned zoo out there," she puffed, dropping the newspapers on the coffee table. "I passed a convoy of motor homes heading to Scotchman's Hill, and that was before I saw all the media vans."

"Scotchman's Hill, huh?" I asked. "Why there?"

"Beats me. Maybe because it's the one place in Greenfield offering a clear view of the sky," she said. "It seems as good a place as any when you're looking to win a million dollars from a supermarket tabloid."

I sat up on the couch and stretched. It had been a crazy day of magic and revelations that had taken their toll on everyone. I watched Stella disappear into the kitchen and listened as she put on the kettle. She was a good woman. Both of them were good women, regardless of the secrets they'd kept from me. I looked out the window as the setting sun began disappearing below the horizon. The clouds reflected the last remnants of the day in a beautiful shade of pink, and the sound of Stella's wind chimes filled my ears with a haunting chorus.

Yes, there were secrets that had led to my meeting Stella and Ruby. Yes, I was going to meet an uncertain fate in less than forty-eight hours. Yes, I would confront a creature whose reputation among creatures in the unseen world was just shy of the Devil himself, but it didn't matter. We were entering tribulation, and Grim Geoffrey was simply the first act in a play that had yet to be written. The cast of characters ranged from slightly eccentric to just plain terrifying. What else was in store for me, should I survive?

Stella placed a tray with a tea service on a coffee table and switched on the TV. She sat down in her La-Z-Boy. It groaned under her weight, and then she started surfing the channels with the remote control.

"I wonder if there's anything good on TV tonight?"

"Somehow I doubt it," I said. "Haven't you heard about the discovery of a superhero in Greenfield?"

"I hear he's an asshole," she laughed. "Flies in the face of the great superhero myth about saving damsels in distress, or thwarting the plans of an evil genius."

I smiled warmly. "Nah, I heard he is less of an asshole and more of a cranky middle-aged fart."

Stella switched to *Fox News*.

"This ought to be good," she said. "We'll listen to what the network that is solely responsible for reducing America's collective IQ has to say about you. Ten dollars says they'll accuse you of being a liberal and that all of this is a hoax."

"A miraculous revelation about super beings that live among us, or a terrorist plot?" the host asked in a cynical voice, as the picture from Drudge's website appeared over his left shoulder.

"Lovely," I muttered.

"We're talking today with Dr. Roberta Bruce, a national security analyst with the Institute for American Intelligence. Welcome, Dr. Bruce."

"Glad to be here," she said.

"I have a question," he said. "Is the mysterious flying man that has everyone in an uproar for real?"

She nodded."We've analyzed the image from the Drudge website, and from what we can tell, it appears to be the genuine article."

"But a flying man? Surely that's a scientific impossibility."

"Not necessarily," she replied. "You have to remember that terrorist organizations like Al Qaeda have vast networks of both funding and scientific research. It's an established fact that they're hard at work trying to develop a nuclear weapon, so it stands to reason they'd be researching an effective delivery method that didn't include a ballistic missile."

"Are you saying the man who saved Marilyn Aldrich is a terrorist?"

"It would be irresponsible to rule that out. We think it's a message from Al Qaeda that says, 'Hey America, look at what we've got.' We also think kidnapping Marilyn Aldrich was just a front for them to unveil their latest weapon against our way of life."

Stella changed the channel. "I owe you ten dollars," she said. "Didn't see that coming..."

"Won't they feel stupid if we can't take out Grim Geoffrey, and creatures from the netherworld start running amok," I joked.

"Let's try some local news," she said, as she switched to Greenfield Newsfirst.

"Scotchman's Hill is alive with news media and superhero watchers alike as they scan the evening sky for a glimpse of the mysterious flying man who appeared over the Greenfield County Hospital." The story cut to an interview with a bearded man wearing a *Spider-Man* t-shirt. A 35mm camera with a zoom lens hung from his neck.

"Of course he's real," the man said. "Meta-humans have always lived among us, and technology is the number one reason their secret is out."

"I think he's wicked cool, whoever he is," an inebriated young woman with a Chesterton U sweatshirt purred. "He can save me anytime he wants!"

I got up from the couch and switched off the TV.

"Hey, what are you doing?" Stella griped. "We were getting to the good stuff."

I shook my head. "Yeah, well, you're not the one accused of terrorism."

"It's going to blow over. America has the attention span of a gnat," she said. "Don't forget, this coverage is distracting everyone from what's really happening."

"Yeah. About that," I said, plopping myself back on the sofa. "I thought we were going to draw out Grim Geoffrey's host before the solstice."

"That's was the plan, but there isn't enough time."

"Define that," I said.

Stella stirred a cup of tea and took a sip. She leaned back into the La-Z-Boy and continued stirring her cup. "The spell calls for a precise amount of filtered sunlight at the right intensity," she said. "The apex of the solstice is nine twenty-six PM – that's when Grim Geoffrey will emerge from his portal at Delaney Park, if your vision is correct. I've spent the past three days fashioning a spectral filter the Big Black Book calls for, so we'll be assembling the final ingredients at eight forty-five PM, and casting the spell shortly after that."

"And what do I do?"

"You'll head to Delaney Park and take out his host before Grim Geoffrey emerges."

"Where's Ruby during all this?" I asked, nervous as hell about the tight timeline.

"With me," said Stella. "I'll need her there to recite the incantation. Only a Chieftain or a Vanguard has the power to project their voice across an entire city. Once we've cast the spell, we'll meet you at Delaney Park to help you subdue his host or destroy Grim Geoffrey, whichever comes first."

I slumped back in the sofa, absorbing everything Stella had told me.

It sounded like a workable plan, but there were still many unknown variables. What if the spell didn't work? What if

Grim Geoffrey's host didn't show up as planned? I already knew what would happen if we couldn't destroy the Púca; that was the easy part. A lingering sense of doom twisted my stomach into knots. Ruby and I had been unsuccessful at finding a portal after scouring the area for days, and I'd missed my chance to capture the host the previous night.

Fate would decide the outcome. I had to somehow make peace with this fact.

I made a conscious decision to warn everyone about the cataclysm that was about to unfold should we fail to destroy Grim Geoffrey. If technology was responsible for revealing that a superhero saved Marilyn Aldrich, I'd use the same technology to warn the rest of the country about the dangerous days ahead.

CHAPTER 41

I slept surprisingly well for a guy who was probably going to be dead by the end of the solstice.

I'd initially thought Stella had put some kind of herbal sedative in the tea, but she and Ruby had left for The Curiosity Nook hours before I crawled off the sofa.

I got dressed and hopped in the Tempo, deciding I'd simply sneak back into my apartment to create a blog to warn others. Matters were now out of my hands, and I had to trust Ruby and Stella to come up with one hell of a dark spell to put psychic blinders on the citizens of Greenfield.

As I drove past The Curiosity Nook, I noticed a large crowd had gathered just outside and were peering in the windows. Boris Yeltsin wasn't waving, and a closed sign hung loosely from his hand.

"That makes sense," I muttered. "Where else would all the kooks go if not the kookiest store in town?" I slowed down and considered going in the back entrance, but changed my mind at the last second. Ruby and Stella needed to complete the final preparations for the spell, and I imagined Ruby was cursing up a storm, knowing the geeks and freaks were clamoring to come inside. The last thing they needed was for me to hang around asking stupid questions.

I stepped on the gas, and within minutes I'd pulled into the parking lot outside my building. I looked around for Marnie's white Honda Civic. It was nowhere to be seen, so I decided to park my car in a vacant spot beside a large motor home, thinking she wouldn't see my car.

I snuck in to the building, looking over my shoulder just in case Marnie was around, then went in my apartment. As I closed the door, I noticed a pink envelope on the floor, so I sat down on my easy chair and opened it up. It was a letter from Marnie.

Dear Marshall:

I knew it was you all along. I only wish that we'd trusted each other enough to talk about your secret before you freaked out on me.

Marnie

At least Marnie was admitting that it was she who had taken the picture, not that it mattered.

I folded the letter and slid it into my pocket, then went to the fridge and grabbed a Red Bull. The leftover Thai Food from my dinner with Marnie was still on the table, and I sighed heavily as I went to the spare bedroom to fire up the computer.

I grabbed my credit card and registered Greenfield-superhero.com with a hosting service from outside the country. Within minutes I received an email telling me how to log into my hosting service and set up a web page. I found a simple blog format and installed it on the server.

Then, I started to write.

I kept on writing for the better part of a day, then spent a few hours editing and rewriting over eighty thousand words that gave a detailed account of the events leading up to my discovery on the *Drudge Report*. It felt a lot like I was completing a condensed autobiography, but that wasn't my intent. There was a mass grave containing the bodies of five homeless people the public was unaware of. Grim Geoffrey needed fear and mass hysteria to build his domain in the mortal realm. He had designs on expanding his domain, and people had better forget about the images they'd be seeing on the news showing Greenfield residents hacking one another to pieces if they planned to survive.

After I finished the blog, I prepared a brief news release that pointed to my web address, and then I used my web cam to record a video file of me hovering above the floor of my spare bedroom, glowing eyes and all. This would be the conclusive proof for anyone doubting that I was Greenfield's mysterious flying man.

There was one problem.

I'd uploaded the video file to the server, and the blog was ready to go. What I needed was someone to fire off the news release to the media, I just didn't know who that someone would be. I'd assumed that either Ruby or Stella could do it, but one or both of them might die. I decided there was no way of knowing who, if anyone, would survive the night, so I scrawled the web address to the blog with the login and password onto two sticky notes, one for Ruby and the other for Stella. I stuffed them into the pocket of my leather jacket and glanced at my watch: 7:05 PM.

According to the plan Stella'd hatched, I was to arrive at Delaney Park at 8:45, so I changed into my outfit, went to the kitchen, and nuked a quesadilla, as it was the only thing in my fridge the gremlins hadn't eaten. "Cripes, even guys on death row get a better last meal than this," I grumbled as I munched away.

My stomach was in knots, so I went to the bathroom and splashed cold water on my face, then gulped down a huge mouthful of Pepto Bismol. It didn't help. I switched off the bathroom light and stepped into the front hallway when I heard a familiar sound coming from my living room

"*Meow*," Walter wailed from atop my easy chair. I walked into the living room and plopped myself down on the sofa. Walter jumped onto my lap and started rubbing his head against my chin, purring like an outboard motor.

"Hi, pal. You've come to say goodbye, haven't you?" I asked, scratching behind his ears.

Walter looked up at me and blinked, as if he were saying yes.

Suddenly I was awash in sadness as I pulled Walter to my chest and sobbed.

"Stupid, goddamned cat," I said, choking back the tears. Walter rubbed his head against my face and kneaded my chest. To anyone looking in, it would have been a pathetic spectacle, but it was bittersweet.

I cradled him in my arms as I left my apartment and headed to the parking lot. When I stepped outside the building, I noticed the temperature had dropped, and it smelled like rain. I held Walter in the air, taking one last good look at him. His black legs stuck out of his fat body like the branches on a tree.

"Walt, it's time for you to get outta Dodge," I said.

Walter meowed one last time as I put him down on the ground.

"Scat!" I shouted, and Walter took off into the night.

Since there was still a remote possibility that I would actually defeat Grim Geoffrey, I decided to destroy my car before Sheriff Don Neuman figured out a way to plant the severed head from the mass grave. It would be just my luck to destroy the creature responsible for the unsolved murders and then come home to find a posse of deputies waiting at my doorstep. I wasn't going to leave anything to chance – the Tempo had to go. If I destroyed my car in the parking lot outside my building, someone would probably see me, record it and send it to the news media.

I could already hear the lead-in on *Fox News*: Greenfield Superhero Attacks Ford Tempo While Mythical Creature Oversees Mass Slaughter of Citizens.

It didn't matter.

The wind stirred around my feet as I walked toward my car, and then I heard something.

"Goddammit!" a female voice shouted from the general direction of the Tempo. I jumped behind a minivan and did a quick scan of the parking lot for a white Honda Civic, but I didn't see one. "Shit!" the voice rang out again. It sounded like Marnie Brindle. I crept toward my car, keeping myself hidden behind the chestnut trees that formed the perimeter of the parking lot until I spotted the Tempo. It was Marnie, all right. She'd smashed the passenger window and was rifling through the glove box, still searching for proof. But why? Her note pronounced her belief that I was her rescuer, so why break into my car?

I watched her for another minute and then decided the time had come to reveal myself in my entire unnatural splendor. Well, not really, but it sounded good.

If there was anyone who I wanted to survive what was about to unfold, it was Marnie. It didn't matter how much she'd obsessed over proving I was a superhero, she was still a good person and deserved to live. Then it dawned on me: here was the person who could publish my blog. I looked at my watch again. It was 7:21 PM – more than enough time to grab Marnie and fly her to safety.

"Here goes," I said, as I pulled my hood over my head and stretched out my hands.

I pushed off the ground and slowly lifted above the chestnut trees. My eyes began to glow as I hovered about thirty feet above my car.

"Marnie Brindle… Stop vandalizing that Ford Tempo!" I shouted, trying to sound like the voice of doom.

Startled, Marnie jumped out of the passenger seat and looked up, the color draining from her face.

"M-Marshall?" she squeaked. "Is that you?"

"There isn't time to explain," I said, sounding ominous. "Step back from that car!"

In an instant, Marnie's legs buckled, and she fainted.

CHAPTER 42

I carried Marnie to a safe place under a chestnut tree until she came to, and then turned my attention to the Tempo.

I'd paid less than a thousand dollars for it, so it wasn't like I was destroying something of great value. I couldn't torch it – that would bring the fire department, and the fire might spread to other cars. Instead, I decided to drop it.

You know, from a great height.

I stepped in front of the Tempo and grabbed the bumper, lifting the car up to my waist. Then I squatted down and heaved it up onto its rear bumper so the front end of the car was pointing at the sky. I reached underneath, keeping one hand on the front end, grabbed a handful of the frame, and then slowly raised the car over my head, groaning under the strain.

"M-Marshall – *what are you doing?*" she shouted, astonished.

"Just stay there." I bent my knees. "I'll be right back."

A line of cars had stopped on the street next to my parking lot, and a crowd of people stood on the sidewalk, their collective jaws dropped.

"Nothing to see here!" I shouted, pushing against the ground until I was in the air. I shot straight up to a little more than two hundred feet and started looking for a place to drop the Tempo. I spotted a freshly excavated tract of land where they were going to build a new subdivision. It was empty of any people or vehicles, so it seemed like a good place. I flew for about a minute until I was certain there was nothing below me and then shoved with all my might.

The Tempo plummeted to earth like a meteor, smashing into the ground with a tremendous crash that echoed into the distance. A cloud of dust blew out in all directions as car parts shot into the air. I flew down to take a look and smiled. It had landed on its roof and crumpled under its own weight. The door pillars had caved in, and all that was left of my car was a flattened-out shape that once resembled a reliable automobile.

"Take that, Don Neuman," I sneered, as I took off into the sky and headed back to my building. Marnie was walking around in a daze, so I dove down and grabbed her like a hawk snatching a ground squirrel for a snack.

She screamed as her legs dangled in the air until I scooped her into my arms and jettisoned skyward.

"Don't look down," I said. "Just keep your eyes closed and hold on."

"M-Marshall, are you going to kill me because of the picture I took?"

"No Marnie, I don't kill people I care about," I said.

"Where are you taking me?"

"As far the hell away from Greenfield as possible," I said, reassuringly.

"W-Why did you wreck your car? W-What's going on?"

I turned my head and looked at her. The glow from my eyes lit up her face, giving her an angelic appearance. "A cataclysm that's going to make news of my existence seem like a fart in the breeze," I said.

"C-Cataclysm?"

"Magic, evil juju, mythical creatures and mass hysteria – the stuff of nightmares."

She threw her face into my shoulder and squeezed her arms around my neck so tightly that I thought she'd cut off my circulation.

"I-Is this about the rocks – the spirals?"

"Yep. And eight murders and one big ass demon."

"*Demon?*"

"Don't ask. If you don't hear from me, you'll be hearing about it on the radio."

"This isn't real; it can't be," she said in a stunned voice. "I'm not really here."

"You're here," I said, as my eyes blazed through the sky. "Things were humming along nicely until you outed me. I'm not too happy about that."

"A-Are you going to drop me like you did with your car?" she asked, dead serious.

"Nope. I'm saving your life, because I care about you. That and you're going to be doing something of critical importance," I said, scanning the ground for a good place to land.

"W-What?"

"I'll tell you in a minute," I said.

I spotted a truck stop on about a mile ahead and decided it would do. I'd been following the Interstate for about ten miles, carefully keeping track of the exits to ensure that we were far enough outside Greenfield to guarantee her safety. I leaned into the air current and started a controlled descent toward a fireguard about a quarter mile from the truck stop where I would drop her off and give instructions.

We landed a few hundred yards from where the fireguard met the Interstate, and I put her down. I could hear the sound of transport trucks roaring by, so I knew she'd have a short walk to the truck stop. I reached into my pocket and pulled out one of the sticky notes, then handed it to her.

"What's this?" she asked, still sounding frightened.

"The web address for a blog I've prepared," I said. "Everything the world needs to know about me and what's going to happen tonight in Greenfield is on there."

"What's it for?"

"Partly to explain who the hell I am, thanks to you," I said. "But mostly warnings for people to take shelter, hide, run like hell – whatever. I don't expect I'll live through the night."

"O-Okay." She forced a weak smile. "If you say so."

I reached into my pocket and handed her an envelope. "This is a news release that you will fax to *CNN*. The fax number is inside. You will fax this news release if you don't hear from me by morning. Do you understand?"

"Yes, I'll do it."

"Good," I said, putting my hands on her waist. "I am not some do-gooder from another planet. It's still plain old cranky Marshall underneath the hood and behind the glowing eyes."

Marnie nodded, her eyes welled up with tears.

"I want to apologize for yelling at you the other night. I had to go."

She sniffed and rubbed her eyes with a sleeve. "I understand."

"Good, then," I said. "Before I leave, you need to know that everything I told you about my feelings was true. I might have lied to you about saving you that night at Chesterton, but it was necessary. I'm not a superhero. Half the time I don't even know what the hell I'm doing. What you need to understand is that while I've kept secrets, I never once lied to you about my feelings."

She threw her arms around me and buried her face in my chest. Her body let out a painful series of sobs. Grief and fear poured out of her like water through the spillway of a dam.

"I'm sorry, Marshall. I am so sorry for everything," she sobbed, not holding back. "A-Are you really going to die?"

I pulled her close and tried to sound hopeful, but I had to be honest. There had been more than enough secrets between us, and I didn't want this last moment with the woman who'd touched my heart go to waste.

"I'm not going to lie to you," I whispered. "Nobody will be more surprised than me if I survive this night. I want you to know that until you walked into my life, I was a hollow shell of a man. I was angry at the world for losing Cynthia, and I didn't believe I would ever find love again. You changed all that. Somehow you changed me. Always remember that, no matter what happens."

She looked up at me and tried to smile. "I will," she said, quietly.

"I have to go now," I said.

"I know."

I looked up at the sky and readied myself to take off when she put her hands on my face and kissed me, full and hard, not wanting to let go. I took her hands and slowly brought them to my chest.

"Stand back now." I said, as I bent my knees and gently lifted off the ground, hovering higher and higher until I was just above the treetops.

"I'm in love with you, Marshall Conrad!" Marnie shouted, jumping up and down.

And then I was gone.

CHAPTER 43

The rain started falling, softly at first, then in a constant stream that stung my eyes.

I looked at my watch: 7:43 PM. Marnie would be well on her way to the truck stop. Now all I had to do was head over to Delaney Park and wait.

Rolling terrain passed below me as I dodged air pockets and swirling downdrafts that smashed against the top of my body, dropping me dozens of feet in an instant. I'd adjust my trajectory, pushing my body through columns of steel-colored clouds, supercharged electric energy that threatened to lash out at me as I forced my way through the gathering storm.

I decided to fly low, just above the treetops and follow the contour of the topography until I reached the city limits. I forced myself into a dive and dropped like a stone until I was just a few feet above the spruce trees.

The air was warmer down here, and the heavy rain became a light mist coating my body as I glided eastward. Soon I was back in Greenfield, so I increased my altitude, hoping to avoid the deluge of amateur photographers and news media scattered throughout the city.

It was a bizarre spectacle.

People stood on top of their homes, chatting amiably with next-door neighbors who searched the horizon, hoping to catch a glimpse of me. I spotted a convoy of at least two dozen motor homes heading toward the Greenfield fairgrounds honking their horns like a wedding party on its way to the reception. Pedestrians waved and cheered as the convoy snaked its way forward past vendors who peddled everything from t-shirts to cotton candy.

When I approached the fairground, my jaw dropped.

Recreational vehicles of every description filled the entire ten-acre parking lot. Loud speakers pumped out country music as thin blue streams of smoke from hundreds of barbecues floated into the evening sky. Men, women and children danced with perfect strangers dressed in superhero costumes of every description, while others sat quietly on top of their motor homes looking at the sky.

They spotted me, of course.

Almost immediately, the sound of hundreds of honking horns blasted through the air as people pointed and waved. Dozens and dozens of flashes sparkled below me as people snapped pictures or recorded me with video cameras. Young women lifted their shirts and exposed their breasts to the heavens as throngs of young men cheered them on.

And that was before I noticed the spectacle on Scotchman's Hill.

At first glance, I couldn't tell if it was a recreational spot or a high tech fortress.

Hundreds of antennae masts jutted out of the tops of media vans and trucks parked beside one another with almost military precision. Countless satellite dishes of every size pointed in all directions from atop cube vans emblazoned with the logos of major networks or smaller local news stations. Men and women dressed in jeans and t-shirts aimed expensive TV cameras or manipulated boom microphones at well-dressed reporters who stood in front of bright white lights aimed at the tops of their bodies. Behind them was a virtual tent city as tourists ate, drank and partied together.

Then, the unexpected happened.

A pain of unimaginable proportions seized my body and thundered into my brain like an atom bomb on steroids. I doubled over in midair, plummeting to earth as a single image burned into my mind.

A massive gray fist mashed into Ruby Thiessen's face.

I crashed through dozens of spruce branches that whipped my body, scratching and scraping my hands and face. The sound of breaking branches filled my ears, and I hit the ground like a wet sandbag. I rolled over on my side, clutching my midsection as a wave of nausea splashed through my stomach. I had to move; I had to get up. Something was about to kill Ruby, and there was no time to waste.

I got to my knees and tried to block out fear and revulsion. I hoisted myself up, gripping a broken tree branch that dangled above my head. Sticky pine sap oozed between my fingers, and I screamed as a searing pain shot from the base of my left leg straight up the side of my body.

I'd broken my ankle.

"Son of a bitch!" I took a hesitant step forward to check the damage. I could feel my ankle start to balloon inside my boot with sharp throbbing pulses of red-hot pain.

There was no time for first-aid. Something was in the backroom of The Curiosity Nook. Something with an enormous gray fist that was going to connect with Ruby's face in what would surely be a lethal blow.

I hobbled to a clearing in the woods and leaped into the air, screaming as the force of my jump compressed the crushed bones in my ankle. I blasted into the sky like a rifle shot, a loud crack slicing through the air and echoing through the woods below. I leaned my body westward, clenching my fists in front of my face, willing my body faster, reaching out, lunging towards Stella's store.

I couldn't be late.

I had to get there on time.

I needed Ruby like I needed air to breathe. She possessed the courage I lacked.

Within a minute, I spotted the large hole in the roof of The Curiosity Nook caused by Ruby's fall only days ago. I leaned earthward and landed clumsily on the roof, wincing at the pain in my ankle. I poked my head inside and my jaw dropped in horror.

An enormous creature made entirely of sticky wet muck held Ruby against the wall with a giant hand wrapped around her body. Its right hand formed a massive fist and it was just about to deliver a devastating blow to Ruby's already mashed face.

"*Ruby!*" I shouted.

The creature glanced over its shoulder and spotted me through the hole in the ceiling. Its thick fat lips curled up into a grin of baneful and simmering evil, and then its right hand connected with Ruby's face, splattering blood and muck against the cinderblock wall.

"*Nooooo!*" I screamed as my eyes detonated into blinding white light, staggering the creature. It let go of Ruby. Her limp body fell to the floor like a bag of cement as the creature shielded its face from my raging glare.

My reaction was immediate.

I threw myself at the creature, seething with hatred.

Blood lust coursed through my veins as my fists slammed into the creature's legs, flipping it into the air so it landed flat on its back. I ripped a metal pipe out of the wall, sending a torrent of frigid water splashing to the floor, and then I rushed at the creature that was already getting back up.

I swung the pipe at its face like a baseball bat, connecting with a loud slapping sound that sent a spray of muck in all directions. The creature sailed through the air, crashing through a metal shelf and landing against the back door. I didn't give it time to move.

I flew across the room, clawing and tearing at the creature's midsection. I pulled out large clumps of mud and gore as the creature shrieked in agony. I dug deeper, harder; my hands were claws that ripped through bone and slime, its evil stench filling my nostrils and fueling my rage.

It kicked and flailed about, struggling to save itself. I mashed its face with my good foot and pummeled the creature's chest with both hands, smashing through its ribs as it writhed in agony. Finally, I raised both hands above my head and drove them straight through the creature's chest and pulled with all my strength, tearing out its football-sized heart.

It twitched for a few seconds and then died.

I dropped to my knees, panting heavily as its gore dripped off my hands and onto the floor. I hadn't killed the creature so much as butchered it with my bare hands, my utter rage fueled by a horrifying lust for vengeance.

Something had gone terribly wrong.

I looked around the backroom for Stella, but she was nowhere to be seen. Then I heard a weak moan from across the room.

"Ruby!" I cried.

I hobbled over and gently cradled her broken body in my arms. Her battered face was almost unrecognizable, but from the look of the back room, she'd fought a heroic battle. Small impact craters the size of dinner plates were scattered about the cement floor. The doorway leading to the hall looked like it had been blasted away with high explosives. There was a giant hole in the wall above the sink, and the dinette table had been smashed into hundreds of pieces.

And there was no sign of Stella.

Ruby reached for my face with her tiny, gloved hand and coughed heavily. Blood sprayed out of her mouth and against my leather jacket. Her eyes opened slowly from somewhere behind the puffed mash that was once her face.

"*G-Golem dead?*" her voice gurgled, almost in a whisper.

"Yes, Ruby" I whispered.

"S-Stop Stella..." She trailed off. "Stop..."

Her body went limp. Her right arm flopped to the floor and something rolled out of her hand.

It was a shard of Sentient Quartz.

CHAPTER 44

Ruby was gone.

I carried her body to Stella's office and laid her on the desk. There was no time for mourning; something had gone wrong while she and Stella had prepared the spell.

Stop Stella. Those were her last words.

I stuffed the shard of sentient quartz in my pocket and leaped into the air through the hole in the ceiling. There was no way of knowing what Ruby's cryptic warning meant. Had Stella suddenly taken leave of her senses? Maybe she'd played both sides of the fence, finally choosing Grim Geoffrey at the eleventh hour.

I tried to remind myself that it was Stella who had to be dragged into using the Big Black Book kicking and screaming, because dark magic was forbidden. It was only after we'd exhausted every reasonable strategy to increase our chances against Grim Geoffrey that she'd reluctantly agreed.

Then I remembered.

She'd warned that the Big Black Book was far from perfect, because many of the spells were unproven. I remembered the night I talked to the rocks. Stella took every possible precaution to protect against something from the netherworld entering her store, and we weren't even using pure magic. It was also possible that Grim Geoffrey had simply waited until the right moment to throw a wrench into our plans. Maybe he'd dispatched this Golem to distract Ruby long enough for Stella to become enchanted.

It didn't matter.

Ruby Thiessen was dead, and now I had the daunting task of facing Grim Geoffrey at the apex of the solstice without the benefit of any protective measures.

Within minutes, I was hovering over Delaney Park. I had hoped I would spot the man in white coveralls busily preparing the gazebo for Grim Geoffrey's arrival, but the park looked empty.

"This doesn't make sense," I muttered. "Something's not right."

I decided to investigate on foot, so I landed behind a fountain about a hundred yards from the gazebo and listened.

Aside from the occasional car driving up Shelby Avenue with the stereo blasting, the only sounds came from water splashing in the fountain and ducks chattering away in the pond to my left. I took a cautious step forward, expecting the host to jump out from the bushes. A twig snapped. I froze, realizing I might have given away my position. I held my breath and waited for what seemed like an eternity. Still nothing.

I was just about to leap in the air and search the park from high above when I heard a muffled crunching sound, as if someone was dragging a heavy object across a gravel surface. Then I heard a female voice, and it was singing.

"You'd better not pout, you'd better not cry
You'd better not shout, I'm telling you why
Geoffrey's near, he'll soon be here in town..."

"Stella," I whispered, and I raced in the direction of the singing voice. I dove behind a large oak tree and slowly poked my head around the side of its massive trunk. My heart stopped.

She was dragging the body of the man from my vision. The man with the stringy blond hair who'd kissed Marilyn Aldrich's forehead. The man in white – *Grim Geoffrey's host.*

Only he wasn't dressed in white, he wore plain old street clothes.

Stella, on the other hand, was clad in a garish white nightgown that clung tightly to her overweight body, leaving little for the imagination.

"Oh my God," I gasped, in quiet horror. "She's somehow become Grim Geoffrey's host."

I ducked my head back behind the tree. I needed time to think.

Soon a large, pulsating mass would appear in the middle of the gazebo. A mass that would act as a portal, allowing Grim Geoffrey to enter the near world, followed by an army of spectral followers that would feed on the souls of Greenfield residents. They would gorge themselves on the terror emanating from mass hysteria as friends and neighbors hacked one another to pieces. An image of the haunting, purple sky and towering pillars of smoke flashed into my mind. I could almost taste death in the air.

I took another quick peek at the gazebo. The man's body was outstretched in a cruciform shape, but he wasn't moving. Had Stella killed him? I couldn't be sure.

She knelt over his body and brandished a small knife, which she thrust it into the side of his neck, before pulling it out and holding it overhead. A stream of black blood slowly flowed from the wound in his carotid artery, forming a large pool about ten feet away.

Then it dawned on me.

Grim Geoffrey needed a human sacrifice to create a portal to the near world. Human sacrifice meant that he needed a sorceress like Stella. She would cast a terrible dark spell, transforming the pool of blood into the large pulsating mass.

I glanced at the man. He wasn't moving. Blood wasn't pumping from the man's neck with every beat of his heart; it was just a slow steady stream.

He was already dead.

I stood up, grinding my teeth as the pain from my ankle throbbed up my leg. If I could get Stella away from the gazebo, she wouldn't have a chance to cast the spell that would create the portal. If I could keep her at bay beyond the apex of the solstice at 9:24 PM, Grim Geoffrey would lose his chance to enter our realm, and Greenfield would survive the night.

I stepped out from behind the oak tree and prepared to fly at Stella.

She flashed a maniacal grin and cackled wildly, then swept her arm in front of her body, aiming her hands at me.

"*APERIO OCCULTUS!*" she roared, in an unearthly voice.

There was a millisecond of blinding white light. Then an explosion as a lightning bolt hit the ground in front of me, sending me careening through the air and crashing into the fountain behind me.

"*APRERIO OCCULTUS!*" she screamed again, and another blast of lightning landed at my feet. I flew head first into the duck pond, landing with a huge splash. The force of the blast left me feeling dazed as I struggled to get up. Chunks of earth clogged my nostrils, making it difficult to breathe as I splashed through the cold green water. The weight of my soaked leather outfit threatened to pull me back under. I flailed away like a drowning man, willing myself to the edge of the pond.

She was powerful.

I looked up at the gazebo as Stella walked to the steps and stretched out her arms to an invisible audience. An icy wind descended from the sky, whipping her gray hair into long tendrils that flowed behind her head, blowing her nightgown off her body.

Then she opened her mouth.

In a voice that shook the earth, Stella projected a dark incantation that summoned a furious breeze, blowing branches off trees and overturning park benches, sending them tumbling against the wrought iron fence surrounding the park.

"Thou art immune to their hate, bring forth thy malice. Thou shalt feed on thine enemy. Thy words and thoughts are no bane to thine deeds."

I looked in horror as the black pool of blood swirled up from the floor of the gazebo, forming into an organic mass. The petals of its orifice opened and closed, making a sticky slapping sound as Stella stretched her arm deep inside.

"That's enough!" I bellowed. My voice shook the ground with a force equally as powerful as the spell Stella had just cast. My eyes exploded with crimson rage, and I thrust myself forward at the gazebo in a dizzying streak of light, smashing

into Stella's fat body and forcing us both straight through the orifice.

Together, in a spinning jumble of tangled limbs, we fell into the darkness.

CHAPTER 45

I opened my eyes.

My head struck something when I landed – was it Stella?

A trickle of blood ran from my forehead and down the bridge of my nose, dripping into the blackness. I couldn't see the blood. In fact, I couldn't see anything at all. A shroud of darkness surrounded me as I reached out, hoping to latch onto something, anything that would help me get back on my feet.

But there was nothing.

"Hello?" I called out. My voice echoed strangely, as if I'd shouted through a hollow paper tube. No reply. I crawled forward, feeling every inch in front of me, but I found nothing. Nerve endings on the tips of my fingers should have registered even the tiniest sensation, but nothing happened. It was like reaching through air, but the air was somehow solid.

And my eyes didn't glow.

Everything about the place oozed menace, but my eyes gave off no light. Were they glowing? Perhaps the blackness was so dense that no light could penetrate it.

Panic rose in my stomach and shot up my throat. I could feel my heart pounding in my temples as fear gripped my mind in a deathly vice.

"This is his realm," I whispered. "But where is he?"

Silence.

"You might be dead," a voice whispered back

Terrified, I spun around, flailing my arms at the voice. I kicked out my legs, desperately trying to injure something, anything.

"*Show yourself!*" I screamed.

Silence.

"But I am already here," the voice replied. "Your eyes have chosen not to see. Were your senses conditioned to this place, you would indeed see a great many things."

A cold hand touched the back of my neck, and I yelped and scurried away from where my senses told me someone should be standing.

"Do you want to see me?" the voice asked. This time its tone registered in my brain. "Are you safe?"

"*Where am I?*"

"You know where you are, Vanguard," the voice giggled, sounding like a young child. "Are you safe?"

"*I don't know!*" I bellowed, filled with rage.

"I agree," it said, as something that bore a close resemblance to steel-toed boot connected with my cheek and laid me flat on my back. A stinging pain radiated from the side of my face and down through my neck. I blinked, then focused every ounce of my concentration into producing enough light to penetrate the darkness. Within seconds, a dim gray surface the size of my hand appeared before me.

It was working.

"Are you quite certain you wish to see me?" the child's voice asked.

"*I will see you!*" I screamed, as I tried to force my brain to see what my eyes inexplicably refused. Beads of sweat formed on my injured forehead, causing a corrosive sensation inside the wound.

Silence.

"*Then look upon me!*" the voice boomed, sending me tumbling backward and crashing into a solid object.

Suddenly, an unearthly crimson light flared up and revealed that I was in an enormous stone chamber. I spun around to see Stella's naked and unconscious body lying against a massive boulder with a glowing red spiral. I looked up. The walls were composed of a chalk-like substance with a bramble of veins stretching out in all directions. The ground beneath me was a fleshy substance that felt like velvet against my hands but was hard as granite. My eyes followed the floor to a cluster of boulders fashioned into what looked like a large chair, each with a glowing red spiral.

Seated in the chair was the figure of a small boy.

"Hello, Vanguard," the boy said in an innocent sounding voice. "You were expecting someone taller, yes?"

I rose to my feet and kept a healthy distance. He appeared to be about six years old. He had thin shoulders and a narrow chest with skin the color of ivory. He was bald and had a sickly appearance, which immediately made me think he looked like a child going through chemotherapy. His thin lips curled upward into an amused smile as he sized me up with a pair of sunken black eyes that glinted in the crimson light.

And he meant business.

"You have delayed our plans," he said, standing up. "I'll admit that I didn't foresee your kind's reaction when they learned of your existence."

"Sorry to disappoint," I said sarcastically. "Where's your army of followers?"

"Here," he said calmly. "With us."

I looked around, expecting to see a host of God knows what, but we were alone.

"Oh, you cannot see them?" he asked innocently, his eyes filled with menace.

Something crashed into me and sent me reeling into the chamber wall. I landed with a loud *thump*, and then dropped to my knees.

"But they can see you."

I looked up, and he was gone from his place in front of the chair. Then a razor sharp pain seized the small of my back as he lifted me off the ground and hurled me like a rag doll against the boulder beside Stella.

"What makes you believe you can destroy me, Vanguard?" he asked, kicking me in the ribs. "Others have tried, yet I am still here. Curious, don't you think?"

He grabbed a handful of my hair, and I shrieked as he dragged me across the floor. I wrapped my hands around his thin wrist and tried to pull him off, but his grip was too strong. It was like trying to pull a tree out of the ground.

"How does this end?" he asked, his voice sweet as syrup. "Do I destroy your soul and let my hoards feast on your flesh, or should I keep you here as a pet?"

"*Screw you!*" I spat, swinging my body around with all my strength, connecting squarely against his face with a roundhouse. He sailed through the air and was about to crash into a wall when he suddenly stopped.

"Clever," he smiled and stretched his palms outward. Then, in a hurling motion, he sent a ball of blue energy rocketing across the chamber and slamming into my chest. The impact blew me out of my boots, and I sailed into the stone chair, landing with a bone-jarring crunch.

"Goddammit!" I huffed, trying to get up. The kid was laying the slippers to me, and somehow he'd created a barrier of psychic energy that kept me from fueling my powers from the evil surrounding him.

"What's wrong?" he asked. "Your powers don't work? Pity."

"Bite me," I shot back.

"Yes, well, you can never be too careful when a Vanguard is close by," he sneered. "Your father wasn't a careful Vanguard, and neither are you. Perhaps it runs in the family."

"*What about my father!*" I screamed, seething with rage.

"Nothing you don't already know," he said calmly. "Perhaps you're thinking I sent one of my minions to kill him, like I killed the old hag."

I'd had enough.

The kid might have built a protective barrier, but this was a realm of dark magic and my body could absorb evil intent like a sponge. It was time to kick some ass.

I closed my eyes and stared at the boulder in front of me. I made a mental image of him jettisoning across his chamber and crashing into the boulder next to Stella. Then I concentrated. I poured my anger and frustration at losing Ruby, at the deaths of eight innocent people and spun around.

"*I hate kids!*" I roared, and he sailed across the chamber, smashing into the boulder.

I charged at him, throwing the entirety of my nearly two-hundred pounds straight into his midsection and he flew off the floor, crashing into a pillar.

He quickly got up and brushed himself off.

"Death, is it?" he sneered. "You care to exchange blows with me, then? Yes?"

"It's not my first choice, but you don't look like the kind of guy who negotiates!" I shouted, hurling a boulder at his body.

He smiled, his shining black eyes sizing me up. "Your powers are returning. You've found a weakness in the barrier."

"Maybe I'm just a helluva lot more powerful than you expected, asshole!"

He raised a tiny index finger over his lips and tilted his head. "Shh. Let's test your theory!"

Suddenly, he doubled over onto his hands and knees. I recoiled in horror as I saw a bloody fissure form over his spine, splitting his back wide open. His ivory skin drooped loosely over his shoulders while a heavily muscled back covered with pulsing veins pushed up through the opening. An arm the size of a tree trunk reached outward, straining to free itself from the skin surrounding it. I heard a sickening tearing sound as his muscular back arched, and Grim Geoffrey's head twisted its way out of the skin in a hideous parody of birth.

Then he rose to his full height, ripping the skin cocoon from his body and throwing it against the chamber wall. A pair of large yellow eyes fixed on me, and the tight red flesh of his massive face pulled back, revealing a grinning set of razor sharp teeth. Two long, black horns protruded from either side of his skull, and each horn contained numerous spiral engravings that glowed like molten rock.

He had no neck. Instead, his head was fixed firmly between two massive shoulders. One of his clawed hands, similar to an eagle's talons, pointed toward a bright light suspended between two pillars that opened and closed like a freakish mouth.

"That is where my kind and I will enter your realm, Vanguard," it grumbled in a baritone voice that shook the ground. "Nothing can stop that now."

He took a step forward with a large cloven foot. I heard the scurrying of countless creatures moving in unison and took a step backward. He reached behind his head and pulled out the largest two-sided axe I'd ever seen.

Then he came for me.

"Now this ends," he hissed, wrapping a talon around the wooden handle. Instantly, the edges of the axe burst into flame with a loud *whump*, and he made a powerful swing at my torso. I darted to my left and the axe grazed my jacket, then crashed into a boulder with explosive force, splitting it in two. There was a searing pain in my side, and I reached around to feel a large gash cut through my jacket through to my skin. Unfazed, he spun the axe around a second time, missing my head by a fraction of an inch. I made a throwing motion and sent a lash of energy toward him. He swung the axe like it was a baseball bat and deflected the blast, sending it harmlessly into the air.

Grim Geoffrey was powerful; there was no question.

But he was also slow.

He lumbered forward, raising the axe above his head, then swung downward, like he was splitting a rail. I jumped to avoid the blade, and it smashed into the ground, creating a tremor that sent me flying headfirst into a pillar.

I got to my feet, dazed, while he bore down on me. His eyes were like fire, and he wore a grin that could scare death itself as he brought the axe above his head. I raised my hands above my head and made a snatching motion, tearing the giant axe from his clawed hands and sending it end over end until it lodged in a chamber wall. He stared at his hands with a surprised look and then swung at me with one of his large, clawed hands.

It connected with my chest, tearing a large hole in my leather jacket and ripping the flesh beneath.

I screamed in agony and doubled over, clutching my chest. Blood poured from the wound, and I could feel the bones of my rib cage against my fingers. He swung at me again, this time connecting with my back and tearing a large chunk of flesh.

"Enter the portal, minions!" he bellowed. *"Fill your bellies on mortal souls!"*

The air filled with the sounds of screeching creatures, and the ground shook as thousands of feet raced toward the portal. I felt the life draining from my body, my stamina almost at an end. I spotted the large boulder beside Stella, then squeezed my eyes shut and reached out, willing the boulder to move with every ounce of energy I possessed.

"What?" Grim Geoffrey howled.

I opened my eyes and thrust my arms toward the portal, sending the boulder jettisoning through the air and crashing at the portal's base.

"Move the stone!" he commanded, his voice insane with fury. His minions raced forward, revealing their true forms

in a living mist of twisted limbs and distorted faces. They enveloped the boulder, sliding it across the chamber floor.

My energy spent, I fell to the floor face first.

Grim Geoffrey wrapped a talon around my body and lifted me up like a child snatching a marble. A razor sharp claw hooked the skin of my neck as his hollow eyes bore down on me.

The end was coming.

His wrapped a talong around my neck and squeezed. *"Now you will die, Vanguard!"*

Then out of nowhere, a weak female voice.

"M-Marshall?" Stella whispered, weakly.

"Eh?" Grim Geoffrey twisted his head to see where the voice was coming from, so with what I was certain would be the last movement I made in this or any life, I reached into my pocket and pulled out the shard of sentient quartz.

"Eat me, you slimy piece of shit," I snarled, as I thrust the sentient quartz into his chest.

Instantly, I sailed through the air, landing in a heap about twenty feet away. Grim Geoffrey screamed in a voice that would shrivel God's testicles. His skin became translucent, and my nostrils filled with the stench of burning flesh and brimstone. He scraped and clawed at his chest, ripping out chunks of bloody pulp trying desperately to get at the shard of sentient quartz.

Then his body split open, releasing a blinding storm of spectral fire and ash. A blast furnace of wind raged like a hurricane as Grim Geoffrey's essence formed a funnel cloud of light and smoke that fell into the shard with a blinding flash.

Silence.

I opened my eyes and looked up at the moon. Puffy black and gray clouds skirted across the sky, and a damp breeze blew against my smoldering body. Ice-cold drops of water splattered against my face, and I opened my parched mouth, drinking in the evening rain.

In the distance, I heard a familiar voice.

"Storch, where are you? Storch?"

I got to my feet and spotted the gazebo. The lifeless body of a man lay on the wooden floor, just as it had before I entered Grim Geoffrey's realm.

"Storch, dammit, get out of that tree," Stella warned.

I staggered to, taking off my leather jacket and wrapping it around her naked body. Walter jumped out of the tree and landed at my feet with a loud chirp. I spotted a flickering green light through the corner of my eye and hobbled toward it.

The shard of sentient quartz rested in a smoldering circle of burned blood. I picked it up and ground it into a powder, then wiped the residue from my hands.

We were alive.

EPILOGUE

I'd like to report that life in Greenfield returned to normal after my little scrap with Grim Geoffrey. I was lucky... end of story. Sure, I could say that I'm some kind of hero, because I destroyed him, along with the portal into the near world, thereby saving the city from becoming a happy hunting ground for his followers. Of course, it nearly killed me, and it cost the life of Ruby Thiessen.

I'm not a hero, and I never wanted to be one.

Stella and I made it back to The Curiosity Nook after I'd raided a nearby clothesline and swiped a comforter for Stella, who'd finally noticed that she was as naked as the day she was born. If I'd had my clothes blasted off my body, I would have flushed with embarrassment, but not Stella. She was livid as she recounted that the last thing she remembered was a corporeal entity flying through the hole in the roof of her store, straight into her body.

"I warned her," Stella chided, as we walked in the front door. "I warned Ruby that dark magic was forbidden."

She was still dazed but had regained her faculties enough to know that something had gone horribly wrong when she and Ruby had prepared the dark spell in the back room of The Curiosity Nook. As we surveyed the damage, she told me the slimy creature lying against the back door was a *Slave Golem* that Grim Geoffrey had dispatched to prevent the spell. I asked her how he would have learned about the spell, and she shrugged her shoulders.

"I suspect he knew what we were planning all along," she said, pointing at the spiral-engraved rock on her desk next to Ruby's broken body. "If the rocks were a beacon, then Grim Geoffrey was likely privy to everything that happened from the day I met you."

I nodded my head as I wrapped a bandage around my torso. I must have experienced a kind of accelerated healing after I'd come through the portal. I was no longer bleeding, and scabs had formed around the tears in my skin. Stella told me I'd received spectral wounds, and since I'd destroyed the creature responsible for inflicting them, they'd eventually disappear.

"She was an amazing woman," I said, covering Ruby's body with a blanket. "I only wish I could have saved her."

Stella put a reassuring hand on my shoulder. "She saved herself, Marshall. That's why she came to Greenfield. She wanted to make amends for past mistakes."

"So what happens now?" I asked.

"She was a witch." Stella said. "She's still entitled to the rite of sacred cremation. I'll contact my coven, and they'll arrive before morning."

"And the Golem?"

"They'll want to study its anatomy."

That made sense.

I looked at my watch. I had to meet Marnie at the truck stop before morning. Stella gave me a change of clothes, and I took to the sky through the hole in the ceiling, arriving at the fireguard within minutes. I hobbled along the Interstate for a half mile and then went into the restaurant. Marnie sat at a table with a worried look on her face, chewing on a french fry. I waved, and she ran to the entrance, throwing her arms around me.

"What happened?" she asked, elated that I was alive.

"I survived," I said wearily. "You didn't fax that news release, did you?"

She shook her head. "No, I was going to wait until morning, just like you told me."

"Thank the stars," I exhaled, relieved. "Do you have enough money to call us a cab?"

"Sure do."

"Good, let's go home."

We sat in silence as the taxi drove up the Interstate and headed back into town. I'd fall asleep for a few minutes, and then the cab would hit a pothole, and I'd wake up, look around, then fall asleep again. When we got back to my building, Marnie helped me into my apartment, and I collapsed on my bed in a heap.

"You need to get your ankle looked at," she said.

"It's just a sprain," I said, too tired for the pain to register in my brain.

She chewed her lip. "Are you going to tell me what happened tonight?"

I yawned, waving her out of my room. "Eventually...
right now I need to sleep."

Marnie headed to the door. "I'll check on you in the
morning," she said. "I'll destroy the the news release. Don't
worry about anything, okay?"

I gave her a weak smile. "Thanks."

And then I went to sleep.

When I woke up, I was dressed in clean pajamas, and there
was a cast around my left ankle. The sun beamed through my
bedroom window, bleaching the entire room in brilliant white
light. I looked at my watch; the calendar said it was June 23rd.
I'd slept for over a day and a half. My mouth was parched,
and my bladder was full as I raised myself onto my elbows
and tried to get my bearings.

"It lives!" Stella announced, standing in the doorway. "We
thought you might need a magic kiss from a dashing Prince
Charming to wake you up."

"Thanks," I said in a hoarse voice.

"Your friend here came to my store yesterday morning and
told me that you'd broken your ankle," Stella said, gesturing
with her thumb.

Marnie poked her head around the doorframe, beaming.

"Who set my ankle?" I asked.

"Oh, just a coven of busy-bodies," said Stella. "We didn't
have to resort to a potion to keep you unconscious. Boy, do
you ever snore."

I glanced at Marnie and then back at Stella with a confused
look on my face.

"She knows; try to relax."

I plopped back down on my bed and stared at the ceiling.

I should have been relieved that somehow I had prevented all hell from breaking loose. Instead, I felt a bit like a lost soul.

Ruby had told me the chickens were coming home to roost in the days leading up to her death. Retribution arrived in the form of a huge creature composed of mud and pure evil that pummeled the life out her. I knew she would never have gone down without a fight, and a part of me questioned whether she knew Grim Geoffrey would send something to kill her. If she did know, she hid the truth to protect Stella and me, and that was a truly heroic gesture.

Maybe she knew that coming to Greenfield would be the end of the road. Perhaps somewhere deep down inside that hard-drinking, wrinkly exterior, she wanted to make peace with whatever demons she'd carried all her long life. I'd like to think Ruby lived and died on her own terms, and at least she hadn't died behind a curtain in a hospital bed, not that it mattered much. Despite a plethora of factors that were out of my control, I still felt somehow responsible for her death. It was a bitter lesson.

The media furor surrounding my discovery was as intense as ever in the days after my battle with Grim Geoffrey. You'd think the discovery of a dead man on the gazebo at Delaney Park might possibly grab their attention. Surely the notebook that investigators found in the pocket of his trousers containing the names of eight murder victims written in their own blood might knock me from the front pages. Hell, you'd think someone, *anyone*, would notice when police announced they'd found a mass grave containing the mutilated corpses of five homeless people beside the barn with the checkerboard roof, but no.

No, of course not.

Talk of dead bodies is a downer when everyone is flapping their gums about how they caught a glimpse of Greenfield's mysterious flying man or "*Hooded Specter*" as they now called me.

God, humanity pisses me off.

I laid low for a couple of weeks to give my ankle some time to heal, staying in my apartment and keeping track of the world through the Internet. Marnie visited me every day, bringing godawful concoctions that she swore up and down came from the pages of her Betty Crocker cookbook.

At least I learned to overcome my phobia about other people's cooking.

The media grew tired of waiting for another appearance of Hooded Vanguard and eventually left town.

Walter decided I was worth visiting from time to time, appearing in my apartment in the mornings and just before bed. He even brought me a dead bird.

He's thoughtful that way.

Stella bought him a new collar encrusted with green rhinestones that were actually small flakes of sentient quartz for protection from anything that might want to get at her through her familiar. Her coven was kept busy shooing away everything from malevolent gnomes to mischievous faeries. And me? Well, I was enjoying a well-deserved rest. Until, of course, I opened my email one morning and read the following:

Dear Marshall Conrad:

Your actions over the course of the last few weeks have jeopardized the Guild's security.

We are sending a representative to provide you with a membership package as well as an orientation briefing. Your base of operations has yet to be determined, therefore, we recommend that you arrange to have your possessions put in storage until completion of training. Be advised that your refusal to become a member can only be regarded as a security threat and as such, we will take measures to safeguard the organization. It is our sincere hope that you recognize your obligation to serve within our ranks. Our work in the promotion of peace, order and justice is of critical importance to global harmony. As you are no doubt aware, The Signet Pact of 1972 requires those displaying meta-human qualities to function under the auspices of the Guild. We look forward to working with you in the near future, and we will continue to monitor your activities while we await your response."

For a body of meta-humans, they sure as hell seemed pushy. Naturally, I felt compelled to respond, writing:

Dear "The Guild":

I've never heard of "The Signet Pact" but it occurs to me that if the Guild were a functional organization, I wouldn't have fallen through the cracks. Incidentally, I didn't ask to become a Vanguard, and God knows I have more productive things to do with my time than to hang with a bunch of bureaucrats wearing capes. I'm not interested in joining your Guild so, you know, get bent.

Lovingly,

Marshall Conrad

It would be just a matter of time before I faced a reprisal for my refusal to join. Not that I was worried about it. I had other things on my mind, like news that a shape shifter was making inquiries about my health to some of Stella Weinberg's unseen world associates.

The next day I found myself standing atop the roof of The Curiosity Nook. Stella and Marnie sat in lawn chairs as the warmth of the mid-morning sun took hold. In my right hand was a modest ceramic urn containing Ruby's ashes, and in my left hand was her infamous pewter flask.

"Are you sure she'd want us to scatter her ashes where she died?" I asked, holding the urn in the air.

Stella smiled. "Of course! The Curiosity Nook used to be called *Pilgrim's Tavern* before I moved in. I'd like to think she'd be pleased as punch to know that we scattered her ashes from the roof of a former drinking establishment."

"Good call," I said.

Marnie put her arm around my waist and squeezed. "You ready?"

I nodded silently as I flipped over the urn, spilling her ashes into strong west wind. "Goodbye, Ruby Thiessen, you miserable old crank," I said quietly, trying to maintain my composure.

"Bye, Ruby," Stella whispered. "See you on the other side."

I unscrewed the cap of her pewter flash and sniffed, then recoiled.

"Jeez, that's some rancid smelling rye!" I coughed.

"I thought she was a twelve-year-old scotch kind of woman." Stella said. "A toast, then?"

"Yes, a toast," I said, remembering the first time I met Ruby. "Whiskey is the Devil's drink, and may the Devil remain scared shitless of me!"

I took a sip and cringed, handing the bottle to Stella.

She chuckled. "That's quite a toast, Marshall. Did you just make it up?"

"Nope," I said quietly, as I watched Ruby's ashes disappear in the breeze. "I stole it from a little old lady."

A SNEAK PEAK FROM

DARK BARGAINS

NEXT IN THE MARSHALL
CONRAD SERIES

I grabbed Walter by the scruff of his flabby neck and ran like hell as he let out a wail in protest.

"Stupid freaking cat," I growled, as I glanced over my left shoulder only to see the pair of smouldering red eyes cutting through the blackness of the pine forest. Walter wasn't helping any as he dug his claws into my chest, making me curse the day I bought my overweight feline at a garage sale for ten dollars.

The psychic visual I'd received had led me to an abandoned cabin nestled, which was supposed to be where I'd find eight-year-old Victoria Jenkins, reported missing by her parents four days ago. The Greenfield Sheriff's Department was treating her disappearance by following standard protocol, first issuing an Amber Alert within two hours of the time she was supposed to arrive at her after school program. Her mother issued a tearful plea for her safe return at a news conference the following morning and me? I'd spent two straight nights combing the streets from up on high, keeping a vigilant eye out for a red Chevrolet Venture minivan that she was reported to have climbed into by a substitute teacher who assumed it was one of Victoria's parents picking her up from school.

The migraine, like all the migraines that are a tell-tale sign of a Vanguard's ability to foresee a crime before it is perpetrated hit me just as Marnie Brindle and I were settling down to watch a chick flick on DVD. (So sue me, I'm expanding my horizons.) It offered two clues: One was the abandoned cabin, and the other was that Victoria would be locked up inside an old refrigerator and left to suffocate. It didn't tell me about a largely hairless monster with claws that could tear through the magical shield I'd invoked to protect Walter and me, and it sure as hell didn't say the refrigerator inside the cabin would be empty, or that I'd be rescuing my cat instead.

Walter hissed loudly as he dug his claws deeper into my chest; naturally, this only acted to piss off the pit-bull terrier demon thing that was the size of a Volkswagen Beetle. Instead of barking at my now traumatized cat as it chased us up a winding path, it belched out a jet of corrosive dog vomit that nearly took my head off just as I dove behind a fallen log.

Evil? You bet! Bent on tearing out my throat? Why not?

Such is the life of Greenfield's only resident meta-human and part-time destroyer supernatural beasties.

Like demonic dogs, for example.

The creature crashed through the log, sending splinters of dried wood in every direction and throwing me about thirty feet in the air. Walter landed against the trunk of a giant blue spruce and skirted straight up out of harm's way. Did I mention he's a treacherous bastard?

"Goddammit," I snarled as I landed flat on my back. "Why the hell aren't my eyes glowing?"

The pit-bull thing gave its head a shake and bared its teeth as it readied to pounce. Shiny threads of saliva dribbled down from its three-inch fangs as a deep, throaty growl sliced through the relative silence of the woods and straight into my bowels. I scrambled behind a large boulder and spotted an opening in the forest canopy where I could take to the skies. The pit-bull let out a mind-numbing howl that I could feel in my fillings as it charged.

Of course I was going to cut and run; I might look like an idiot most days, but I have the good enough sense not to duke it out with giant, hairless K-9's on their own turf. I'd have a better shot at taking the beast down from the sky. The creature leaped into the air and snapped at my boot heels just as I pushed off the ground.

"Not so tough now, huh, Fido?" I snapped as I floated to a safe distance. The creature blinked a couple of times, and then it let out a loud sneeze. Its crimson eyes narrowed as the it coiled back on a pair of rear legs that glistened in the moonlight.

And that's when the unexpected happened.

The demon launched its body off the ground and straight at me. I pushed higher to avoid having one of my legs ripped off, and then gravity decided to play a trick on me.

Instead of falling back to the earth, the creature continued its ascent. The damned thing could *fly*.

"Walter!" I shrieked, as the fat fur ball dove into my arms. I clenched my teeth and shot into the clear black sky like a rocket. I didn't even bother to look behind me this time – I didn't have to, because I could hear the demon cutting through the wind current behind me.

Oh, and he let out another corrosive hork of dog vomit.

ABOUT THE AUTHOR

Sean Cummings is a comic book fan, zombie nut and a classic car lover. When he's not writing about curmudgeonly superheroes or netherworld invasions, he likes to spend time enjoying East Indian cuisine and can usually be found with his nose in the latest X-Men comic. He lives in Saskatoon, Canada.

ACKNOWLEDGMENTS

I'd like to thank Erin Kellison and Wayne Simmons for their very kind words about Unseen World. My thanks to Anna Torborg, who, as usual, pulled off a fantastic design for the cover and had a keen eye during the editing stage. Thanks to Cheryl, who thought the world was ready for a curmudgeonly, forty-something superhero, and to my mother, who threatened to disown me if anything bad were to happen to Walter the cat. Don't worry, Mom, I'd never allow any harm to come to our feline friends; you know, unless they're possessed by demons or something. Thanks to Hayley and Joanne, who listen to me rant every last Wednesday of each month, and to Snowbooks for all their continued support.

BUT WAIT — THERE'S MORE!

TURN THE PAGE TO READ ABOUT
Sean Cummings' OTHER URBAN FANTASY
SERIES, STARRING Valerie Stevens!

SHADE FRIGHT

A VALERIE STEVENS NOVEL

"GRABS YOU FROM PAGE ONE AND DOESN'T LET GO UNTIL
YOU'VE READ THE FINAL SENTENCE" *NANCY HOLZNER*

SEAN CUMMINGS

SHADE FRIGHT

FIRST IN THE VALERIE STEVENS SERIES

"I fell into this job quite by accident, when I discovered that I possessed the ability to see the preternatural world. There are a handful of people with similar abilities, and part of my job is to locate them, since Government Services and Infrastructure Canada like to keep track of these things. Don't ask me why."

There's a malevolent force in town, and it's quite literally Valerie Stevens' job to determine who's behind it and why they want to destroy the world, starting with Calgary.

She'll have help, in the form of her best friend (now more or less a zombie, unfortunately), a powerful dwarf troll, and the ghost of former Canadian PrimeMinister William Lyon Mackenzie King (but he goes by 'Bill' these days). But that's not all – Valerie has some tricks up her sleeve and, she hopes, luck on her side. Oh, and her boyfriend, Dave. He drives a dump truck.

FUNERAL PALLOR

SECOND IN THE VALERIE STEVENS SERIES

There's a nest of rotting husks in an old Calgary warehouse, and they've got a hankering for human flesh, but that's the least of Valerie Stevens' problems. While necromancers are a dime a dozen, these mindless killing machines all share one thing in common: they're the former occupants of every funeral home in the city.

The evidence points to the zombie Caroline, especially now that she's been experiencing short term memory loss and an inability to account for her whereabouts. If Valerie plans to clear her best friend's name, she'll have to move fast: someone's dispatched a zombie assassin, and Caroline's only hope may rest with a pair of middle-aged metal heads who've got a few secrets of their own.